THE GOOD PARENTS

JESSICA HUNTLEY

INKUBATOR
BOOKS

Published by Inkubator Books
www.inkubatorbooks.com

Copyright © 2025 by Jessica Huntley

Jessica Huntley has asserted her right to be identified as the author of this work.

ISBN (eBook): 978-1-83756-526-9
ISBN (Paperback): 978-1-83756-527-6
ISBN (Hardback): 978-1-83756-528-3

THE GOOD PARENTS is a work of fiction. People, places, events, and situations are the product of the author's imagination. Any resemblance to actual persons, living or dead is entirely coincidental.

No part of this book may be reproduced, stored in any retrieval system, or transmitted by any means without the prior written permission of the publisher.

PROLOGUE

The cool tiles under my bare feet almost tickle as I tiptoe across the kitchen in the dark of the night. There is underfloor heating across the whole ground floor, but it hasn't clicked on yet. I believe it's set to come on at five o'clock in the morning, but if the temperature doesn't drop below a certain point, then it won't come on at all. A fancy heating system that thinks and acts for itself is something that still astonishes me. Not to mention the huge coffee machine that brews automatically, ready for the morning, when the owners of the villa come down to start their day. It even dusts chocolate over the top in the shape of a coffee bean.

My eyes flick up to the huge metal clock that's illuminated gently by the cool white backlighting on the wall. It's two minutes to midnight. Another day is about to start. I wonder what it will bring. Answers, I hope. Perhaps, some sleep.

I should be doing exactly that: sleeping, but sleep has been an elusive, slippery creature lately. In fact, it's not only been lately I haven't been able to drift off into dreamland.

Insomnia of varying magnitudes has plagued me for the past two years, ever since that awful day I was told the news, changing my life forever. Sleep is something that I'm learning to live without, among other things.

I stop in the middle of the kitchen floor, watching the clock. I used to do this a lot as a kid; watch time tick by second by second. It helped calm me when I felt overwhelmed or anxious about anything. The passing of time is something that can never be stopped, never be changed, slowed or sped up. It's constant and I think, especially lately, I'm finding the passing of time a gift. I think a lot of people take it for granted; I know I've been guilty of that in the past. So, for now, I watch the clock and listen as the seconds tick by, for no other reason than to re-focus and remind myself of what's important in my life now.

My eyes glaze over from exhaustion, so I reach to the side, grasping the edge of the granite worktop to steady myself, keeping my eyes zoned in on the clock.

Breathe.

The seconds tick by, slowly, towards midnight.

I know that time never changes, but I swear it really does move slower when you're focusing on it. It seems like it does anyway. Then again, time seems to have passed in the blink of an eye, and I've done nothing but focus on time because I didn't know how much of it I'd have left with her.

A sharp pain stabs me in my lower abdomen, then shoots down to my crotch. It forces me to lean forwards, almost bending me over double. I close my eyes and take several deep breaths until it passes, then stand up straight, clutching my stomach. I don't think I'll ever get used to that.

I can't remember why I'm even in the kitchen. It's weird; my memory is as slippery as sleep lately, hard to grasp onto at times. I lick my dry lips. Ah yes, I remember now. I need a drink of water and a new glass because I accidentally knocked my usual one over as I sat up in bed and reached for it as a coughing fit shook my body.

My body doesn't feel like my own lately, and I guess, in a way, it's not. Perhaps, it never will be again. I've put it through an awful lot and now it feels as if it's punishing me. All the aches and pains I've never experienced before are not only freaking me out but pushing me to the edge, closer and closer, to the point I'm wondering if I'll ever go back to the way I was before all this happened. The lack of sleep is turning me into a walking zombie, one night at a time. It's not for too much longer though. Then, I can get all the sleep I want, if my body allows it. If I can stop thinking about her.

The glass cabinet is directly in front of me and as I reach up and open the door, the clock chimes, signalling the arrival of midnight. I've never understood why people have clocks that chime on the hour throughout the night, but then again, this villa is so large that I doubt anyone can hear it. The staff quarters are right on the other side of the villa and the owners live in the far south wing.

I could have gone to the staff kitchen for a fresh glass, but there's something about this kitchen I like, especially in the dead of night while everyone is asleep. It's not often I get the chance to walk around without anyone in the vicinity. It's large and creepy, yes, but I quite like it. The moonlight is beaming in through the huge bi-fold doors and down through the skylight above the enormous dining room table, accentuating the furniture, creating shadows and movement everywhere.

I fill my glass from the fancy kitchen tap that takes me several attempts to work out how to turn on, take a drink, followed by a deep breath as the water soothes my dry mouth. I finish the glass, refill it and take it with me back across the kitchen the way I came. I suppose I should head back to my room, back to bed, back to the staff quarters, back to the seemingly never-ending night where I just stare at the ceiling and hope sleep takes me away.

Leaving the vast kitchen behind, I walk slowly and steadily towards the spiral staircase that leads to the staff area of the villa; a separate annex. Grasping the banister in one hand, I take each stair one at a time, still unaccustomed to my unbalanced and stiff frame.

By the time I reach the top, I'm slightly out of breath and stop to compose myself.

That's when I hear a creak of a floorboard up ahead.

I look up, towards the sound, but all I see is the gloomy darkness. I can just about make out the swirly patterns on the tiles in the hallway leading to the staff bedrooms. There's a large window at the far end hall, which overlooks the pool and patio area. There are lights surrounding the pool, which are on throughout the night, casting strange shadows through the window onto the tiles.

But it's not the shadows that catch my attention or make the hairs on my arms prickle.

It's another creaking sound, like someone is opening a door and the hinges need to be lubricated. This time, it's behind me, downstairs. I lean and glance over the banister, holding my breath to listen out for any other sound, but there's nothing.

'Hello?' I call out. 'Is anyone there?'

The glass I'm holding shakes as I wait for an answer.

None comes.

I turn and head down the hall to my room, but as I do, a

black shadow darts across the tiles in front of me. I stumble backwards, the hand holding the glass losing grip. The glass slips from my fingers and smashes at my feet, soaking me and the area I'm standing on.

'Hello?' My voice is a little firmer this time, from fear, not annoyance.

My heart rate is so fast that I can't breathe. I put a hand over my heart, praying it calms down because it feels like it could explode. I've been warned several times now that my blood pressure needs to stay low.

Dizziness washes over me and my foot slips on the wet tiles beneath me.

I reach out to grab the banister, steadying myself. That was close.

I'm still off balance as a shadow lunges towards me. I don't even have time to open my mouth and scream because I'm already tumbling down the stairs.

A snap pierces the darkness as my leg breaks, erupting in white-hot pain.

I land with a heavy thud at the bottom and listen to the heartbeat of the villa; the ticking of that damn metal clock on the wall in the kitchen.

But all I can think about is the pain in my leg, that and the dark humanoid shape standing and looking down over the banister at me.

Finally, darkness engulfs me.

PART 1

CHAPTER ONE

EIGHT AND A HALF MONTHS BEFORE

I love my job. Not a lot of people can say that. I work long hours, and the pay isn't exactly great. Early mornings and late nights are the norm, but I thrive on the high pressure of the kitchen. A pastry chef is all I've ever wanted to be. I grew up watching *MasterChef: The Professionals* when it first aired in 2008. At age ten, I watched the first series and was instantly drawn into the world of being a high-profile and expertly skilled chef. More accurately, a pastry chef. Ice cream, pastry, chocolate, sugar and caramel were my staples in life. They made everything not only taste better but feel better too. The perfect caramel cream was enough to sooth any stress or worry. That's what I thought anyway.

I attended Le Cordon Bleu for nine months at the age of twenty, completing their globally recognised and respected culinary qualification in pastry and baking just over four years ago after finishing an apprenticeship in a top London hotel. My speciality is chocolate, but I enjoy all aspects of being a pastry chef, including confiserie, ice cream, bread and decorating.

Today, I'm working at one of the finest Michelin-star restaurants in London, alongside a highly renowned head chef: Chef Andre. He's super strict and an arrogant twat, but I can't deny his expertise and knowledge. I've learned a lot from him, but his attitude towards me and some of the other chefs in the kitchen leaves a lot to be desired.

Today is no different.

I'm three minutes ahead of schedule in plating up my desserts, which means, according to Chef Andre, I've rushed my presentation of the dish and need to do it again, despite it being perfect. He has his timings down to the last second and if you're late it means you're not working fast or hard enough and if you're early then you haven't put in enough effort required for perfection.

'Chef, with all due respect, my dessert *is* perfect,' I say, adding the finishing dust of edible gold powder to the top of the miniature crème brûlée. 'Me being three minutes early will not affect its presentation or taste.'

A collective inhale of breath sounds from the various chefs in the kitchen who are within earshot. I don't mean to come across as rude, but I know for a fact he's only telling me to re-do the dishes because he wants to belittle me in front of everyone. It's what he does. I think it makes him feel powerful, or whatever.

Chef Andre is a small man, the same height as me, at five foot seven. He often wears thick heels on his shoes, thinking no one notices, but the *clop, clop, clop* across the kitchen tiles is a dead giveaway. His face is beetroot red as he squares up to me, puffing out his chest. He most likely has a small penis too. Just a guess.

'Are you questioning me, pastry chef?'

'No, Chef.' In this kitchen, everyone addresses Chef

Andre as Chef. He usually calls us by our titles or ranks within the kitchen. We don't have names here.

'Good. Then re-do the plates. Now. I won't ask you again. You have two minutes.'

I take a deep breath in through my nose and out through my mouth, dampening my growing frustration. I'm now going to be late getting the dessert plates out because there's no way in hell I'm going to be able to plate up six desserts in two minutes; not at the standard that's required. I, too, have my timings down to a T, and I know exactly how long it takes to plate up a dessert.

Five minutes later, Chef Andre inspects the plates. He picks one up and tosses it into the nearby sink where it smashes and crème brûlée flies everywhere.

'Do another,' he says.

I do another, all the while biting back a vile retort.

I love my job. I love my job.

I've worked here for three years. When I started, I was the commis chef, the junior chef in the kitchen. My main job was to assist the other chefs by preparing food, cleaning work areas and providing any tools or utensils they required at a moment's notice. It was hard work. At the time, Chef Andre was the pastry chef, the same title I now hold. I learned a lot from him, including how to create the perfect sugar work, but I also learned that he was a vile, sexist pig who liked to pick on the junior, female members of the team.

It doesn't matter how hard I work, how many extra hours I spend in the kitchen perfecting my recipes or how many times I practice a dessert to get it right, it's never enough for him to give me any sort of praise or admiration. So, I've stopped needing or wanting it. I don't need his approval.

The other chefs keep their heads down, taking his abuse

day in and day out. I've witnessed several instances of Chef Andre acting inappropriately towards the female chefs and waitresses. Not to mention when we had an Indian chef come to work here, Chef Andre wasted no time in throwing around racist comments that made everyone uncomfortable. No one ever said anything for fear of losing their jobs. I'm the only one who fights back, but when I do, I'm punished for it. I know I'm a brilliant pastry chef, and one day I'm going to prove it by owning and running my own Michelin-star restaurant.

The aim is to keep working and saving hard until I'm thirty to put away a big chunk of money for a deposit, then ask the bank for a loan for the rest of the funds I'll need. That's just four more years of working in this kitchen and putting up with crap from a self-indulgent chef who thinks he's above everyone else just because he went to one of the best culinary schools in France and once had dinner with Gordon Ramsay, who apparently called his food *pleasant;* high praise indeed.

I turn back to my workstation and begin the next round of serving plates. I have a junior chef to assist me with making sure I have everything I need, but I like to plate up myself because design and presentation of the food I serve is something I pay intricate attention to.

As I wipe a tiny drop of chocolate that shouldn't be there off the white plate, my junior chef nudges me gently in the side. His name's Luke.

'Incoming,' he whispers.

I look up just in time to see Chef Andre approaching. 'You're required in the main restaurant,' he says with an air of boredom. 'It seems someone would like to speak to you regarding your dessert.'

'Yes, Chef,' I respond. 'Is it a complaint?'

'Most likely, yes. Table eight.'

My heart sinks. Complaints do happen from time to time. Usually, Chef Andre deals with them himself, but when it comes to the dessert, he always makes me deal with it, which I suppose is fair enough, but it means my next set of plates are going to be late going out too.

'Can you plate the next three?' I ask Luke.

'Yes, pastry chef.'

Luke has worked here for a year and still has a lot to learn, but he's watched me plate up every day and has practiced a lot of the techniques too. He's young, fit and eager to learn, often following me around the kitchen like a lovesick puppy. I'm three years older than him, but it feels like he has a massive crush on me the way I catch him staring at me sometimes. Or maybe he just likes watching me while I bake and prepare food.

'Leave the quenelles to me though, yeah?' I add.

'Yes, pastry chef.' He still hasn't been able to match my quenelle technique. Even Chef Andre never critiques them. It's my thing.

I quickly remove my apron from around my waist and straighten my chef whites. I work very cleanly; very rarely do I have a dirty jacket. I tuck a stray strand of hair that's come loose from my bun behind my ear, then head into the busy restaurant.

I always find stepping into the main restaurant is like stepping into an alien world. Chefs very rarely see this side of the job and whenever I get the chance to visit, I feel out of my depth. I've always preferred to be in the back, in the kitchen, where the magic happens, creating and designing the dishes, rather than watch them be demolished before my eyes, surrounded by all the loud chatter of diners.

I weave through the tables towards number eight, which is in the far corner by the window, perfectly placed to look out over the back garden area of the restaurant. It's winter now, January, so the garden is not in use, but during the summer it's the most spectacular place to be, surrounded by greenery and flowers, along with a water feature that sparkles in the sunlight.

The restaurant is heaving, as it is most nights. Most diners have had to wait more than six months for a table. People don't come here just for the food, but for the experience, the journey into a different world, as they taste something they've never experienced before.

The couple on table eight are in their early fifties, expertly turned out. Wealthy, no doubt. They look as if they demand respect and attention wherever they go. As I walk towards them, my stomach clenches and my mouth turns dry. I lick my lips so I don't stutter over their names, which I checked before I walked over here.

'Good evening, Mr and Mrs Gibson. My name is Brittany Young. I'm the head pastry chef.'

The woman looks up. I can't help but notice their dessert plates are clean, as in they've eaten everything I prepared, so it can't have tasted that bad.

'Ah, so you're the young lady who I need to thank for the most exquisite dessert I've ever tasted!'

My stomach flips in relief and my shoulders visibly relax. 'Thank you. I'm so glad you enjoyed it.'

'Enjoyed it?' says Mrs Gibson with a laugh. 'I *enjoy* a bowl of chocolate ice cream. This dessert was pure perfection. I've never tasted anything like it.'

My cheeks heat up. I'm never one to take compliments well. 'That's very nice of you. Thank you.'

'I shall be putting in a good word about you with my friends at the Royal Academy of Culinary Arts. The Annual Awards of Excellence are coming up.'

'Thank you. I really appreciate that,' I say as calmly as possible. All I want to do is squeal like an excited schoolgirl and jump up and down.

After a few more minutes of pleasantries, I return to the kitchen to see whether any of the dessert plates that Luke has presented are salvageable. To my astonishment, he's done a brilliant job and all I need to do is add the quenelle of toffee butter puree to each plate.

'How did it go?' Luke asks me, handing me a dessert spoon.

'Fine. It wasn't a complaint, but someone who wanted to tell me how much they enjoyed the dessert. Oh, and they may talk me up to the Royal Academy of Culinary Arts.'

'That's brilliant. Oh my God, if you get a nomination ahead of Chef Andre, please let me be there when you tell him. I'll even pay you.'

'Let's not get ahead of ourselves,' I say with a sly smile. 'Besides, if that happens, I'll be inviting the whole restaurant to that particular revelation, free of charge.'

Luke hides a smirk.

I work fast to get back on track with the timings and turn out all fifteen dessert plates, complete with perfect quenelles ready for inspection, in time for Chef Andre to approach. He casts a quick glance over the plates.

'Good, pastry chef. How did the tongue-lashing go?'

'It wasn't a complaint, Chef,' I say.

'Oh... Well, that's good, I suppose. Service!'

Luke and I flinch at his booming voice. It always makes everyone in the kitchen jump, often dropping whatever food item or utensil they're holding.

THE REST of the evening goes smoothly, despite one of the waiters dropping two dessert plates on the way to the restaurant and me having to whip up replacements within seconds. Working in a Michelin-star kitchen is a high-pressure job. My doctor always tells me that my blood pressure is on the high side whenever I go for a check-up, and my periods have stopped completely thanks to stress and exhaustion, but I wouldn't have it any other way. This is what I was born to do. It's like a drug to me. The stress, the expectation to be the best, the strict time pressure I'm constantly under to deliver, it's all helping me develop and learn so that I can run my own kitchen one day.

I don't finish until eleven that night. After service has ended, it doesn't stop there. I have to prepare for tomorrow too, which involves making a new batch of ice cream and setting the chocolate tuiles in the fridge. Finally, I take off my chef whites and put them in the laundry bin, then head to my locker to grab my bag and jacket.

It's Friday night and I know that some of the junior chefs are heading out for a drink now. They're all congregating by the changing rooms, chattering and laughing. A hush descends as I walk past.

'Have a good evening, everyone,' I say.

'Oh, um... pastry chef, um... Brittany, do you want to join us?' asks Luke.

I turn and smile at him. I've always told him to call me by my first name once we're out of the kitchen environment.

A few of the others swap looks and roll their eyes. 'Thank you, but I can't. I have to get back to my sister.'

'Okay, see you tomorrow... Brittany.'

'Goodnight, Luke.'

I watch as they walk out into the night. I used to be one of them not long ago. I'm only twenty-six, but I feel like I'm their babysitter sometimes. Luke was only asking me to come out of pity and politeness. No one wants me tagging along.

I shift my bag onto my other shoulder as I slip my phone from my pocket, checking my messages. One from my twin sister, Clara.

> Hey, Britt. I'm turning in now. Hope you have a good night. I got the results back from the hospital today. I'll tell you everything tomorrow. Not exactly something to tell your sister over text message. Love you. Night Xx

It was sent at 21:47 p.m.

She'll be fast asleep by now.

The results we've both been dreading for weeks now are in.

I'm not sure if I want to rush home. She won't be able to tell me till tomorrow morning when she wakes up, but the idea of going home, back to the flat we share, fills me with dread. More than dread. Fear. Pure, mind-numbing fear about what those stupid test results say.

I walk through the busy London streets, hopping on and off tubes, on autopilot, staring at my feet, which instinctively take me towards home, but my mind is elsewhere. I get on the last tube and sit down.

My mind isn't on work. Not anymore. When I'm there, I have to focus on it, otherwise everything falls apart, but when I don't have work to distract me, my mind is on only one thing.

My sister.

On the reality that no matter what those test results say, our lives will change forever.

CHAPTER TWO

The London top-floor flat that Clara and I share is situated in Shoreditch, only a stone's throw away from the main park. There are tall buildings covered in graffiti, hordes of people, and more coffee shops than pigeons. It's not far on the tube to work, but far enough away to distance myself from the middle of the city. Most of the time, I walk to and from work, since the tube is always ridiculously busy, and I can do without sweaty commuters pressing themselves against me.

Our grandmother owned a house outside of the city, having bought it sixty-odd years ago when the average house cost less than five thousand pounds. She raised her daughter there, our mother, but we had to help her sell it five years ago to pay for her ongoing care. Neither Clara nor I earned enough to pay for everything, and the bills just got too much. She was happy to sell it and give us whatever was left, but thanks to inheritance tax, we didn't end up getting as much as we thought. She died five years ago at the age of seventy-eight from a nasty bout of pneumonia that made the rounds around her care home. That, on top of her progressing dementia, unfortunately, was too much for her frail body to handle. The care home was amazing and looked after her well, but the costs ate into the money from the house sale, not leaving a great deal for Clara and me once everything was paid off.

After care home costs, funeral costs and inheritance tax, we didn't have enough to buy a tiny flat to share, so we've had to resort to renting instead, which is basically daylight robbery at its finest. We could have moved out of London, of course, moved somewhere a hell of a lot cheaper, but Clara wanted me to stay close to the capital due to my job and dream of working in high-profile kitchens. She also has this weird fixation on London, same as our grandmother, who grew up performing in the West End (way before we were born) and always told us that London was the place to make dreams come true. London was the place to be, so London was where we stayed. To be perfectly honest, I'd have preferred to move somewhere cheaper, but over the past two years, it has come in handy to be so close to amenities, jobs and health care. Maybe I'll float the idea to Clara soon about moving elsewhere, especially since things seem to be calming down now with her treatment and we're finally seeing the light at the end of the tunnel.

We just about get by, but money is tight. Okay, maybe it's more than tight. Clara doesn't know about the three credit cards I've maxed out to pay the rent, nor the late repayments on the electricity and gas bills. She doesn't know that her treatment and medication have been a combination of private and on the NHS. She doesn't know that I sold our grandmother's wedding ring to help pay for costs, and she has no idea that I've been to the bank and practically begged the loan officer to give me not one, not two, but five extensions on our loan. I'm pretty sure he won't extend it any further. I can't tell Clara though. She has enough to worry about.

There are three flights of stairs to walk up to our flat. I could easily take the lift, but the little extra tastings of dessert soon add up to a lot of calories, and I don't have the time or the money to go to the gym. Therefore, walking up three flights of stairs every day is the least I can do to burn off those pesky extra calories. Although with the high stress of the job, not to mention being on my feet all day, it's enough to see I don't pile on the pounds. Sometimes, I forget to eat lunch or skip dinner, but I always eat breakfast. My grandmother constantly told Clara and me that breakfast was the most important meal of the day and to never skip it.

Reaching the final steps, I blow out a long breath before sliding my key into the lock. I'm as quiet as possible as I tiptoe through the hallway and place my shoulder bag on the side table. Clara's medication is laid out ready for her to take tomorrow on the kitchen worktop and the letter from the hospital is resting beside it. My stomach flips. Should I read it now and find out the results sooner, or should I wait for her to tell me? I know what I *should* do, but...

As I stare at the opened envelope, I think back to when we first found out that my identical twin sister had chronic kidney disease. She was first diagnosed two years ago after suffering through ever-growing symptoms, including general weakness, tiredness, nausea, loss of appetite, swelling of the hands and feet and difficulty sleeping.

The moment the doctor told us the bad news, my world fell apart, but she took it all in her stride. She's always been so much more positive than me. We were told she was in stage 3b, and, with the right treatment, she could stay in this stage and never progress to stage 4. If she ever reached stage 5, requiring dialysis and a possible kidney transplant, then it would basically be the end of the line.

A year ago, she had to give up her job of being a tattoo artist because she didn't have the strength to hold a tattoo gun, hence why money is extra scarce lately. I'm basically earning for the both of us, another reason why I work long hours and have a mountain of debt up to my eyeballs.

Unfortunately, life sucks and is unfair as hell, and she didn't stay in stage 3b, quickly progressing to stage 4. However, after six months of touch-and-go, things started getting better and her health improved, along with her energy. The doctors told us that she was responding well to treatment and for a while we both looked forward to the day when she could return to work and start enjoying her life again.

But then, a couple of weeks ago, she seemed to decline, so she went back to the hospital for more tests. And now, the envelope resting on the table in front of me will reveal the results of those tests.

I can't take it any longer.

Pulling out a stool from under the worktop, I perch on it and drag the envelope towards me. I stare at it for almost a full minute before sliding the letter out and reading it.

As the words sink in, my world breaks apart even further. I'm surprised an audible crack can't be heard as my heart snaps in two.

My sister is in stage 5 kidney failure and is now on the list for a kidney transplant, which could take up to three years.

Tears blur my vision as I tuck the letter back inside the envelope.

'Couldn't resist, huh?'

I look up to see Clara standing in the doorway to the kitchen in her dressing gown and fluffy pink slippers. She may look a bit goth with her half-shaved head and tattoos, but she loves a bit of pink. Her face is gaunt and pale, her short, black hair lifeless and flat.

I stand up, walk up to her and wrap my arms around her frail body. Tears spill from my eyes, soaking her shoulder. She hugs me back as tightly as her weak arms allow, and strokes my hair.

'It'll be okay,' she says. She reminds me of our grandmother so much, the way she used to stroke our heads when we were sick or upset.

'You said that two years ago,' I say, lifting my head off her shoulder. 'You keep getting worse.'

'Well, at least now I'm in stage 5 I can get a new kidney,' she replies, her voice upbeat and perky, the opposite of what it should be.

'That could take years.'

Clara shrugs. 'Then we wait years.'

'What if you don't last that long?'

Clara laughs. 'Gee, thanks for your faith in me, sis!'

I roll my eyes and smirk. 'You know what I mean. Now you're in stage 5 your symptoms will only get worse, and you'll have to spend more and more time at the hospital on dialysis.'

'You know, I actually don't mind that. Jessica, my nurse, is super cute and I'm pretty sure she fancies me.'

'Well, why wouldn't she? You've always been the gorgeous one.'

We share a smile. Clara walks across to the worktop and sits down on the stool I was sitting on earlier. She plays with the envelope in her hands, turning it over and over.

'I wish I could go with you more often,' I say, even though she knows it's a lie. 'To the hospital, I mean. I don't like the thought of you going through dialysis on your own.' It's not that I don't want to be there for her, but she knows I've been terrified of hospitals since I was a kid after waking up from a routine operation to have my appendix out and finding out my best friend had died suddenly during hers. Amazingly, she'd been there to have her appendix out too. We called ourselves the appendix duo. But something had gone wrong during her surgery, and she never woke up. It's traumatized me ever since.

Then, our grandmother was transferred from the care home to a hospital and died there too. Hospitals, to me, are a place where people go to die. When I step inside one, all I can see and smell is death.

'Don't worry, I'm not going to force you to come with me. You'd hate it there, trust me. There's nothing to do and the Wi-Fi is proper shit. Besides, you need to work. We can't live off thin air, you know. Plus, I told you when all this started that you weren't giving up on your dream career just to stay home and look after me as I wither away. I can take care of myself.' I try and smile at my sister's morbid sense of humour, but I can't find the energy to turn my mouth into a smile. It's not that she makes jokes about dying, but I think she intentionally makes light of the situation so it doesn't feel so soul-crushingly devastating.

'Yes, but...' I stop, realising how pointless it is to argue with my sister. She's so strong and stubborn. She's always pushed me towards my dreams, always told me to reach for the stars, never once complained about her illness or the fact she's had to give up work. That's why I can't bear to admit that I'm failing, that I can't afford all the bills and payments that are coming out of my ears.

'I saw Paula today,' I say solemnly, needing to change the subject, even though it's only marginally better.

'How is she?'

'She was with another woman.' There's no point in me lying to her about that. I don't want Clara to have false hope when it comes to her ex-girlfriend.

Clara sighs. 'Well, I guess that was inevitable. I'm glad she's happy.'

I roll my eyes. 'God, Clara, you can't ever speak bad about anyone, can you? Even Paula, who promised to stick by you when you were first diagnosed but then dumped you as soon as you started getting worse and required more care and couldn't go out drinking with her anymore.'

'I don't blame her. You know that.'

'But you should,' I snap. 'She did a shitty thing to you.'

'I didn't want her to watch me decline. She deserves to live her life, not sit by my bed as I puke into a bucket or am hooked up to a dialysis machine for four hours at a time, three times a week.'

My eyes automatically glance at the machine in the corner of the room. Clara said she'd rather have her treatment at home lately, but now she's in stage 5 she may have to go into hospital for it. It's something we'll have to speak to the doctor about. The thought of more regular trips to the hospital makes my insides squirm.

'Well, *she's* the one who doesn't deserve *you*,' I say, turning to the kettle. 'Tea?'

'No, thanks. I'm going to go back to bed. I have a hospital appointment on Thursday at ten to talk about the results.'

I don't answer straight away. My mind immediately goes to a dark place. My first reaction to going to the hospital is always no, but I can't do that to her. She doesn't even ask me anymore whether I want to go. She just assumes I'll say no because I have to work or come up with some other excuse. The worst thing is that she never makes a big deal about it. She never forces me to go. The only time I went with her was right at the start when we were first given the bad news. After that, I never went back.

'I'll be there,' I say, putting the kettle under the running water to fill.

'Are you sure?'

'Yes,' I reply without pausing. 'I'm coming with you.'

'You're not going to have a panic attack and run out of the hospital screaming that everyone in there is going to die, are you?'

'That only happened once, I'll have you know.' We share a smirk.

Clara stands up. 'You know I love you, right?'

'You know I love you too, left?'

'You're such a dweeb.' Clara shuffles out of the kitchen and back down the hall to her room.

I stay up for another hour, winding down from the chaotic day at work, as well as the results from the hospital. I sip my tea and wonder why my sister is the one who's sick and not me. Why her? Why not me? What's she done to deserve this? I wish there was some way I could take away her pain. Twins are supposed to share everything, and I'd do anything to alleviate her pain.

Anything.

Even if I had to live at a hospital for the rest of my life, if it meant she'd get to live, I'd do it.

CHAPTER THREE

I practically beg Chef Andre to give me the time off to go with Clara to her hospital appointment. It's too important to miss, considering we're talking about possible donors and what her options are for the future. A part of me even wishes he'd say no, that I have no choice but to miss it. I hate myself for thinking like that, too scared to go to a freaking hospital with my sister who needs my support. What the hell is wrong with me? This isn't about me. This is about Clara and making sure she grows old with me so we can have matching walking canes and bitch and moan about the weather while we're sitting in our matching wheelchairs with a warm blanket over our laps. I don't want to grow old alone.

In the end, Chef Andre relents and agrees for me to attend the appointment, but it means poor Luke has to come into work early and do all my prep work for the evening shift. He doesn't mind because he's a decent human being and isn't a sadistic, vile butthole like Chef Andre. I said I'd buy Luke a drink next time we go out somewhere, although the chances of that happening are slim, considering I don't go out anywhere, but I like to give the guy hope.

Clara is notably quiet in the taxi on the way to the hospital, as am I, but for different reasons. She stares out of the window, watching the tall buildings rush past, her hands folded neatly on her lap, a clean tissue clasped in her left palm; a security habit she's had since she was six. She even goes to bed holding a tissue. Sometimes during the night she'll let go of it and then I'll find numerous screwed-up tissues behind the bed or tucked under the pillows, but mostly she holds onto the tissue all the way through the night, never letting it go until the morning.

'You okay?' I ask, even though I know it's a stupid question.

Clara takes a deep breath, turns to me and grasps my hand. 'Thank you for coming with me,' she says, ignoring my stupid question. She's used to my stupidness by now. 'I know how difficult this is for you.' She reaches out and tucks a strand of my black hair behind my left ear. I have long hair. That's the main difference between us. She chopped hers off when she was twelve after one of our many squabbles. I think the words, 'I don't want to look like you anymore!' were shouted and then the scissors came out. I may have been the one to hand them to her, but she was the one who hacked off her hair without making any attempt to ensure it was level. Our grandmother was furious and marched Clara straight to the hairdressers to get her wonky chop sorted out. She's had short hair ever since, but it suits her, and long hair suits me. Weird.

'I wouldn't want to be anywhere else,' I reply with a smile.

'Maybe lying on a beach in Spain with a cocktail?'

'Hmm, yeah, actually I'd rather be there. If I had a chance to go there right now, I'd leave you behind in a heartbeat.'

We share a giggle and spend the rest of the journey to the hospital in silence, holding hands. My heart feels like it's trying to break through my sternum and I'm focusing really hard to not hyperventilate. There doesn't seem to be enough air to fill my lungs. I even open a car window, but it doesn't help.

As the signs for the hospital start popping up, I think I might throw up. All I can think about is myself and how I'm feeling. God, I'm the worst sister in the world. I'm afraid, too scared to face the reality of the situation. Being in this place just reminds me that my sister is dying, and I'd rather just forget that fact, thank you very much. Hospitals are where people go to die.

Clara is the one who's going through this, who is slowly withering away and has to put up with all the tests and needles and horrible symptoms, yet I'm the one who makes such a fuss about it. I wish I was as strong as she is.

The taxi drops us off at the front doors. My legs are so jelly-like, it's a wonder I can even put one foot in front of the other. The smell hits me like a punch to the gut as I walk into reception. The first thing I see is someone in a wheelchair with blood on their forehead.

Nope.

I spin on my heels and rush outside as a wave of panic washes over me, taking my breath away. I find a bin and lean against it for support. Clara appears at my side moments later. I feel like I'm failing her as my eyes swim with tears.

'I'm sorry,' I manage to choke out.

'Don't be sorry. It's not your fault.'

Sometimes I wish Clara would be more aggressive with me. She's always been the calm one and I've always been hot-headed. It's not like I'm always up for an argument, but for once I wish she'd tell me off.

'Do you want me to get you a wheelchair and shove you through those doors or...' She breaks off from her joke as I raise my head and give her a weak smile.

'No, thanks. I'm okay.'

'Are you sure? Because you look almost as bad as the time you ate that weird-smelling fish you brought home from the restaurant after promising there was nothing wrong with it.'

I straighten up and take a deep breath, only just realising how bad the bin I've been leaning against smells. I move away and wipe my hands on my jeans. 'Okay, I'm ready.'

Clara extends her hand and holds it out for me. I take it and she leads me through the maze of corridors to the waiting area.

HERE WE ARE, sitting in the waiting room of death. I've already paced up and down the corridor at least twenty times before a random patient gave me the evils, so I scurried back to the chair next to Clara. She's reading a book on her Kindle, some fantasy romance, I think, about dragons that's apparently all the rage, whereas I can't stop staring at the poster on the wall opposite.

So, you have chronic kidney disease... Let's face it together.

Then the poster lists all the various ways the hospital can

support its patients. There's no mention of the word *dying* or anything morbid like that. It's full of positivity and uplifting options, designed to make people feel supported and understood, but perhaps I'm reading it wrong because all it does is make me want to lunge forward, rip the goddamn poster off the wall and rip it into a dozen pieces, then set fire to them and watch them burn.

'Britt, you coming?'

I look up to see Clara and a doctor looking at me inquisitively. 'Sorry,' I say. 'Yes.'

I stand up on wobbly legs and follow along behind them as the doctor and Clara swap pleasantries and share a laugh. Sometimes my sister's upbeat attitude is unfathomable. In fact, it's also annoying. Why can't she be miserable and moody like most people would be in her situation? Somehow, I manage to keep my panic at bay as an alarm sounds from somewhere. Wait... does that mean someone has died? I scan the area, searching for the answer, but before I know it, we're at the door.

CHAPTER FOUR

We enter the small office, and the doctor closes the door. She's the same doctor Clara's been seeing for the past two years. Doctor Layton. Middle-aged, attractive, and with a brilliant bedside manner. I've only met her once though.

'Good to see you, Brittany,' she says with a smile.

'And you,' I respond, although I'd prefer it if I never saw her again.

Clara takes a seat, and I do the same next to her. My palms are so sweaty that I'm leaving damp patches on my light-blue jeans whenever I wipe them. Doctor Layton sits at her desk and types a couple of words on her keyboard, activating the computer.

'So,' she finally says, 'unfortunately, Clara's tests have confirmed that her chronic kidney disease has now escalated to level 5, and while we're not surprised this is the case, it's certainly not the situation we were hoping for. However, we've already put you on the donor list and—'

'How quickly can you find a donor?' I interject.

Doctor Layton smiles, most likely expecting this question from me. 'At the moment, the typical waiting time from a deceased donor is two to three years.'

I almost laugh but manage to cover it up with a cough. 'Two to three *years?*' I glance at Clara, who hasn't made a sound yet. 'That seems like such a long time. How long does my sister have until her kidneys completely shut down and kill her?'

'It's difficult to say, but I believe we can control Clara's symptoms with dialysis three times per week and upping and adjusting her medication.'

I slump back in my chair. My heartbeat is pounding in my ears, and I can barely think straight.

'However, there is a quicker way to receive a kidney transplant,' says Doctor Layton.

I sit up straight as if I've just been electrocuted. She could have led with that comment. 'What is it?'

'To find a suitable living donor. In that case, it can take only between three and six months to go through the tests and procedures to prepare for the transplant.'

'Okay, so let's do that,' I say abruptly.

Doctor Layton puts her hand up, signalling me to calm down. I want to slap it away. 'I understand you want this to be done quickly, but we must do what is in the best interest of Clara.' Doctor Layton looks at her.

'Surely, what's in the best interest of Clara is to live,' I answer quickly.

'Okay, Britt, I think you've said enough,' says Clara, leaning forwards and placing a hand on my arm.

'Sorry,' I say quietly. I don't mean to be rude, but why does no one seem to be taking this as seriously as me?

'Now, as I was saying, finding a living donor will speed things up, but finding a match is quite complicated and difficult, unless...' Doctor Layton glances from me to Clara then back to me. 'You're an identical twin.'

My breath catches in my throat. 'M-Me?'

'Yes. Research shows that having an identical twin provides a unique circumstance in which post-transplantation immunosuppression can be withdrawn because there's little risk of organ rejection due to the donor and recipient organ antigens being identical. In other words, there's minimal risk that the organ will be rejected. Obviously, this is a big operation for both the donor and the recipient and will consist of several months' worth of tests, but because of you being identical twins, this may mean we can reduce the waiting time even further. Now, I can't force you to go along this route, but it is the quickest way that Clara will receive a kidney.'

Silence fills the small room. I'm supposed to say something. I'm supposed to leap out of my chair and say, 'I'll do it!' But my body isn't responding. It's just frozen to the chair. This is it. This is the answer to Clara getting better. Me. I have a chance to save my sister from suffering.

Clara nudges me. 'Britt? Are you—'

'I'll do it,' I say, cutting her off yet again before my brain catches up to what's just come out of my mouth.

Clara squeezes my arm. 'I think what my sister means to say is that we'll go away and think about it and—'

'What's there to think about? I'm a perfect match for you. Let's start the tests today. Right now.' I look at Clara and back at the doctor, perplexed at why neither of them is jumping at this chance.

'Brittany, you need to understand the risks involved with the operation and living with one kidney, as well as knowing the consequences of anything going wrong,' says Doctor Layton.

I know what that means. She's just not saying the actual words.

My eyes swim with tears and my voice shakes as I say, 'I get it, okay. I get it, but my sister is dying and if I can give her a kidney and stop her from dying rather than watch her suffer for the next two or three years waiting for another donor who may or may not be as perfect a match as me, then I will do it.'

Clara sighs. 'Britt, think about this. Please. This is a massive operation, and I know how hospitals make you feel. You'll need time off work. You can't afford to give up on your career right now.'

'I don't care about my career.'

'Yes, you do. And so do I.'

'Why are we even arguing about this?' I turn to the doctor. 'You agree that this is the best way forward, yes?'

Doctor Layton smiles at us. 'Let me give you all the information sheets for you to both read through. I agree with Clara that this decision can't be rushed, and obviously both parties must be on board before we can proceed.'

'But I'm saying I'm on board.'

'But I'm not,' responds Clara.

I have never wanted to slap my sister so hard in my life. Not even when she broke the head off my favourite Barbie doll.

'May we have a moment to speak alone?' I ask the doctor.

'Of course. I'll be back in a few minutes.' Doctor Layton stands up and gives Clara what looks like a sympathetic smile before walking out of the room. The moment the door is closed I turn to my sister.

'What's going on? Why don't you want my kidney?'

'It's not that I don't want it, I just think you haven't thought about it for long enough. It's a big operation. It will set you back for several months while you recover. It could impact your health in the future and even put you at risk of not being able to have children, not to mention your intense phobia of hospitals and operations.'

I pause for a moment. 'I'll be fine. I'll get over it.'

'You're just saying that—'

'No, I'm not just saying that. Please, Clara. Please. It's not going to affect my health. I'm perfectly healthy. I'm not going to be missing out on anything like drinking because I don't go out partying as it is, and I could do with a few weeks off work.' At this point, the mounting debt on my shoulders doesn't even appear as a blip on my radar screen.

Clara sighs. 'That may be, but your career means everything to you—'

'No, *you* mean everything to me. You're dying, Clara. Who knows how much time you have left, but if you agree to this you can have a new kidney within the next few months instead of possibly waiting years and getting so sick and weak that your body rejects the kidney when you finally get it. At least this way, you know your body will accept it. If you won't do it for yourself, then do it for me. I can't live without you, okay? I'm selfish. There, I said it. I don't want my sister to die and leave me all alone in this world. Trust me, I wouldn't last long. I'd probably forget to eat and die from starvation within two weeks. Yes, I'm scared of having the operation. I'll admit it. But I'm nowhere near as scared as I am of losing you. Please.'

Silence envelopes the room; the only noise is the ticking

clock on the wall above the doctor's desk. I watch the clock, willing time to hurry up.

A knock appears at the door.

'Come in,' says Clara.

Doctor Layton pops her head round the door. 'Everything okay in here?'

'Yes. We've come to a decision,' says Clara. 'I accept Brittany's kidney.'

CHAPTER FIVE

Time moves quickly on the lead-up to the transplant. Over the next four months, Clara and I go through various blood tests, EKGs, cancer screening, x-rays, lung-function tests, dental evaluation as well as mental and emotional health tests to ensure we're both prepared for the operation. I can honestly say it's the most stressful, terrifying and arduous ordeal I've ever experienced, but I stay strong for Clara, only breaking down in floods of tears behind closed doors at the thought of going through complex surgery.

So many unwanted and ridiculous thoughts race through my mind. What if I don't wake up? What if Clara doesn't wake up? Hell, what if we both don't wake up? What if something goes wrong and the whole procedure doesn't even work? What if they remove something other than my kidney?

During the emotional health tests, I keep it together and basically lie on every form, saying that I'm happy to have the procedure, I have no concerns and am of a sound mind. It's all a front. I'm surprised the mental health nurse who questions me doesn't see through my lies. She just smiles and reassures me, putting my excessive sweating and shaking down to nerves about my sister.

However, other than my blood pressure being a little high (which isn't shocking, considering, and it's still high even though they re-test a few times, putting it down to nerves because I'm perfectly healthy otherwise) and I need a replacement filling (again, not surprising considering the number of sweet treats I eat at work), I'm in excellent health and the doctor has no concerns regarding the transplant. Both Clara and I pass the health tests and progress through the other various stages and screenings with no issues.

We keep hearing from multiple doctors and nurses that we're lucky we're identical twins because it's very rare to find such a perfect donor match, although I want to reply that if we were that lucky, we wouldn't have to be going through this procedure in the first place.

My work (and by work, I mean, Chef Andre) has been less than helpful regarding my numerous hospital visits and tests, making the whole experience even more stressful to the point I get dizzy before every hospital test. He ensures I work extra time to make up for any hours taken to go to hospital, and constantly mentions how much of a drain it is that I keep disappearing at important moments.

Luke reckons I should report him, but the procedure for workplace bullying and harassment is to speak to either the HR department or the boss, neither of which I can do, because we don't have an HR department in this restaurant and Chef Andre is the boss. I have no other option, and even if I did, I honestly can't deal with the drama right now, so I bite my tongue and get on with it, silently seething.

However, as the day of the transplant draws closer, Chef

Andre kicks things up a notch by calling me into his small back office at the restaurant. I'm already a bag of nerves, barely eating due to stress and constantly feeling as if I'm sprinting around a racetrack, unable to catch my breath, so his sudden wish to speak to me does nothing but make me feel worse.

'I'll get straight to the point, pastry chef. I am afraid that I do not have the capacity to have you off sick for the next few weeks while you recover. We have a very busy schedule ahead with numerous bookings. We're full to the brim for the next month, and there's no one who can take over your duties. Luke is not ready to handle that type of responsibility.'

I frown, staring at him like he's just spoken a different language. I've done my best over the past four months to get Luke up to scratch so he can deal with my workload. He's improved a lot, but his standard just isn't quite there yet.

'I'm sorry, Chef, but what are you saying?'

'I'd rather not have to say it.'

I clench my teeth. 'You're refusing to give me time off?'

He doesn't reply.

'You can't be serious!'

'I can assure you, I am.'

'That's immoral! It isn't like I'm taking sick leave to have a nose job. I'm donating a kidney to save my dying sister.' How can this be happening now, having spent the past four months preparing for this day, and now my arrogant boss thinks he can swoop in and just say no?

'Yes, but unfortunately under UK employment law, an employee is not legally entitled to paid time off work specifically for a planned operation unless it is medically necessary and falls under the standard rules for sick leave. Your operation may not be cosmetic, but it is elective, and so, there is no legal right to time off work for it.' It sounds to me like Chef Andre has been a snivelling weasel and has been researching the rules to throw it in my face at the opportune time. Dick.

I want to argue with him that it might be elective for me to have this operation, but it's not for my sister, who needs my kidney to live, but if I say that, I know what his response will be; Clara doesn't work here and, therefore, doesn't fall under his employee law.

'I am very sorry about your situation. You leave me no other choice. I must find a replacement for you, which means you won't have a job here when you have recovered.' His words may sound sincere, but I know for a fact he's enjoying every moment of this, watching me squirm, just waiting for me to have a go at him so he has cause to fire me on the spot.

'This is outrageous!' I want to scream expletives at him, but I manage to choke them down in time.

Chef Andre stands up a little taller. 'Pastry chef, if you don't calm down, I will fire you on the spot without providing you any paid sick leave or giving you a reference. Do you understand?'

I take a breath and bite my lip so hard that it hurts.

'Now,' he says, 'I'd be happy to keep you on if perhaps you can rearrange your little operation for a couple of months' time when we're less busy.'

'My sister is dying, you mother-fu—'

A knock at the door luckily saves me from spitting every vicious word I know at my boss. Luke pops his head round the door. 'I'm sorry, Chef, but there's something you should see to in the kitchen.'

Chef Andre nods. 'Thank you, junior chef. We're done here.'

'Actually, no, we're not,' I snap. Luke pales at my stern voice, having never heard it before, and ducks out of the room while Chef Andre turns the colour of beetroot.

I storm out of the office, past Luke and into the busy kitchen. Luke and Chef Andre follow behind.

'Everyone, I'd like your attention for a moment, please,' I say to the room.

All heads turn in my direction, the kitchen as silent as it's ever been before. You could easily hear a grain of salt dropping to the floor.

'As you know, my twin sister has terminal chronic kidney disease, and she has no other choice but to get a kidney transplant. I am donating her my kidney in two days' time to save her life. However, Chef Andre has just taken me aside and has told me that I cannot have the time off for this operation, which has been scheduled for nearly four months now. He is forcing me to choose between keeping my job here or saving my sister's life.' At this point, several of the chefs audibly gasp, cover their mouths in horror or turn and stare open-mouthed at Chef Andre, who is shrinking further and further into a nearby corner. I'm not finished quite yet, so I continue, my voice loud and commandeering across the kitchen even though my knees feel like they're about to buckle.

'Now, I haven't yet given him my answer, but I'm sure you can all imagine what it is.' I turn and glare at Chef Andre as I say, 'You can take this job and shove it up where the sun doesn't shine.' I feel somewhat proud of this line, as it was something my grandmother used to say instead of the more vulgar version.

More gasps erupt, followed by several head nods and murmurs of 'Oh my God, I can't believe she just said that.'

I'm on a roll. Nothing can stop me now. The floodgates are open and there's no stopping me.

'While I'm on the subject, I would rather stick hot pokers in my eyes than work for you any longer. You are a sexist, racist bully, and if anyone else feels the same way, then feel free to follow me out the door.' With that, and before my throat seizes up completely and I lose my nerve, I turn and storm out of the kitchen. As I do, a round of applause erupts, which makes my heart swell with pride.

I don't care to turn and look back.

I should have done that a long time ago.

I rush into the changing area and start grabbing my things. Polly, Lucy and Genieve, three young female chefs, join me, giving me another clap as the doors swing close.

'Well done, girl!' exclaims Polly, enveloping me into a hug.

My face burns hot. 'It felt good, I won't lie. Have you all just left your jobs too?'

All three of them nod.

Now I feel bad.

'I'm really sorry. I got a bit carried away. I didn't mean for anyone else to lose their jobs.'

Lucy waves my comment off. 'Pfft, I've been secretly applying for other jobs for weeks now. I got a call back the other day and they offered me the position. I haven't accepted yet, but now, guess who's going to be the new sous chef at The Bistro?'

Poppy and Genieve gather around Lucy and congratulate her.

'That's great news. Congratulations,' I say.

'I can't believe that dickhead made you choose between

your job and your sister,' says Poppy, shaking her head. 'He's seriously sick.'

'He needs to be reported to HR or something,' adds Geneive.

'We don't have an HR department here,' I reply.

'Yes, but... surely there's something we can do.'

I sigh. 'I know I should look into it, but I've got a lot going on with the transplant coming up and now having to search for a new job. Hopefully, me outing him like that will be enough to put him back in his box.'

The girls all nod their agreement.

'I hope the transplant goes okay,' says Lucy, giving me another hug. 'I'll keep an eye out for any pastry chef jobs going and let you know.'

'Thanks, I appreciate that.'

'You've got my number, yeah?'

'Yeah, thanks.'

Darcy pops her head round the changing room doors. 'Um, word of warning, Chef Andre is on a rampage. I suggest you make yourself scarce. Well done, girls. You're all braver than I am. Brittany... you're a badass bitch. I love it.' She disappears again.

I quickly say goodbye to the other three at the door and then walk home. My heart rate still hasn't slowed. I'm functioning solely on adrenaline. My words jumble around in my head on repeat. Did I seriously just call my boss a sexist and a racist? Oh, and a bully? He is all those things and more, but what the hell have I just got myself into? I know what he's like. He's vindictive and manipulative. I know for a fact he won't let me get away with humiliating him like that.

Then, the reality of what I've done hits me like a freight

train and it makes me stop mid-stride in the middle of the pavement.

I have no job and no way of paying any of the bills, rent or food for the foreseeable future until I'm recovered enough to start working again. The adrenaline of the confrontation is wearing off, revealing just how much I have screwed myself over with my outburst.

But how else could I have handled it? He made it clear he wasn't giving me paid time off work and I wouldn't have a job upon my return. There was no other way of dealing with it, not from my point of view, but now I'm severely screwed.

I have no job.

I doubt he'll give me a reference to help get another.

In a few days' time, I'm going to be undergoing a kidney transplant to save my sister's life.

I might not wake up.

She might not wake up.

And I'm terrified about what the future will bring.

CHAPTER SIX

It's the night before we're due to go into hospital to begin the final lead-up to the transplant, scheduled for the day after tomorrow at noon. Tomorrow, we'll both be admitted to the hospital where we'll undergo a series of tests, meet with our transplant team, discuss the procedure in detail, receive instructions on fasting before surgery, and potentially have a catheter inserted (something I am in no way looking forward to). The focus of tomorrow is to ensure we are both medically ready for the transplant and to address any final concerns we may have.

To be honest, I could come up with a list as tall as me about the concerns I have, but I can't think that way right now. Clara and I are trying to enjoy our last night together in our flat for the next week or so and are watching a cheesy romantic comedy film, but neither of us is really focusing on it. I made us a healthy dinner of rice, vegetables and grilled chicken, but Clara has only managed a few nibbles, and I've left most of it too. My stomach is in knots, and I'd kill for a glass of wine right now just to settle my nerves, but I've had to cut out all sorts of food and drinks for the past four months, including alcohol and excess salt and sugar, focusing on whole foods and lots of vegetables instead. I've also had to increase my water intake, something I'm exceptionally bad at keeping up with, then wonder why I have a headache at the end of the day. This is also our last meal before we're forced to eat hospital food, which I know for a fact is always bad.

The thought of the operation is bad enough, but staying in the hospital overnight, for more than one night, is almost worse than the procedure itself. While I'm there, what if someone dies? If an alarm goes off, what does that mean?

Clara smiles at a funny part of the film, but then sighs.

'You okay?' I ask, my mouth so dry I have to take a sip of water.

'I miss Paula. That's all. Kind of wish she were here right now.' She looks up at me and gasps. 'Not that I don't appreciate you being here, but... you know, you're going through it too. We're both going to be out of commission for a few weeks while we recover, and we don't have anyone to help us.'

'We don't need help. I'll be able to handle everything.'

Clara smiles. 'I know you will. You're my hero. You know, I've been thinking about a lot of things lately, including what we're going to do once all this is over. I know you're focused on your career right now, and I don't want you to ever give up on that, but...' Clara bites her lip, her telltale sign that she's struggling to get her words out. She's afraid of telling me.

'But what?' I ask.

'But I want to have children one day, Brittany. I know

you don't, and that's absolutely fine, but I do. I doubt my body will ever be in the position to carry a child, but I think I'd like to adopt one.'

I avoid eye contact with my sister while she's talking about my career because I haven't told her I walked out of my job a few days ago. I told her I was given extra leave to prepare for the transplant. I've no idea what to do when the time comes to go back to work, but it's on my to-do list to find a new job while I'm recovering. I have no idea what's going to happen or how I'm going to pay the bills, but I have to focus on one thing at a time, the first being getting us both through this operation and surviving a stay in hospital.

'I think that's great, Clara. I really do. If you want to adopt kids, then go for it. I'll support you with whatever you want. And, once I run and own my own restaurant, you can always eat for free when you come to visit with the kids.'

Clara laughs. 'That's perfect. Agreed, but I need you to promise me something.'

'Anything.'

'Promise me, no matter what happens tomorrow, or in the future, that you'll reach for the stars. You'll do whatever it takes to make your dreams come true. I want you to be happy, Britt.'

'I'll never be happy without you in my life. You know that, right?'

'Of course you will.'

'Why are you making it sound as if you're dying tomorrow?'

'I'm not saying that. I'm just... I guess I just want you to be prepared for whatever happens. That's all.'

A silence stretches between us. It's so big that I feel as if we're standing on different sides of a vast canyon. Clara turns her attention back to the film, but I can't focus on a single word. Why does it feel as if my sister just said goodbye to me?

CHAPTER SEVEN

As expected, I don't sleep at all. Every time I'm about to give in to exhaustion, my body jolts itself awake as if I'm falling off a cliff. I listen to the cars zooming past, horns blaring, the chatter of drunken residents stumbling back home after a night out and, eventually, the chirping of the birds who have made their home in the large oak tree next to our building.

At five o'clock, I decide I've been lying awake long enough, so I get up and take a long, hot shower to distract myself from my caffeine cravings and empty stomach. I can still eat today, but the thought of eating isn't one I relish, considering I can't keep anything down.

I can't believe that it'll all be over soon. It feels as if Clara and I have been on this transplant journey for years, but it's only been four months. After tomorrow, Clara and I can begin to rebuild our lives. We have each other and that's all that matters.

But I don't know if everything will be okay. Clara keeps saying that it will be and is already talking about her plans to return to work, but I can't think that far ahead because, when

I do, all I see is a murky haze. There's nothing in my future, other than the impending doom of this operation and the very real risk of not walking out of the hospital after tomorrow.

I don't know how I'll survive if anything happens to Clara. If I die, she'll be fine because she's strong and she'll have a brand-new, working kidney to see her out for the rest of her life. She can start a family. Whether that's with a partner or not, I don't know, but Clara's always been very independent. She's never needed me whereas I've always needed her. Even as kids, Clara was always the first one to break apart and speak to new people, make friends and socialise. I clung to her for as long as I could, but eventually I had to let her go. Our grandmother told me that Clara loved me but it wasn't healthy for us to be joined at the hip forever. I disagreed. She even pushed me to make friends of my own, but no matter how hard I tried, my friends were never as close to me as Clara was.

Clara and I leave on time and arrive at the hospital where I somehow manage to make it through the doors without having a panic attack. We're directed to a private room to change while we wait for the doctor to do his rounds. Our blood pressure is taken, we're asked a few questions relating to our overall health and well-being, and the transplant procedure is explained again in detail.

Clara is told there's a high chance her new kidney will begin working within a day of the transplant, something which is less likely to happen with a deceased donor's kidney. The doctor is very positive about the transplant, explaining that due to my good health, there's less risk of infection or any unforeseen diseases transferring from me to Clara. Her two non-working kidneys will not be removed, which seems crazy to me, but since they aren't causing pain or infection, they will eventually grow smaller after being disconnected from the blood supply.

We will be in separate operating theatres. My left kidney will be removed via a small incision made in my lower abdomen and then transplanted into Clara straight away. The whole procedure will take between two and four hours. The doctor talks about the various blood vessels that are to be connected, and the multiple procedures involved, then goes through the details regarding post-op. We'll need to stay in hospital between three and six days, depending on any unforeseen issues or recovery.

As he talks, I begin to feel a bit light-headed, most likely due to lack of food because despite being offered food here, I can't stomach it.

Once the doctor has left, Clara and I wait in our room on separate beds. There are other patients here behind drawn curtains, and every cough or monitor alarm makes my blood pressure skyrocket. It takes every ounce of resolve not to sprint from the room and down the corridor in my hospital gown.

We're dressed in the normal ugly hospital gowns, and we share a laugh, saying that it's the first time we've dressed the same since we were twelve.

That night, I manage to get maybe two hours of sleep, but it's broken and full of the most awful dreams imaginable. In the end, I lie awake and read Clara's Kindle, which I pinch from her bedside table while she snores.

The next morning, it's go time. We're not allowed any food now until after the operation. I haven't eaten for nearly forty-eight hours, but it means that when I do retch out of pure fear, nothing but bile or water comes up.

Clara is lying on her bed, reading her Kindle, whereas I'm pacing up and down in front of her, following a green line on the floor.

'Britt, you're actually making me dizzy,' says Clara. 'Will you sit down and relax, please?'

'Sorry.' I slide my bum onto the edge of her bed next to her feet, but my knees bounce up and down. If I stay still, the fear threatens to take over.

'It's fine. I know you're nervous.'

'And you're not?'

'Of course I am, but everything will be okay. We're in safe hands.'

I nod and smile at my sister's enthusiasm and positive outlook. 'I just can't wait for all this to be over,' I say with a sigh.

'Same. I'd kill for a cheeseburger right now.'

We share a giggle just as a nurse opens the door and walks in. 'Brittany, it's time to head to theatre now. Clara, another nurse will be along soon to take you.'

'Thank you.' Clara looks at me, leaning forwards to grab my trembling hands. 'See you on the other side,' she says.

My eyes swim with tears as I get up and lean across the bed, hugging my sister as tight as I'm allowed. She hugs me back. We cling to each other, neither one of us wanting to be the one to break the contact. But eventually, like always, she's the first to break away.

'See you soon,' I say with a wobbly voice.

'You know I love you, right?' she says.

'You know I love you too, left?'

We share a smile. I take one last look at my twin, then follow the nurse out the door towards operating theatre one, wondering if it's the last time I'll ever see her.

CHAPTER EIGHT

In the blink of an eye, it's over. I'm groggy as hell when I come to, but the lights are dim, and a soothing voice welcomes me back to reality. The kind nurse who held my hand while the general anaesthetic was being administered sits next to me, talking to me and checking my vital statistics.

A gentle beeping emanates from the machine next to me. I blink my eyes several times, attempting to focus my vision, but keeping my eyes open feels like a monumental effort. My body feels heavy, weak. I'm not sure I can even lift my arm to scratch the itch on my nose. The nurse is speaking to me, but I miss half of what she says because all my brain is thinking about is Clara.

Is she out of theatre yet? Is she okay?

Oh my God, I'm alive. I made it. I didn't die on the operating table, but I can't rest or relax until I know that Clara made it too.

I open my eyes and then lick my lips, summoning some much-needed moisture. The nurse picks up a glass of water and a straw and holds the tip of the straw to my cracked lips. I take a small sip. The water feels so freaking good. My mouth feels as if something has died in it. I'm in serious need of a toothbrush and mouthwash.

'C-Clara,' I say.

'She's fine, love. She's literally just come out of surgery now and is still under anaesthetic, but the transplant went well. The doctor is very happy. She will be monitored closely over the next few days, but everything went according to plan, as did your procedure. How are you feeling?'

I shuffle on the bed, attempting to move my body. 'Heavy and stiff,' I say, 'but pretty good, considering.'

'It will take a few hours for the anaesthetic to wear off, so you'll feel groggy for a while. You've been put on some strong painkillers. If you're in a lot of pain still, then press the blue call button on the side and either I or another nurse will come and look at you. The doctor should be around in the next hour or so to do your post-op check.'

'Thank you,' I say. 'Can you tell me when Clara's awake?'

'Of course.'

I still don't relax fully, but it's a step in the right direction and the crushing weight of fear lessens ever so slightly, enabling me to close my eyes and snooze.

THREE HOURS LATER, I've managed to eat some dry toast and keep it down. I remember when I had my appendix out, I'd suffered a bad reaction to general anaesthetic. I was nauseous for several hours after the operation, but luckily, this time the anti-sickness that was administered seems to be working. Plus, I don't have the added stress of finding out my friend died on the operating table. I just need to see Clara, then all will be well.

Clara is awake and I've been told I can see her soon, so I'm just waiting for the go-ahead from the doctor. My eyes are closed. I'm still drowsy from the drugs as I listen to the busy sounds of the hospital around me. The beeping of machines, low voices of doctors and nurses and footsteps up and down the corridors. It used to fill me with dread and mind-numbing fear, but my body and mind are slowly accepting the noises and smells are normal things, and they're more like background noise now.

But then, a loud alarm sounds, jolting me out of my relaxed state and catapulting my anxiety to almighty levels. It takes my breath away and I can't get it back.

Loud, quick footsteps echo down the corridor.

My eyes fling open.

What's going on?

A couple of nurses and a doctor rush past my room as the alarm continues to sound, but a few seconds later, it switches off, plummeting the hospital into an eerie silence as everyone contemplates what the alarm might mean.

I take a deep breath and lean back against the pillows, the sound still vibrating through my body. I try and relax again, try and get some rest, but something deep inside my soul is wrong. I can't relax, not after that. The background noise of the hospital is now on high-volume, and I can't block it out no matter how hard I try.

Something doesn't feel right.

My heart is beating so fast that my monitor alarm goes off and a nurse I don't recognise rushes in to check my vital signs.

'Everything okay?' she asks. 'Your heart is racing.'

'The alarm that just sounded. What's going on?'

The nurse checks my blood pressure and adjusts something on the monitor. 'I'm sure it's nothing to worry about.'

'Can you check on my sister, Clara Young?'

The nurse's eyes blink several times, and she avoids eye contact with me. 'Of course. Try and relax, okay?'

The nurse leaves the room, and I focus my attention on the monitor I'm hooked up to, watching my pulse beep in time to my heartbeat. I wait several minutes for the nurse to return and tell me how Clara is doing, but she doesn't, so I push the call button, my pulse almost deafening in my ears.

Four long minutes later, another nurse comes in.

'I need someone to tell me if my sister is okay,' I say, a harsh tone to my voice, despite it wobbling.

The nurse smiles. 'I'm sure everything's fine,' she says.

'People keep telling me that, but I'd rather *know* if everything is fine.' I take a deep breath. It's not the nurse's fault if she doesn't know and I mustn't take out my frustration on her. 'Please,' I say with emphasis. 'Can I go and see her? The doctor said I could.'

'Um, I'm not sure that's possible at the moment, but I'll get someone to come and... and... I'll be right back.'

I sigh heavily as she scurries out of the room. I need to see Clara. The anxiety of being apart from her is growing by the second and I can't quell it. I lift my arm, grasp the thin blanket covering my legs and pull it off, but my legs are weak, and I only make it as far as sitting on the edge of the bed with my feet on the floor before the doctor walks in.

'Where do you think you're going?' he asks, picking up my chart from the bottom of the bed.

'I have asked two different nurses to tell me if my sister is okay, but no one is saying anything.'

The doctor sighs, replacing the chart. 'Brittany, I'm afraid I have some bad news regarding your sister.'

'Bad news? What bad news? I was told the operation was a success and she was in recovery three hours ago. Was that what the alarm was?'

'The transplant was a complete success. Your sister came round from the anaesthetic, but then, I'm afraid to say, she had a massive brain haemorrhage. It's extremely rare, but it can happen, as you remember from the risk sheet we gave you both.'

My mouth is dry again and no matter how many times I lick my lips, I can't summon enough moisture. I gulp and cough, eventually managing to ask, 'Is she okay?'

The doctor looks at me, places a hand on my leg and sighs. 'Brittany, I'm terribly sorry to tell you, but... Clara passed away twenty-one minutes ago. She had a DNR on her medical records. I'm very sorry. It was a tragic and unexpected reaction to the transplant. The new kidney was working perfectly. Her death had nothing to do with your kidney.'

The room swims in and out of focus. All the oxygen is sucked out. I stare at the doctor. He can't have just said that. Clara can't be dead. If Clara is dead, then why am I still here? Why am I alive? Without Clara, my other half... I should have died with her. It makes no sense as to why I'm still breathing. She's my lifeline, my soulmate.

'Doctor, I... I don't understand. My sister is dead?'

'I'm sorry.'

'But... But... you said... everyone said there was little risk involved, that because we're identical twins there's a higher-than-average chance of nothing going wrong. This doesn't make sense. It doesn't make any sense!' My voice has risen, the panic clear. I grasp the bed covers either side of me and squeeze them between clenched fists. What I feared would happen has happened. Did I cause this by worrying about it too much? Did I sentence her to death by my own stupid phobia?

'You're lying,' I say quietly. 'You have to be lying.'

The doctor stands up. 'Brittany, I'm very sorry.'

'Why didn't you try and save her?'

'The DNR means—'

'I know what it means,' I snap. I'm doing it again. Getting angry at people even though it's not their fault. My grandmother and Clara taught me better than this, but it's hard to do right now when my whole reason for living has been taken away.

I gulp in some air, but it's not enough. The alarm on the monitor next to me starts beeping as my heart rate and blood pressure shoot up. A nurse rushes in to assist the doctor, who asks her to bring some sedatives to help calm me down.

'No! No, I want to see Clara. I want to see my sister right now.' I fling back the covers again and manoeuvre my legs off the side of the bed, my bare feet skimming the cold floor. I go to stand but as soon as I put weight through my legs, a sharp pain erupts in my lower abdomen.

The nurse rushes forwards and places a hand on my shoulder, gently pushing me down. 'Brittany, I think it's important that you remain in bed. You're in shock and still in recovery.'

'I need to see my sister,' I repeat slowly as if speaking to a child. 'Please, just... fetch me a wheelchair.'

The nurse glances at the doctor, who nods.

'I'll be right back,' she says, leaving the room.

The doctor and I are alone in the room. 'Again, I'm very sorry.'

I refuse to look at him. 'Would this have happened if she'd had a kidney from someone else?'

'It's impossible to say. With your kidney, she had the highest chance of survival and recovery. As I said, the kidney was working perfectly. She died from a brain bleed that was unforeseen. It had nothing to do with your kidney.'

The nurse returns, pushing a wheelchair. Wordlessly, she helps me into it, then pushes me out the door and down the hospital corridor. All around me people mill about. Some are doctors and nurses, others are patients or family members. No one seems to care that I have just lost a piece of my soul. The fact I'm still breathing is baffling me. That's why I'm certain there's been some sort of mistake. Clara can't be dead. I need to see her for myself.

The nurse stops outside a room. 'She's in here underneath a sheet. We have left her in here for now, but she'll be moved shortly to the hospital mortuary. I'll wheel you in and leave you to say goodbye, then come and collect you in five minutes.'

I don't respond. I just stare blankly at the door handle, convinced this is all some sort of sick joke. She pushes open the door, then wheels me inside the room. The smell hits me without warning. It's something I've experienced before. I know it well. Death. Yet again, a hospital has taken someone important to me but left me alive to suffer through the pain alone.

A white sheet is draped across a body lying on the bed. The outline of her shape is quite clear. I can tell it's her under there, but it's not enough. The nurse parks my wheelchair on the left side of the bed, then silently leaves the room.

I sit for a few seconds, fighting back nausea and dizziness. It's most likely due to being up and about so soon after waking up from surgery, but also because of the smell in here. Its thick and claws at the back of my throat as I attempt to take a deep breath.

I need to see her.

I shuffle to stand up, having to grasp the side of the bed to stop my legs from buckling. As I pull the sheet down her face, her beautiful short, black hair is the first thing I see. I let go of the sheet once her face is revealed, then sit back down.

I watch her, looking for any slight movement. It looks as if she's merely sleeping. So peaceful. Her eyes are closed, but I know that underneath her eyelids are the most gorgeous eyes; hazel with flecks of brown.

I pull back the sheet at her side, finding her soft hand and sliding mine into hers. She's cool to the touch, but not yet stiff. I hold her hand in silence for over a minute before I find the courage to speak.

'You can wake up now, Clara.'

I'm met with silence. I'm not stupid. I know she's gone.

'I'm sorry,' I say. 'This is all my fault. I shouldn't have pushed you into doing this transplant.'

I bite my lip hard, forcing myself not to cry. Tears spill from my eyes anyway. 'I don't know how I'm supposed to survive without you.' I force back a sob. 'How could you do this to me? It hurts, Clara. It hurts deep down inside. I feel like my insides are on fire. I can't... I can't...'

Finally, my body succumbs to the shock and grief. Huge, body-shaking sobs take over me, so I rest my forehead against her hand, still grasping it, as I allow the tears to fall.

I can never come back from this.
Never.
I'll never be the person I was without my sister.
How am I supposed to survive each day without her?
What am I supposed to do now?

CHAPTER NINE

The recovery from the operation is slow and painful, slower and more painful than I expected it to be, but it's nowhere near as bad as the recovery from my sister dying so suddenly. In fact, the more time that passes, the more painful it becomes.

Five weeks have passed, and my body may have healed, and I may be ready to return to work, but my mind, my spirit, my soul is broken, split straight down the middle with no chance of recovery. No number of painkillers numb the gut-wrenching agony of losing my twin sister. When Clara and I lost our grandmother five years ago, it hurt and we grieved for weeks, months, but it was nothing compared to this. When she died, Clara and I had each other to lean on. If one of us was having a particularly bad day, then the other was always there to offer a hug or to talk, but with Clara gone, I have no one to turn to. I'm completely alone with my grief and it's suffocating me.

The hospital offered and provided me with grief counselling sessions, but I refused them. My doctor prescribed therapy and anti-depressants, but I declined both. I don't want to move on from her death because if I do, it means I feel okay about her passing, and that's never going to be true. If I accept that she's gone it means she really is, and that's not acceptable.

Each day that passes feels like a year. All I think about is surviving the day, then the night comes, then another day starts, but it's another day without Clara and another day where nothing makes any sense. It feels as if I'm living in a bubble where nothing exists in the outside world. All the days and nights blend into each other and I have no idea what day or time it is. It's warmer now, mid-May I think, but it means nothing to me.

During my recovery, I arranged her funeral, but only five people attended, including me; my doctor, the nurse from the hospital, and her ex-girlfriend Paula and her new partner. I sat at the front of the church while the pastor droned on and on about how she was in a better place and that we were lucky to have had such a wonderful person in our lives. But I barely heard a word. He didn't know Clara. He was just some pastor I hired to take the service. I had to give him details of her life the day before and he was reading from a notebook. Clara deserved better, but I didn't have it in me to do any more.

Paula came up to me after the service and gave me a hug, but I was so numb I didn't feel it. All I felt was anger towards her because how dare she grieve for Clara. She was the one who left her when she got too ill to care for. What gave her the right to mourn her and cry at her funeral, and bring her new girlfriend along too? She may as well have stuck a knife directly into my heart and twisted it. I don't even remember most of the funeral. As soon as it was over, I left, refusing to hold a wake.

I cry a lot. Sometimes I just burst into tears randomly. Three days ago, I was found by a staff member at the local Tesco crying in the frozen food aisle, clutching a bag of chips because that bag of chips reminded me of eating chips with Clara on the lounge floor out of a bowl and arguing over the crispy ones at the end. She'll never hog all the crispy bits ever again. I can now eat as many of the crispy bits as I want, and she'll never care. What's the point in ever eating chips again?

I have no one to help me pick up the pieces of my life. Yes, I could go to therapy and take medication, but I don't want to. I don't want to dull the pain and grief I'm feeling. I want to feel it all because it's my fault she's dead. I deserve it. I shouldn't have survived. Why did she have to die? Why couldn't I have been the one to die? She'd have fared much better without me than I will without her.

I spend most of my days on the sofa, staring at the television. I don't see the shows or hear any words. I've attempted to look for a job, but apparently my outburst at Chef Andre has now come back to bite me in the butt because every job I apply for, they won't even offer me an interview. When I ask why, because I'm more than qualified, they give me a random answer, like saying I'm too over-qualified. I text Luke for answers. That's when I find out that Chef Andre has been bad-mouthing me all over London, at all the top restaurants with job openings.

I'm screwed on the job front. One hundred per cent screwed.

The bills have increased, now piled high on the side of the kitchen worktop. There are angry red stamps all over them. Final warning! Urgent!

I know I need to do something about them, but I haven't worked for the past five weeks. I have about a hundred quid in my bank account and the rent is due in a week's time. I can't deal with it all. It's too much. I can barely remember how to draw a breath.

Luke texts me several times, asking how I'm doing after the transplant. I haven't told him about Clara. I don't know why. Perhaps it's because I don't want his sympathy. I don't want anyone to give me sympathy or special treatment. I don't deserve it.

But he is relentless. He keeps texting me. Now, as his name pops up on screen, to my horror, I see that he's calling me. Eventually, I cave and answer.

'Hi, Luke,' I mumble. At this point, I realise it's the first time I've spoken out loud in nearly five weeks.

'Oh, good. You're alive.'

I flinch at how close to home his comment hits. 'Sorry,' I say. I clear my throat, lubricating my vocal chords. 'I've had a lot going on.'

'I know about Clara.'

'Y-You do? How?'

'Genieve told me.'

'How did she find out?'

'I don't know. I didn't ask. I just wanted to make sure you were okay. I'm really sorry, Brittany. I can't even imagine—'

'Stop. Please.' I cover my eyes with my spare hand and lean into the darkness it brings.

'Okay, well... I just wanted to reach out and... I don't know... I don't know what I can say or do to help but just know I'm here for whatever you need.'

I gulp back the huge lump in my throat. I barely know Luke, not personally anyway. We've spent many hours together in the kitchen, slaving away, rolling pastry, decorating cakes and whipping cream, but outside of work, I've never spoken to him before, apart from that time I ran into him in the supermarket at the fish counter, so him calling me like this feels odd.

'Thank you, Luke, but I'm fine.'

'No, you're not, and you're not expected to be fine. Not after what happened.'

'I meant I'm fine physically.' Although that's a lie too because I'm weak from not eating.

'Have you found a new job?'

'No, because no one will hire me or even offer me an interview.' My eyes flick to the mound of envelopes on the counter.

'Yeah, that was a really shitty thing he did. I hear Cafe Bourgeois is hiring a few new waiters. If you're clear to carry things and be on your feet, then maybe you could try there?'

I sigh as I squeeze the bridge of my nose then rub my left eye. I've had a pounding headache for the past two days, most likely due to dehydration. I keep forgetting to eat. Didn't I warn Clara that without her I'd forget to eat and drink and eventually die of starvation? I've lost so much weight that most of my clothes are hanging off me.

'Thanks. I'll give it a try. I guess it's better than having no job at all.'

'Let me know how you get on, yeah?'

'Luke, you don't have to do this.'

'What?'

'You don't have to pretend to care about me.'

'I'm not pretending. I do care about you.'

'Well, you shouldn't,' I snap, then a stab of guilt hits me. 'Sorry, I'm just...'

'Brittany, you don't have to apologise. I understand. I mean, I don't understand, obviously, but... I get it. Just... check in with me, yeah?'

'Sure, I'll do that. Bye, Luke.' I hang up and cry for the next two hours.

CHAPTER TEN

That night, once I stop weeping, I apply for that stupid waitressing job at Cafe Bourgeois. The next day, I get an interview. The day after that, I drag myself into the shower, wash my hair for the first time in three weeks and pull on something that isn't pyjama bottoms or an oversized t-shirt, then attend said interview, even plastering on a fake smile. It's a trial run, consisting of two hours' work in the restaurant at lunchtime. It takes every ounce of my energy to put one foot in front of the other. To be honest, I have no idea how I make it through the shift without bursting into tears or collapsing on the floor.

Miraculously, I get the job, despite getting a couple of orders mixed up, but the other girl who was being interviewed dropped a load of glasses and spilled red wine down a woman's white dress. No, it's not my dream job, but I need to pay the bills, which are now piled so high on the kitchen worksurface that they finally toppled off and spread across the floor yesterday.

Unfortunately, Cafe Bourgeois is situated just around

the corner from where I used to work, so it means there's a high risk of running into my previous colleagues, or worse, Chef Andre. In a weird way, I'm glad to be in employment. I suppose there was only so long I could sit at home and wallow in my own grief, but the effort it takes is exhausting. Being on my feet, carrying plates and taking orders distracts me from the fact that I'm missing a piece of myself, but sometimes it feels like I'm merely going through the motions. I don't have a purpose in life anymore. I've lost my career and my sister. What's left for me to live for?

During my breaks, I keep checking my phone, expecting a message from her, checking up on how my day is, but there's nothing. My phone remains silent. I have no one in my life who is likely to call me.

My doctor leaves me a voicemail to call him back, but I don't. My scar has healed nicely, and I have no physical issues after the operation. He calls me again the next day, again leaving a voicemail.

'Hello, Brittany. I understand that you may not want to discuss this, but I really think it would be beneficial for you to see a grief counsellor or a trained therapist to help you deal with this huge upset. Please do call me back so we can get you the help you need.'

I hang up. I delete the voicemail and don't return his call.

The first week of my new job flies by in a flash. Sundays and Wednesdays are my days off, which I spend on the sofa watching the soppy romantic comedies I used to watch with Clara. I practically cry through every film. The worst thing is, thanks to now only having one kidney, I can't drink alcohol to numb the grief. Well, I can, but it's not recommended, and if I do have a drink, then I can only have one, which is utterly pointless because one drink doesn't even get me tipsy. It doesn't do anything to numb the pain.

I may not wish to take anti-depressants or talk about my feelings in a long-winded therapy session, but I have no issue with destroying my brain cells with alcohol.

One of the other waitresses seems nice enough and asks me what my previous job was. When I tell her I was a head pastry chef, she almost laughs.

'What the hell are you doing slumming it with us then?' she asks while we're polishing wine glasses.

'It's a long story,' I say with a sigh. 'I'm desperate and need the money.'

'A good story?'

'No.'

The waitress gives me a weak smile, quite possibly feeling sorry for me. I don't offer her any further information.

'You fancy coming out for a drink with us tonight? Me and Charlotte are going to Bar One. We're meeting there at nine.'

I inwardly groan, really wishing I could tell people without having to actually tell people that I have no interest in socialising with anyone outside of the working environment. Plus, I can't afford it.

'Oh, um... thank you, but... I can't.'

'Well, if you change your mind, you know where we'll be.'

I smile, but the effort exhausts me. All I want to do is drag myself home, grabbing a cheap chippy on the way, and fall asleep in front of the television. Tomorrow is Sunday, my day off. I have no food in the house other than bread and butter and a can of baked beans, so I'll need to go shopping with the twenty quid I have left, but even the act of walking around a shop is something that fills me with dread. Clara and I used to do the shopping together. Even when she was sick and weak, I'd push her around in her wheelchair while she balanced a basket on her lap and read out the items from the shopping list. We were a team, working together effortlessly. Without her, I don't work at all. I'm broken. It was something we did together, always. Now, I'm forced to do it alone and it's yet another thing I hate. I keep forgetting to buy things I need because she's not there to tell me. My whole life revolved around Clara. Without her, it's empty and pointless.

BY NINE THAT EVENING, I'm contemplating going to bed because there's nothing else to do, but what's the point? It's not like my body will allow me to sleep. I stand up and shuffle across the lounge towards the bookcase. Clara always enjoyed reading. It kept her occupied while she was having her treatment in hospital. I pick up a book and flick through the pages, then read the blurb. It doesn't grab my attention, so I pick up another. This one I recognise because it's the book Clara was reading during her final day here. She was also reading a book on her Kindle and liked to switch between the two, but sometimes a paperback was too heavy for her to hold for long periods of time. She never finished this book. A bookmark is placed roughly halfway through the pages. I take the book back to the sofa, deciding to finish it for her. It's a romance; not my favourite genre, but Clara loved getting lost in the pages of a romantic novel.

Clearly, I've missed half the plot, and I have no idea who the characters are, but I'm so engrossed in the words that for the first time since Clara died, I don't dwell on how much pain and guilt I'm suffering through. However, as I turn the last page and read the last word, the emotion comes pouring out. Clara will never get to finish this book, never find out that the couple don't get together, but find new love with other people, then, decades later, when their other halves pass away, they find each other again. Tears stream down my face, soaking the pages.

I can't do this anymore.

I need alcohol.

I just need a temporary release because if I don't, I fear I may do something stupid. Clara once had a friend who took their own life at university. I'd never seen her so distraught. She blamed herself because she hadn't seen the signs. After the funeral, she took me aside and made me promise I'd never do that. Not that I had any intention of doing it back then, and I told her so, but she said anything could happen and if it ever got so bad that I thought it was the only way out, then I'd talk to someone about it and get help.

I'm sure she didn't expect to get kidney disease, for me to donate her my kidney and then her die only hours later. Does she still expect me to keep my promise? My eyes flick to the sharp knives in the block on the worktop.

No.

Think of something else.

Alcohol.

I open a nearby cupboard and see what I'm looking for. I grab myself a mug and open the bottle of white wine, not caring that it's room temperature.

I'm sorry for what I'm about to do to my one remaining kidney, but it's better than taking one of those knives and inflicting a different sort of self-harm.

. . .

AN HOUR LATER, I go in search of another bottle of wine but only find vodka. It's been sat in the cupboard for approximately two years, ever since Clara was first diagnosed. She loved the stuff. Personally, I can't even sniff it without gagging, but she swore that vodka was the best drink to get you drunk... fast. I grab the half-empty bottle and fill up the mug, bringing it to my lips.

I immediately retch into the sink, grasping the sides for dear life. Somehow, I manage to keep the liquid down. I don't feel so good as I stagger back to the sofa with the bottle.

My phone lights up with a text message from Luke asking how I am.

My woozy brain immediately conjures up another idea. At least this plan doesn't involve anything that will destroy my body or mind. In fact, it may just provide me the distraction and release it needs. Something to make me feel better. An endorphin rush is just what I need right now.

I pick up the phone and press the call button.

'Hey, Luke... You fancy coming over for a drink tonight?'

He takes several moments to respond, probably shocked that I'd called him back rather than texted. 'Brittany? Are you okay?'

'Yes, I'm fine. So... you want to come over?'

'Sure, I'd love to.'

The rest of the night passes by in a haze; a good, drunken haze, and for the first time in five weeks, I sleep soundly and dream of absolutely nothing.

CHAPTER ELEVEN

The next morning is almost the complete opposite. As soon as my eyes open, the pain and guilt hurtle back at full speed, almost smacking me in the face. I quickly close my eyes again, hoping it has all just been a crazy dream and I haven't had drunken sex with my ex-colleague. The flashbacks play out like a movie in my head.

I have never in my life had a drunken one-night stand with someone. In fact, Luke is only the third man I've slept with. The first two were boyfriends. Neither of them lasted long though, because I didn't have the time or inclination to have a serious relationship with anyone. I missed dates, I cancelled last minute, and I wanted sex to be over as soon as possible. I wasn't girlfriend material. Now, apparently, I'm the type of girl who drunkenly phones her ex-colleagues and asks them to come over before pouncing on them like a starving lion as soon as they walk in the door holding a bunch of flowers, which are now looking a little drab after being discarded on the worktop all night with no water.

Luke is lying on his stomach next to me, the covers

pulled up to his waist. He has a tribal tattoo on his right shoulder blade. Dear God, what have I done? Who am I? I'm not this person. Grief has changed me into someone I don't even recognise.

Nausea floods my body as my brain connects the dots of last night and remembers how much I drank, and I barely make it to the bathroom before bile and remains of vodka splash into the toilet bowl. I kneel, grasping the edge while I wait for my body to void itself of all the toxins I drank last night. Then the guilt surfaces; the guilt that I only have one kidney left and I spent the night poisoning it. I owe it to Clara to look after myself, but it hurts too damn much.

Angry tears spill from my eyes and down my cheeks. I don't think I've ever loathed myself more than I do in this moment. And, worst of all, I've led Luke to believe that I like him. I mean, I do like him. He's attractive, but… I barely know him.

A knock sounds at the bathroom door. 'Everything okay?' he asks.

I pull off a piece of toilet roll and wipe my mouth before flushing. I wash my hands, splash water on my face and then open the door to find Luke on the other side wearing his boxers and holding a glass of water in front of him.

'Thought you might need this.'

I take it. 'Thanks,' I say sheepishly as I walk past him and sit on the edge of the bed. I'm wearing an oversized t-shirt and nothing else, but at least it's big and long enough to cover my modesty.

Luke sits next to me.

'Listen,' I say. 'Last night was great, but it shouldn't have happened. I'm sorry. I was drunk and depressed and feeling a bit stupid. I just want you to know, I am not the type of girl who has one-night stands, and I'm really sorry. I shouldn't have called you.'

Luke stares ahead for a moment. He's going to hate me, isn't he? Then he looks at me and shrugs and I can't help but notice the way his deltoids flex. 'Hey, we've all been there, right?'

I give him a weak smile. 'Still friends?'

'Still friends,' he answers. 'Besides, I also must apologise because I was the horny idiot who took advantage of a drunk, depressed, stupid woman when what she really needed was someone to talk to and a shoulder to cry on. I should have turned you down, but... maybe it was what you needed at the time, and if it was, then I'm glad I could have been of service.'

'Yeah, I'm not so great with the whole talking thing. Maybe the drunken sex was the better idea.'

He chuckles. At least the tension has broken, and I don't quite feel as ready to crawl under the duvet and never venture outside in case I run into him.

I take a sip of water. 'Drinking neat vodka was a bad idea.'

'Well, it's never a good idea,' answers Luke. 'You have to look after that remaining kidney of yours, yeah?'

'It seems such a waste, you know. I donated my kidney to my sister thinking we'd suffer through the rest of our lives by not being able to get wasted ever again, yet here I am... One kidney down, one sister down, and nothing to show for it except a scar and the fact I can only have one small drink at a time.' I take another sip of water, feeling a little self-conscious because it's the most words I've spoken to a real person for over five weeks. 'Sorry,' I add.

Luke shrugs. 'Hey, my offer still stands. I'm here if you

ever need to chat shit, cry on my shoulder, be your punching bag or your sex slave. Whatever works for you.'

I can't stop the stupid grin that spreads across my face. 'Just knowing you're there for me is enough for now. Thanks.'

Luke nods. 'Okay, well... listen, I don't want to come across as a heartless bastard right now, but... I have to leave and get ready for work.'

I give him a look.

'What? I do!' He holds his hands up, palms facing me in defence.

'It's fine. You don't have to tiptoe around me. I'm a big girl.'

'Oh yeah? Had one-night stands before, have you?'

'No, actually you're my first.' *Wait... that sounds like...* 'I don't mean you're my first... I meant you're my first casual... Oh, whatever, can you just go and save me from further humiliation?'

Luke smirks as he says, 'Well, I'm honoured to be your first one-night stand, but I'm afraid I can't say the same about you. I'll have you know I'm a total pro at them. You're my fifth this week.'

I punch him in the arm, then stand up. 'I'm going to go and stand under a very hot shower for a very long time until I stop feeling like death warmed up. I take it you can see yourself out?'

Luke nods and salutes me and that's when I realise just how young he is. He's got such a baby face. 'Text me later, yeah? Let me know how you're feeling.'

I nod, but I already know I won't.

CHAPTER TWELVE

The next day, I'm working at the restaurant during the evening service. It's exceptionally busy and we're fully booked up until ten. I have seven tables to wait on, one of which is a table of eight, who are rowdy businessmen, all of whom seem to be on a mission to drink as much whiskey as possible in the shortest amount of time. I've already been leered at and slapped on the bottom as I walked past with a tray of drinks. If it happens again, I'll have to inform the manager because this is not that kind of place. It's a respectable, high-profile restaurant, and people like them cheapen it. I'm also worried I'm going to smash one of them over the head with a glass.

'Brittany, could you possibly take table eighteen for me? I'm swamped,' says Chris, one of the other waiters.

'Um... sure. No problem.'

'Thanks. They've had drinks. Just need to take their order.'

'I'm on it.'

Chris disappears through the swinging doors into the

kitchen. I need to get to table seven and take their order too, but I'll do that as soon as I've taken table eighteen's. Smiling, I make my way over to the small table at the far end of the restaurant.

As soon as I set my eyes on the couple, something inside my gut clenches and I'm not sure if it's to do with them or the effects of working too hard only six weeks after having surgery. The closer I get the worse it hurts, and by the time I've arrived at their table I can barely take a breath. I resist the urge to lean over, but I can't help it. I stumble forwards, knocking into the table just as a wave of pain envelops me.

'I'm so sorry,' I say, pushing myself away from the table and picking up a knocked-over glass, which luckily was empty.

The couple look at me for a moment as I feel my face turn hot.

'Goodness me, are you okay?' asks the woman. 'Are you ill?'

'I... No, ma'am. I'm fine. Just... it's nothing. Are you ready to order?' I force a smile on my face, almost biting through my tongue to stop from reacting.

'Are you sure you're okay?' she asks again.

'Yes, ma'am. Thank you.'

The man hasn't said anything yet and is just looking at me with an odd expression on his face. I can't quite read him. His hair is jet black, most likely dyed. He looks to be in his mid-forties and has a very noticeable scar running from his left eye across his cheek and down to his jawline. My eyes focus on it a moment too long, and I catch him watching me, so I quickly turn my attention to the woman, who is, quite possibly, one of the most beautiful women I've ever seen in real life. I'm talking Hollywood beauty, but it doesn't look paid for. I'm no expert, but I'd say she looks after herself, especially her skin, which is as smooth as porcelain, not a single pore or blemish anywhere. She is quite thin though; her collarbone sticks out sharply.

'What do you recommend?' she asks.

I'm momentarily taken aback, never having been asked that question before. 'Oh, well, if you're a fan of fish, then the salmon is the best you'll find anywhere. The chef here is very skilled and manages to instil a variety of flavours in the fish without taking anything away.'

'Sounds delicious. I'll have the salmon then. John, would you like the salmon too?' The woman turns to her husband.

'No, I'll have the roasted pheasant,' he says quite sternly.

I nod, jotting it down on my pad. 'Excellent choice,' I say. 'Would you like any sides?'

'No, thank you,' says the woman. 'You say the chef here is very talented?'

'Yes. I mean, I haven't worked here long, but I've worked in my share of kitchens and she's one of the best I've seen.'

'You've worked in kitchens before?'

'Yes, ma'am. I'm actually a pastry chef myself.'

Her eyebrows shoot up to her hairline. 'A pastry chef! Goodness, then what are you doing taking our orders? Shouldn't you be back there making desserts?'

I glance nervously over my shoulder, aware I'm taking too long and table seven needs attention. 'I've taken a break from the kitchen for a while,' I say. I take a step backwards. 'I'll get your order to the kitchen as soon as possible.'

The woman smiles and nods, then leans over and whispers something in her husband's ear. I quickly see to table seven, place the orders with the kitchen and then rush to the bathroom to freshen up. The pain is still there, but it's not as bad as before. I take a deep breath, compose myself and then return to service.

I KEEP an eye on table eighteen for the rest of the evening. The woman cleans her plate and gushes over the salmon, thanking me for my recommendation. Even John, the husband, clears his plate and seems satisfied with his meal when I return to pick up the dirty plates.

'Would you mind asking the chef to come to our table?' asks the woman. 'We'd like to thank them personally and offer them an opportunity to work for us.'

This time it's my eyebrows that shoot up to my hairline. 'Of course, ma'am. I'll fetch her right away.'

They want to offer the head chef a job? I head to the kitchen to deliver the news. I know nothing about the couple or even who they are, but they must own some sort of eatery if they're looking for a chef to join their team.

The head chef rushes out to speak to them as soon as I tell her the news. I'm overcome with a pang of envy. I realise, at that moment, that it's the first time my mind hasn't been solely focused on Clara. For a moment, the old spark I had for my career ignites again. It hasn't died out completely after all, but guilt quickly rears its ugly head, forcing its way back to the forefront of my mind. How could I be thinking of my career right now? I feel as if I've just betrayed Clara.

I get back to clearing tables and fetching drinks while keeping an eye on table eighteen. The chef is standing next to the table, nodding and smiling. The woman is doing most of the talking and I see her hand the chef a white business card. The chef then heads back into the kitchen. The woman catches me watching them and raises her hand, signalling me to come over.

'Can I get you anything else?' I ask.

The woman dips her hand into her glamorous handbag and brings out another business card. 'What's your name?'

'Brittany Young, ma'am.'

'Brittany, we'd like you to attend a job interview tomorrow at noon. The address is on the card.'

My mouth drops open. 'Me, ma'am?'

'You said you're a pastry chef. Is that right?'

'Yes, but...'

'I have no idea why you're working as a waitress, but I'd like to see what skills you have in the kitchen,' she says. 'You never know, you may surprise us.'

I take the card with a shaking hand. 'Thank you, ma'am. I'm honoured.'

'Good. We'll see you tomorrow then. May we have the bill?'

'Right away.' I turn and scurry away as fast as I can in case this is all a mistake and they call me back and take the card back off me. I slip it into my apron pocket. The guilt still niggles away in the back of my mind, but there's a familiar warmth settling in, almost as if Clara is giving me a sign.

When the couple leave and I go to clear their table, I find two fifty-pound notes tucked under the silver tray which I used to deliver their bill. They'd paid via credit card, so I assume this is a tip for me. I pick it up and slide it into my apron pocket. That will help pay for food for the next few weeks.

CHAPTER THIRTEEN

Evening service draws to a close. The restaurant is empty of guests and I and the other waiting staff are wiping down the tables and re-setting them for tomorrow's service. I say goodnight and then begin my trek home, the business card and cash practically burning a hole in my pocket. I resist the urge to take the card out until I get home, then promptly flick the kettle on, grab my phone and do some googling on the couple.

John and Angela Dalton.

They live in the south of France, on Cote d'Azur, at a multi-million-pound villa. They also have a private superyacht, which they often take on around-the-world trips. They own five luxury restaurants in various countries, give millions to charity every year, as well as having investments in huge organisations and businesses across the globe. Angela Dalton is an heiress to her father's vast fortune. John Dalton is a respected private surgeon who also owns a technology business overseas.

I can only assume they're in London to hire a chef, but

I'm not sure where the chef would be required to work. Gosh, imagine if they needed a chef to work at their New York restaurant? Or perhaps one of the two Michelin-star restaurants they own in Spain? They do have one in London too, so perhaps they need one for there.

Either way, clearly Chef Andre and his lies haven't spread to their ears. It's not that I don't enjoy waitressing (whom am I kidding; it sucks butthole), but the fact is I'm a highly skilled pastry chef, have trained with Michelin-star chefs, and I'm going to waste serving people their food rather than creating it. I miss the thrill and the buzz of the kitchen. I don't miss Chef Andre's sharp voice in my ear the whole time though.

I loved my job, despite the stress and long hours. Before Clara died, I had goals, desires, dreams. Now, they've dwindled away, been forgotten while I've wallowed in grief and self-pity. Perhaps this job interview is the kick up the butt I need to get my life back on track. I'm never going to get over Clara's death, but I know for a fact she'd want me to keep reaching for the stars no matter what. I did make her a promise after all.

It's time I kept it.

I've made a lot of mistakes lately—most recently sleeping with Luke—but I think it was the wake-up call I needed to kick myself into the right gear. Now, with this job interview on the horizon, I have something to focus on, to work towards. I need to get out of this dark, deep hole I've dug myself into.

One day at a time.

. . .

I ARRIVE fifteen minutes early to the interview, freshly showered, with a hint of make-up on. My palms and armpits are already damp, and my heart rate is through the roof as I climb the steps at the front of the building and enter the reception area. The address that Google brought me to is a posh hotel, roughly thirty minutes on the tube from my flat.

I take off my jacket, revealing a smart skirt suit I pulled out of Clara's wardrobe. Since we were the same size, we often shared clothes, although we did have different tastes and styles. She bought this suit years ago when she had the idea to go for a stuffy office job as a receptionist. She didn't get the job, so the suit got shoved to the back of the wardrobe and she decided to become a tattoo artist instead. That was Clara though; always making crazy decisions, living life to the fullest and doing whatever she felt like in the spur of the moment.

I sign in for my interview at reception and am asked to wait in a designated area. I sit down on a grey chair. Perhaps they are staggering the interviews, because I don't see anyone else waiting. I sit in silence for several minutes, picking at the loose piece of skin around my thumbnail.

'What the hell are you doing here?'

My head snaps up as I instantly recognise the voice of Chef Andre. He's glaring at me in his usual way, dressed in his chef whites. Oh God, was I supposed to wear chef whites to the interview too?

'Chef Andre,' I say, attempting to calm my shaking voice. If I wasn't nervous already, I certainly am now. 'I'm here for the job interview with John and Angela Dalton.'

'So am I,' he snaps. 'How did *you* get an interview?'

'I guess your badmouthing me didn't reach everyone,' I reply.

Chef Andre plonks himself down on the chair opposite me. 'There's no way you're getting this job over me,' he says.

'Why do you even want this job?' I ask. 'It's a pastry chef position. Wouldn't you be taking a step back?'

'I'd earn double and get to travel the world on a luxury yacht.' I can't argue with that.

'Brittany Young, they're ready for you,' says a female voice.

I stand up and straighten my skirt. 'I would say good luck, but I'm not going to,' I say, ignoring Chef Andre's glare as I follow the woman into the kitchen.

CHAPTER FOURTEEN

As soon as I walk into the kitchen, I see John and Angela sitting on stools by the worktop, which is laden with ingredients, pots and pans and various herbs and spices. Angela spots me first. She gets to her feet, smiles and offers me her hand. When I take it, I notice her hand is trembling ever so slightly and her palm is damp.

'Hi, Brittany. Thank you so much for coming along today.'

'Hi,' I say, swallowing the lump in my throat.

'So, I thought we'd just have a quick chat first to get to know one another, and then we'll ask you to create a dish using the ingredients on the side. No pressure or anything, but we just need to know whether you know your Chantilly cream from your diplomat cream.' She laughs. I laugh. But then she raises her eyebrows at me. It clicks into place.

'Oh, um... Chantilly is a type of whipped cream, which is sweetened and flavoured with vanilla, whereas diplomat is made from crème pâtissier, whipped cream and gelatine and can be flavoured in many ways, such as orange or caramel.'

Angela smiles at me. 'Lovely. So... Brittany, take a seat and we'll get started. Do you have any questions to begin with?'

I shift myself onto the stool and attempt to cross my legs at the ankles the way women are supposed to, but I wobble too much and just perch my feet on the little footrest on the stool instead. The last thing I want is to topple off.

'I guess just to know more about the job and where it's based.'

'Yes, of course. I'm sorry I didn't explain last night. It was foolish of me. My husband and I are looking for a head pastry chef to join our close-knit family of staff in the south of France, at our private villa on the Cote d'Azur. You'd be expected to design and create a range of desserts for the evening meals, as well as delicate treats and pastries when needed. My husband often has a lot of businessmen and colleagues to dine at the villa and we expect a high level of professionalism and attention to detail. While the position is as a private chef, you'll also be expected to accompany us on our yacht if we're to travel anywhere. You'll be provided with the best and freshest ingredients and will have free rein to design and come up with your own desserts. We love to taste and try different things, an array of flavours, and expect a wild combination of tastes and ideas. Does that sound like a job you'd be interested in?'

'It sounds amazing,' I say, attempting to sound as calm and casual as possible. 'It's perfect, actually. I've always enjoyed coming up with my own unique desserts.'

'Good,' replies Angela with a kind smile. 'Now, could you perhaps tell us a little about yourself, such as where you trained and your last job?'

I fidget with my hands while I tell them where I trained

as a pastry chef, my qualifications and where I've worked in the past. I keep all the details of my life purely focused on my career, so when she asks what I like to do for fun and whether I have any friends or family, I don't answer straight away.

'Is something wrong?' she asks.

'No, ma'am. It's just... I don't really do anything for fun because I'm so busy with work, or at least I was before... before...' Then, to my horror, tears fill my eyes, and I can't get another word out. My throat closes and I use every effort to stop from bursting into hysterical tears.

'My goodness,' says Angela, hopping off her stool. She manages to find some kitchen roll and offers me some.

I take it and dab my eyes, then blow my nose. 'Thank you. I'm so sorry. I'm so embarrassed.'

'Don't be silly. I assume something awful has happened recently?'

I nod, unable to look her in the eyes.

'Grief is a very strong emotion, is it not?'

'Yes.'

'It can turn us into very different people from who we used to be.' Her eyes flick towards her husband. 'I understand,' she adds. 'Now, how about you take a few moments to compose yourself, then we'll give you ten minutes to look through the ingredients and come up with a simple yet delicious dessert. Does that sound okay?'

'Yes, thank you.'

During this whole thing, John hasn't said a word. He looks bored with the whole situation, perfectly happy to let his wife take control and lead the interview. I pop to the toilets to salvage my make-up, then return to the kitchen, ready to prove to John and Angela that I'm not a complete loser who cries at the drop of a hat.

I use the ten minutes wisely and choose my ingredients quickly, then spend longer coming up with the recipe and even jot down a quick plan of how I'm going to plate the dessert. I feel like I'm on *MasterChef: The Professionals*. Since I only have thirty minutes to create it, I decide to make something simple, yet sophisticated and delicious. A miniature dissected strawberry and vanilla cheesecake with chocolate flakes and a rich, strawberry and mint drizzling sauce, flavoured with chilli. Yes, it's bold and a bit out there, but I want to show them that I'm not afraid to mix flavours. Chilli and strawberry are delicious together, but most people are put off by the combination of sweet and spicy.

I effortlessly move around the kitchen, even in my skirt and low heels. It's been over a month and a half since I've been in a kitchen and created something, but it's like I never left. I know I belong in this career. Being in the kitchen makes me feel alive. The past few weeks I've been dead inside, my flame dwindling, on the verge of going out completely, but right here, right now, it's roaring to life again, fuelled by the prospect of a new job and life in a different country. I want this job. No, I *need* this job.

It's reckless and impulsive, but it may be exactly what I need to put the past behind me and begin to recover from the trauma of losing Clara. Plus, I roughly know how much private chefs earn, and it will help me greatly in paying off my mammoth bills and backlog of overdue payments.

Thirty minutes later, I place a perfect plate of food in front of John and Angela. She picks up one of the forks, digs in and tastes it. Her eyes light up and she sighs, letting out a small whimper.

'My goodness,' she says. 'John, isn't that the most exquisite dessert you've ever tasted?'

John reaches for the second fork and takes a bite. He nods. 'It is... surprisingly good.'

Angela laughs. 'Oh, ignore him, Brittany. The chilli and strawberry flavour really packs a punch, plus the freshness of the mint on the palate is delightful. Honestly, this is the best dessert I've ever tasted, even better than the one I had last night. Your presentation is unique and perfect and your attention to detail is beyond anything I've seen. You look very much at home in the kitchen.'

'Thank you, ma'am.'

'Now, the reason I asked you before if you had any close friends or family is because if you are given the job, then you'd be expected to leave them behind and I wanted to make sure they'd be happy with you moving to a different country. It's a three-year contract.'

I gulp and nod. 'Yes, ma'am. My apologies. I... I don't have any close friends or family. It won't be a problem. A clean, fresh start is exactly what I need right now.'

'Glad to hear it. Thank you for coming here today, Brittany. I'm very glad you served our table last night and we had the chance to meet. I shall let you know the outcome by tomorrow evening.'

'Thank you, ma'am, sir, for the opportunity to cook for you.'

I walk out of the kitchen with my head held high. Chef Andre locks eyes with me.

'Beat that,' I say, then saunter out of the hotel. I just hope Chef Andre doesn't tell them about what I said to him all those months ago. I wouldn't put it past him.

As I walk home, I feel both elated and disappointed

because on the one hand, I clearly did very well and they enjoyed my dessert, but on the other hand, Chef Andre could have walked in there after me and told them what he's told every other restaurant in the city, ruining my chance of starting a new life.

I now must wait on tenterhooks. If this doesn't work out, then I'm back to square one. I hope my emotional outburst doesn't wreck my chances, but Angela did seem sympathetic towards me. It appears she has some experience with grief, if her comments are anything to go by. It goes to show that even the wealthiest, happiest person can hide their grief and anxiety behind their shiny shield. It's only a matter of time before the shield weakens. I wonder how long Angela has had to remain strong on the outside.

CHAPTER FIFTEEN

Work manages to keep me occupied for the rest of the day and most of the next. During one of my breaks, I check my phone and am delighted to have received a voicemail from Angela, asking me to call her back at my earliest convenience.

That's a good sign, I think. Because, if I hadn't got the job, she would have just told me that via the voicemail, right?

I press the return call button and hold my breath while I wait for her to answer.

'Brittany, thank you so much for calling me back,' she says.

'I'm sorry I missed your call. I'm at work at the moment,' I say.

'Not for much longer, I hope! I'm delighted to say that we'd love for you to come and work for us in the south of France as soon as possible. In fact, we're leaving in two days' time, and we'd like you to accompany us back.'

'Oh, my goodness. I can't believe it. Thank you so much.

I don't know what to say.' I cover my mouth with my free hand.

'I hope you'll say yes!'

'Yes!' I practically scream. My heart is beating so fast that I can barely control my voice. 'Of course I will. I'm honoured you've chosen me.'

'Now, the chef who came in for an interview after you did have some very interesting things to say about you.'

'I thought he might.'

'But I'll have you know that I've never cared for bullies, and that's not who we're looking for to join our close-knit family of staff. All your expenses will be taken care of, including the flight over and any bills or rent you may have to complete wherever it is you're living at the moment. We really want you to feel as if you're at home with us.'

I don't answer for a moment. 'I'm sorry... did you say you'd pay for all my bills and rent on my current flat?'

'Yes. We don't want any of our staff to be weighed down by debt or money troubles. We like them to be happy and stress-free because they, in turn, make better workers. So, just send me all your details, and I'll take care of it.'

My mouth opens, but I can't find the words. 'I... I...' I'm close to tears again. 'T-Thank you, I appreciate that,' I manage to say with a croaky voice.

Do not start crying again, Brittany!

'There is one thing I haven't mentioned to you yet, so I'm hoping it won't affect your decision to take the job, but all of our staff are required to sign a non-disclosure agreement before they arrive.'

'Oh... okay.' I'm stumped for words again, but not nearly as shocked as I was by her announcement that she would take care of all my debt. It's not every day I'm asked to sign a non-disclosure agreement to take a job. 'I mean, it's unusual, but it's not a problem,' I say.

'Great. I'll send it over via email for you to read through and sign, but if you could have it back to me by this evening, then I can get you booked on our flight on Thursday.'

I'm briefly taken aback by her rushed tone but brush it off. 'No problem. Thanks again.'

'I'll send you everything via email once the agreement is signed.'

'Okay.'

We say our goodbyes and I hang up. I don't have long to dwell on my excitement of a new job because my boss signals to me that my break is over, and I get back to work.

BY THE TIME I get home and check my phone again, there's an email from Angela in my inbox. I open it while I chuck a jacket potato in the microwave, fully aware that I'm a highly trained chef yet I can't be bothered to cook myself proper food at home. I used to love cooking for myself and Clara, even if I didn't have time to do it very often, but without her here to eat and enjoy it, it feels like a pointless endeavour. I know I need to eat, and I should be eating healthier food to recover, but it's one of those things that just don't really matter to me anymore. I love cooking for other people, to see the look on their faces as they take their first bite, but I hate cooking for myself. I know I'm a good chef. I just don't see the need to do it for only little old me. I'll add some baked beans and melted butter to the potato when it's cooked. Can't go wrong with that.

While the microwave does its thing, I lean against the

kitchen counter and read through the contract. I'm signing a minimum of a three-year contract to work for them. As she explained, all my expenses will be taken care of, and I am not required to pay rent. It's perfect because with the salary she's paying me, I can save so much money in three years and perhaps put it towards opening my own restaurant, like Clara and I always talked about. I don't even need to use the money I earn to pay off my debts. It feels strangely like some sort of scam because it feels too good to be true. For once, it seems, things are going my way and I can see a faint light at the end of the tunnel.

This job opportunity has kick-started something inside me because I remember what Clara and I spoke about, the night before we left for the hospital. She told me that no matter what happens, to promise her I'd reach for the stars, to live out my dreams, to keep going. So, that's what I'm finally doing, and this job is the steppingstone to doing that. Working as a private chef is a highly respected job and it can catapult me on my way to owning my own restaurant and earning a Michelin star.

I scroll down and get to the non-disclosure agreement part of the contract, which states that I am not allowed to tell anyone outside of the villa anything about what I see or hear within the confines of the estate. I cannot tell anyone the address of the villa due to the fact they are a high-profile couple and they don't want their address being public information. Only they are allowed to disclose that information.

That's pretty much the gist of the contract.

But it leaves a slightly nauseous feeling in my gut because what could possibly be happening within their villa that they wouldn't want people on the outside to know about? It's a red warning flag, but surely, it's a small price to pay for such a glamorous, well-paid job?

Right?

CHAPTER SIXTEEN

I sign the contract after eating and send it back to Angela, along with my rent and debt details. She replies within two minutes with an email outlining the flight details and the hours I'm expected to work. I'm not even on a normal flight. They're putting me on their private jet with them.

I root around in the hallway cupboard for my suitcase and start to pack, but as I remove things from my wardrobe, I come across an item of Clara's that's somehow got mixed up with mine. Her favourite t-shirt with a Mr Men character on it. I hold it to my face and breathe in her scent, but it's not there, washed away the last time it was cleaned. I pack it in my case.

Angela is true to her word and pays off the remainder of my rent up until the end of my contract agreement, which is due to renew in five months. She also pays off my credit cards (all three of them!) and also pays for me to store all my personal items that I must leave behind, most noticeably all of Clara's belongings. Clara's bedroom hasn't been touched since she died. In fact, I haven't even been able to step foot inside it.

I'm not ready for this.

I can't throw anything away. Every single item is going into storage for the next three years and then I'll sort it out afterwards. As I shift her bed away from the wall, I find bunched-up tissues on the floor, covered in dust, and I spend the next forty minutes crying as I hoover and clean the room. I can't even throw the damn tissues away. They go in a packing box.

It feels as if I'm leaving Clara behind, but there's no way I can bring any of her things with me. Only the t-shirt I found and her favourite blanket. In three years, I'll deal with it then. Maybe I'll be ready by then. Or maybe I won't.

THE NEXT DAY happens to be my day off from work. I call them and explain my situation. Luckily, they don't seem too bothered by my short notice period. I then book a moving company to come and take away all the furniture and while they transport everything down to the moving van, I spend the rest of the day sorting through the things I want to take and cleaning the flat, even painting over the huge scorch mark on the ceiling from when Clara tried to flambé a steak and almost burnt down the flat.

My last night, I sleep in Clara's bedroom on the floor, wrapped up in her blanket. The flat feels empty now all the furniture is gone, but if I'm being honest, it's been empty ever since Clara died.

'I'm sorry,' I whisper through my tears.

I'm doing this for her. She'd want me to do this, I'm certain of it. Clara always wanted the best for me and I'm sure if she was here now, she'd be proud of me. Or perhaps she'd tell me I'm being reckless by leaving everything behind and moving to a different country to work for a couple of strangers who made me sign a non-disclosure agreement. For the first time in my life, I don't have her voice in my ear, giving me advice or helping me make a difficult decision. I'm having to make it on my own and it's utterly terrifying.

I'm going to miss this flat. It holds so many memories within its walls; happy ones. It's the place we shared and spent time together, when I wasn't working. When we first rented it, it was unfurnished and we didn't have money to buy beds at the time, so we slept on a double air bed on the floor for the first five months, and had to blow it up each night because it had a slow puncture, and, try as we might, we couldn't find it to fix it.

So many memories, and I'm leaving them all behind.

I ARRIVE at the airport on time and meet Angela and John in their private waiting room where they hand me a glass of champagne with a strawberry perched on top. I don't have the heart to turn it down or tell them about my single kidney. In the health questionnaire they gave me to complete, I skipped over the section regarding any recent surgeries. I don't know why. I guess I just couldn't care to explain the whole situation about Clara.

'Cheers!' says Angela.

'Cheers,' I echo back, clinking glasses with her. John is reading a newspaper nearby and doesn't say anything.

Angela and I fall into a comfortable conversation. It's mostly her talking, telling me about the villa and the wide variety of ingredients she can get for me to experiment with in the kitchen. I listen and take it all in, silently wishing I had someone to share this with. I want to tell Clara everything. If she were alive, I'd be snapping selfies of me drinking fizz and pictures of the private jet and sending them to her, but I have no one to tell, no one to share the experience with.

As Angela settles in her seat on the plane, leaving me in mine, I'm left feeling lonely and vulnerable. I stare out of the window as the plane takes off up the runway, saying a quiet goodbye to my old life. I blink back the tears as we hurtle into the sky.

THE FLIGHT ISN'T a long one, but somehow, I fall asleep and wake up as we're landing. However, as we head down the steps to the ground, I notice Angela has changed her outfit. She's now wearing the most extravagant white outfit I've ever seen; tailored, high-waisted trousers and a white blouse that's cinched in at the waist. She finishes off the look with oversized sunglasses encrusted with jewels on the side.

I watch while their private staff take the luggage from the hold.

John and Angela are standing close together. John leans in and whispers something in her ear, which causes her to nod and root around in her handbag. She pulls out a bottle of pills and pops two in her mouth, swallowing them with a sip of water from her fancy bottle. She then opens her mouth for John to look inside it—I'm assuming to check that she's swallowed them.

Okay, that's a bit weird. Did he just remind her to take her medication? I wonder what she's on. Then I remember that it's none of my business and I look away before either of them catches me staring.

The weather is glorious when we step outside the airport. There's a fancy car waiting for us too. I wait until I'm told which side to get in.

'Oh, actually, Brittany, your car will be along in a moment. John and I have a few things to talk about on the journey home and we'd rather be alone.'

'No problem,' I say with a forced smile.

'We'll see you when you arrive.'

I nod and step back from the kerb, watching as the car drives away, leaving me standing on the pavement at the airport, my suitcase and carry-on luggage at my feet. I look up and down the road. How long am I supposed to wait for my ride?

As the seconds tick by, my heart rate climbs. Have I just made the biggest mistake of my life? Is this some sort of scam after all? The idea of being left alone in a country I've never been to is enough to kick-start my anxiety. I don't have any cash on me. I haven't set up my phone yet to work abroad without using extortionate amounts of data and, come to think of it, I don't have Angela or John's phone numbers. Well, I do, but only the numbers they use in the UK. On the plane, I saw Angela swapping her phone for another. I assume she has one that she uses in France and one for the UK.

This cannot be happening. It takes me straight back to my first day of training at Le Cordon Bleu. I knew no one and I was in the biggest city in the country. For the first time in my life, Clara wasn't there to help me. She was off doing her own thing. But this is worse because I really am alone now. There's no one I can call for help...

CHAPTER SEVENTEEN

Tears fill my eyes as I take a deep breath. I rummage in my bag and pull out my phone just as an expensive black car rolls to a stop in front of me.

'Miss Young?' asks the driver as the window lowers.

'Yes!' I gasp, reaching for the door handle to the back seat. I start lifting my suitcase, but the driver gets out and puts it in the boot for me.

Once my heart rate returns to normal and I settle in the back seat, I finally take a cleansing breath, putting the anxiety of being alone in a foreign country out of my head, then spend the journey to the villa looking at the passing countryside and glorious views of the Cote d'Azur as we drive out of the Nice airport. It doesn't take long for my anxiety to dissipate.

I don't think I've ever seen anything as spectacular as this place. To call it magical seems to do it a disservice. It truly is the most beautiful, idyllic place on earth. The ocean is a dazzling bright blue that sparkles under the southern sun.

I stare open-mouthed at the beauty around me, not quite

believing that I'll be living in such an amazing country for the next three years of my life. I wish Clara could see this. I wish she were here to share this special moment with me. I take pictures for no reason other than my own memories, ensuring my data is off until I can sort it out.

But, in a way, she is with me. I'm living my life the way she wanted me to live it. I'm taking a chance and reaching for the stars. I don't know how this job will pan out, but I know I'm making the right decision because for the first time since she died, a smile appears on my face as I lean back in my seat, staring out across the landscape at the brilliant views.

I knew Angela and John were wealthy—they'd have to be to live here—but I'm not quite ready for the grandeur of their villa estate.

'Holy crap!' I say as we drive up the long driveway towards the majestic villa. The enormous structure is made of white-washed sandstone, glistening in the sun, accentuated by the perfectly manicured hedges, lawns and trees surrounding the gardens. The walls are so bright they're dazzling to look at directly for too long.

The car pulls to a stop and the driver opens the door for me. I get out, keeping my eyes glued to the villa, which looms in front of me in all directions, like a sparkling white castle. There's a swimming pool off to the side, as well as tennis courts and what looks like stables, and a separate building, equally as grand, on the other side of the driveway.

'That's the staff quarters,' says the driver, pointing to the building next door. 'There are twenty-seven staff altogether.'

'Wow,' I say, my mouth suddenly dry. 'This place is enormous.' I truly am lost for words. The villa is situated on a slight hill so when I turn and look back the way we came, I can see the ocean and the spectacular views over the coastlines and then the forests and mountains surrounding the area.

It takes my breath away.

'Brittany! You made it,' comes a familiar voice.

I turn and see Angela rushing towards me from the villa. 'Hi,' I say with a squeaky voice.

'What do you think of your new home?'

I chuckle as I say, 'It's a bit of an upgrade, that's for sure.'

'Follow me. I'll introduce you to my head housekeeper and she'll get you settled into your room and show you around the staff accommodation. Then, you can have a look round your new kitchen.' She gives me a wink. Any chef worth their salt would be super excited to see a state-of-the-art kitchen in a place like this. If it's anything like the outside, then it'll be the most lavish kitchen I've ever worked in. Imagine the desserts I can create and design!

The head housekeeper is called Mrs Dubois and, apparently, I'm to always call her that, nothing else. She's an older lady who is strict but very professional and expertly turned out. She tells me she expects me to always be presentable whether I'm in the kitchen or not. There are no messy chef whites to be worn in the kitchen, which isn't a problem since I pride myself on keeping my whites clean at all times, no matter the ingredients I'm working with.

The staff quarters are simple, yet clean and spacious. I'm given my own room and private bathroom with views across the courtyard where there are fairy lights strung up and around a beautiful gazebo and patio and all the white-stone columns.

I'm given an hour to settle in and unpack and then I'm due to meet Mrs Dubois outside the front of the staff quarters so she can take me to the main house and show me around. I'm beyond excited. I can't seem to get my head around the fact that this is a house where people live. Not dozens of people, but two. A couple. Why do they need so much space? But then, if you had millions of pounds in the bank, what else would you do with it?

I meet Mrs Dubois at the agreed-upon time and place, and she gives me a tour where I bombard her with questions. She answers them curtly and briefly, clearly having done this several times before with new-starters. I'm sure she's used to this place now, but I'm not sure how I can ever get used to it. What if I get lost?

'How many bedrooms does it have?'

'Fifteen,' she answers.

'Do they rent it out for weddings and stuff?'

'Yes, sometimes. It's also been used as a set for a very famous film.'

I make a mental note to google which one as soon as I get some data. She shows me the three interlinked reception rooms with antique furnishings which can seat up to eighty guests for dinners and events; the grand salon with furnishings and an enormous fireplace; the family kitchen, fully equipped, leading to an al-fresco dining terrace and garden; then comes the professional kitchen for use during dinners and events, the one I'll be working in.

The kitchen is beyond my wildest dreams. The refrigerator and separate freezer are big enough to walk into and there are six ovens. As the head pastry chef, I get my own section of the kitchen, complete with all the cooking utensils I could wish for, and glistening kitchenware, all of which I know are exceptionally expensive.

There's an infinity pool, a home gym, a games room, cinema room and a spa area, complete with a sauna, steam room and hot tub. The staff have use of a small pool on the west side of the estate near their accommodation and they can use the games room whenever they like.

Once Mrs Dubois has finished showing me around, we stop outside the main villa.

'Do you have any questions?' she asks.

She's told me everything I need to know regarding the job. I start tomorrow morning, when I'll have free rein to make and design a dessert with whatever ingredients I can find in the kitchen. Once a week, I'll be making the trip to the markets to pick up fresh fruit and other ingredients.

'No, I think I'm good,' I say with a smile.

Mrs Dubois gives me a curt nod and walks inside the villa. The moment she's gone, my eyes flood with tears. I'm not sure what's come over me. I miss Clara. I want to talk to her and tell her everything. She'd be so amazed by this place. She always wanted to travel the world, and the Cote d'Azur was one of the top places she wanted to visit. The outfits, the wealth, the sun, the grandeur of everything.

She should be here. Not me.

The tidal wave of grief I've been holding back for the last few days suddenly crashes into me and I rush to my new room before anyone sees me bawling my eyes out. I slam the door shut, lean against it and sink to the floor, pulling my knees to my chest. I cry so much that it physically hurts. I cry until the tears dry out and a headache forms from dehydration.

What have I done? I've left everything I've ever known to come to the south of France to work for a couple of people I barely even know. I've left my life behind, Clara's belongings and the familiarity of my work, to come here and start afresh. It's suddenly dawned on me how much of a rash decision it was, but I know it was driven by need to create some distance between me and my old life. Everyone I've ever loved and cared about is gone, so I may as well start again in a different country.

I could have ended it all completely, but I owe it to my sister to keep going, to at least piece the shattered parts of my life back together, even if the joins are wonky and rough.

It won't be easy.

How am I supposed to get through this without her?

CHAPTER EIGHTEEN

The next few weeks whizz by in a haze of chocolate, late nights and hastily scribbled notes of recipes I think up at random times. I'm so busy and preoccupied that I don't even have time to stop and grieve for my sister until I'm back in my room late at night after an exhausting but satisfying day. Then, after I've eaten and showered, I'm physically so tired that I fall asleep within minutes of my head hitting the pillow, only waking up when my alarm blares to life at five in the morning, ready to start it all again.

The head chef in the kitchen is called Margo and she's a world apart from my previous boss. She's firm but fair and, so far, I haven't heard any complaints about her from the other chefs. She's a little on the nose and a bit blunt, but I can't fault her style and the way she runs her kitchen. I don't have a junior chef to help me, so I purchase, prepare, design and create every dessert, pastry and bread from scratch myself. It's a huge challenge to get it all done within the time provided, but I'm relishing the freedom it's giving me. I'm taken back to my training days when I had free rein to come up with brand-new recipes and pitch them to high-profile chefs.

John and Angela mostly keep themselves to themselves. I hardly ever see them, and I rarely spend any time in the main part of the villa at all. I'm practically chained to the pastry kitchen. However, during my one day off per week, I decide to treat myself and take advantage of the spa and pool facilities, so I don my swimsuit and grab a crisp, clean towel and head out to the staff pool area.

As I make my way across the courtyard, my flip-flops clip-clopping across the tiles, a raised voice makes all the tiny hairs on the back of my neck stand on end and I freeze in place. For a moment, it feels as if someone is shouting at me. Perhaps I've entered the wrong area.

I look around, frantically searching for the stern voice, but no one appears. It comes again, this time echoing from up above, a nearby balcony. I quickly jog so I'm underneath it, out of sight, and wait by the pillar. Holding my breath, I listen as John's voice booms across the courtyard. It's strange to even hear it because the few times I've seen him, he's barely said a word.

'Stop it, Angela. Just stop it. I've had enough of this. It's gone on for far too long.'

'How could you say that?' comes Angela's tearful reply.

'You have no idea how much effort it takes to keep you safe, do you? No idea!'

Their voices are so loud now. They must be standing directly above me. I dare not move a muscle. In fact, I shrink back even further beneath the balcony in case they happen to look out across the courtyard and see my shadow under them.

'You treat me like an animal, John!' she shrieks.

'Because you're no better than one!'

I cover my mouth as an audible gasp escapes, but luckily most of it is muffled by my hand.

'What was that?' he snaps.

'What? Nothing,' says Angela. 'Please. Can you just...'

'Just what, Angela? I do enough for you, you heartless cow.'

My mind flitters back to the non-disclosure agreement I signed. Is this what they were talking about? On the outside, John and Angela appear to be the perfect couple. They have everything in life they could ever want or need, yet clearly their marriage is strained, broken somehow. Maybe they don't want anyone knowing that they are having problems.

'Mark my words, John,' says Angela, sounding a little sterner, more in control of her tears. 'You'll be sorry you ever took me for granted one day.'

John laughs, then storms off. A door slams and his footsteps fade away. I finally release my hand from my mouth and look up at the underside of the balcony where Angela is now quietly sobbing.

To get to the staff pool area, I need to cross the courtyard in front of me, but if I do, she's bound to see me. Perhaps there's another way around I can use to avoid being seen. I tiptoe a few steps, but my stupid flip-flops make too much noise, so I carefully remove them and then pad barefoot through a nearby stone archway, in search of a different route to the staff area, still carrying my towel and pool bag containing my phone, a book and sun lotion. I did manage to find a phone plan that came with data to use overseas, but I've barely used it. In fact, I only use the Wi-Fi in the villa.

'What are you doing?'

I almost slip on the shiny tiles as I skid to a halt and turn to face Margo, the head chef. I'm momentarily relieved that it isn't Mrs Dubois, Angela or John who's caught me.

'Sorry, I was just trying to get to the staff pool area.'

Margo frowns at me. 'The easiest way is to go back the way you came.'

'Okay, yeah... I know, but...'

'Why do you look like you've just been caught red-handed doing something you shouldn't?'

'Um... Do I?'

'Spill it, pastry chef.'

I glance around my surroundings. 'It's nothing, really. I just overheard something I probably wasn't supposed to, and I was trying to go the long way round to the staff pool area.'

Margo's nose twitches. 'Overheard what?'

'It's nothing.'

Margo sighs heavily. 'You may as well tell me, or I won't give you directions to the staff pool and you'll have to walk back through the courtyard.'

What is her problem?

'Fine. I overheard an argument between John and Angela. I've never heard John raise his voice before and it sort of freaked me out.'

Margo is quiet as her eyes scan the area directly behind me. Then, they focus on me. She steps closer, then keeps her voice low as she says, 'Be careful, okay? John and Angela may act like the perfect couple on the outside, but there's trouble in paradise. Big trouble, and the last thing you want to do is get in the middle of it. Take it from me.'

'I'm not here to cause drama. I just want to work.'

'Good. Just ignore everything you hear, and you'll be fine.'

Somehow that doesn't fill me with confidence. 'They're not... dangerous, are they?' I ask.

Margo doesn't answer straight away. She checks our surroundings again. 'It depends.'

'On what?'

'On what you'd class as *dangerous*.' I'm about to give her an answer, but she continues. 'It's nothing, but... once or twice I've seen bruises.'

'What!' I immediately clamp a hand over my mouth, wishing I could take my loud outburst back. Margo shoots me a warning look. 'Sorry,' I whisper, pulling my hand away. 'Are you saying John hits her?'

'Who said anything about John hitting her?'

'But...'

'Look, we shouldn't be talking about this. Forget I said anything, okay?'

'How am I supposed to do that when you've just told me you think they're dangerous?'

Margo shrugs her shoulders. 'Anyway, happy swimming. If you head left and walk around the outside of the villa, there's a back gate to the pool area. You can't miss it.'

'Um, thanks,' I mutter.

I watch her until she disappears.

There's no way that Angela hits John. She's the nicest woman I've ever worked for. John is clearly a bit temperamental, considering his temper just now, but Angela seems harmless. Unless...

I feel as if Clara is sending me alarm bells from beyond the grave. Her voice is in my head.

Don't trust her. Not Angela.

Margo. Don't trust Margo.

CHAPTER NINETEEN

Another week goes by and I, thankfully, don't hear or witness any other arguments between John and Angela. In fact, the couple are more than polite and kind to me whenever I see them, even praising my desserts and cooking, describing them as unique and exceptionally crafted. Even John compliments me after one meal, saying he thoroughly enjoyed the miniature chocolate truffles with hints of basil, and he'd like me to make more for Angela's birthday coming up. I'm more than happy to oblige.

After Margo told me about John and Angela and their marital issues behind closed doors, I keep an eye out for bruises on either of them, but none appear. Margo doesn't say anything else that makes me uncomfortable, but I still struggle to trust her. She doesn't mention John and Angela to me again, but she does complain about the long hours on occasion, and she mutters under her breath something about rich, white people with more money than sense.

I cry in my room every night for Clara because I want more than anything to share this experience with her, but I opt for writing it all down in a diary, as if I'm writing her a letter. It soothes me at the end of each day, and even as the tears splash on the paper and smudge the ink while I write, I smile as I scribble away, like I really am talking to her. She doesn't reply, but I can feel her here with me.

While sleeping, I clutch a clean tissue in my palm. It almost feels like I'm holding her hand. It's silly, but the more time that passes, the harder it seems to get. I can't see how I'm ever going to recover from the grief. It's overwhelming, painful and exhausting, but with each day that passes it becomes more bearable somehow, even though I don't know how that's possible.

During another of my days off, I decide to explore the villa a bit more. Angela has told me several times over the past couple of weeks that I should visit the library. I can borrow any book I like as long as I return it in the same condition I took it. So, that's where I'm heading, except, as usual, I'm lost and have walked around in a circle for the past ten minutes.

There are so many rooms, so many corridors, all beautifully presented, but it truly is like a maze. I know the library is located on the first floor somewhere, which is where I think I am, but there's a staircase in front of me now and I either have to go up it and try and find another way down, or I must turn around, go back the way I came and attempt to locate a different corridor to walk down.

I decide to go up the stairs.

Angela has mentioned I can explore as much as I like. The only room we're not allowed in as staff is their master suite, which is on the top floor. As long as I don't find myself up there, I'm safe.

The stairs are creaky, so I quickly go up them, sighing

with relief at the top. I'm not sure why I'm on tenterhooks. It's not like I'm trespassing. I'm taken back to a time when Clara and I were young, around nine I think, and we crept into our grandmother's bedroom because we wanted to play dress-up. We knew we weren't allowed, but we did it anyway. She was asleep downstairs, having one of her Sunday afternoon naps, so she wouldn't be awake for hours. We held our breaths as we opened her wardrobe door and took out two of her prettiest dresses. Then, the giggling began, and it must have woken her up. Boy, were we told off!

There's an open door along the hall. I peer around it, but it's not the library. It's a bedroom; a very tidy, beautiful bedroom. I still can't quite understand why they have such a large villa. So far, I've never seen any guests here. No visitors of any kind.

The door next to the bedroom is closed, but my hand instinctively reaches for the handle, and I push it open. I don't know what comes over me. I suppose my curiosity is taking over. I can't wait to tell Clara all about it later when I write to her.

As the door swings open, I flinch in surprise at what I see.

It's a child's bedroom.

Now that, I wasn't expecting. I didn't know they had children. It never crossed my mind to ask. I've never been interested in children or finding out about other people's children. That was always Clara's domain. She could sit for hours and listen as her friends told her about their precious babies, but not me. My eyes would glaze over. Clara's friends all eventually had kids and separated themselves into their mum groups, and Clara was pushed out because she didn't have kids. Anyway, the point is that children don't interest me in the slightest, so seeing this room fills me with dread. Is there a child wandering around here and I just haven't seen them yet? By the looks of the room, I'd say the child could be around eight or ten, but then, what do I know?

I step further into the room, gazing around at the array of toys and children's items. A single cot bed with pink bedding, along with a stuffed unicorn. A gorgeous dollhouse that has what looks like hand-crafted figurines inside. Dozens of dolls dressed in beautiful dresses adorn several shelves, and teddy bears wearing matching hats are piled in the far corner.

One thing I do notice almost straight away is that there are no pictures on the walls. In fact, now I think about it, there are no pictures anywhere in the villa. No family photographs in hand-made frames, no dreamy wedding photos, nothing.

If they have a child, then where is she? Where are the photos?

Deciding not to risk staying in here any longer, I step backwards out of the room and gently close the door. Then, I continue down the hallway. I end up giving up on finding the library and head back to my room. As I walk around, I keep my eyes open for any sign of a child, but there's nothing.

No toys.
No pictures.
No clothes.
Nothing.

CHAPTER TWENTY

Two days later, I'm in the kitchen preparing tonight's dessert menu. I've finely chopped an array of succulent fruits, including pineapple, mangoes and kiwi, to adorn the top of the miniature meringues.

Margo comes and stands beside me. 'You have great knife skills,' she says.

'Thank you, chef.'

'I heard you last night, you know.'

I continue chopping, attempting to ignore the rising panic. 'What do you mean?'

'Crying.'

'I'm sorry?'

'There's no need to be ashamed. Did you leave someone behind? Do you miss them?'

The hand that's holding the knife trembles, so I put it down. 'Yes. My sister.' I hate these types of conversations because inevitably it always ends with me telling the other person that my sister is dead and then there's an awkward silence where the other person doesn't know what to say, and then I end up saying something stupid to try and break the tension.

'Are you close?' she asks.

I take a deep breath. *Here it comes.* 'Um, yes... we were very close. We were twins.'

'Identical?'

'Yes.' Yet another conversation I hate having. People are fascinated by identical twins, and they almost always ask the question...

'Do you have that weird twin vibe thing where you can read each other's thoughts?'

Exactly that...

'No, that's basically a myth, but we do... I mean we did...' A lump forms in my throat and I can't get another word out. I return to chopping, rattled, and within a second, I slice through my finger. 'Ouch!' The knife clatters to the worktop and I quickly rush to the sink and run the wound under cold water, fighting back the tears.

Margo leans over and winces. 'Ouch, that's a deep cut.'

'Sorry, Chef, I should have been more careful... and just after you complimented my knife skills too,' I add with a chuckle, hoping to dispel the awkwardness.

Margo grabs a clean tea towel ready for when I need to dry my hands. 'I'm afraid you're going to have to start all the fruit again. Can't have any contamination.'

I nod. 'Of course. I understand. Let me just get this cleaned up and...'

'Chef, Angela has asked to see you,' says one of the other chefs, interrupting us. I'm glad the twin conversation is behind us and I don't have to explain any more about Clara.

Margo looks up. 'Where is she?'

'Oh, sorry, Chef, I meant...' The other chef flicks her eyes to me.

'She wants to see me?' I ask, taking the towel from Margo and drying my hands. I put pressure on the wound with the towel to stem the bleeding.

'She's in the outside dining area.'

Margo looks at me and pouts. 'Ooh, someone's special,' she says with a wink. 'Go on. Off you go. Be quick. I'll clean up the fruit, but you're going to have to get that patched up before you return. Those meringues aren't going to make themselves.'

Still using the towel to wrap around my finger, I head up to the outdoor dining area, making sure my chef whites are clean and tidy. There is a splash of blood on my cuff, but hopefully she won't notice. I'm not sure where I can fix up my finger. The blood is still flowing, but not as bad as it was. A big plaster should do the trick, then I'll have to wear plastic gloves to prevent contamination.

When I reach the outdoor area, Angela is lounging on a padded chair in a black swimsuit and a sarong, wearing an oversized sunhat and shades. She's sipping a pink cocktail through a straw and has a platter of perfectly prepared canapés next to her on a tray. As soon as she catches sight of me, she places her cocktail down and stands, embracing me and air-kissing both my cheeks. I freeze like a statue, unsure how I'm supposed to respond, still clutching my injured hand.

'Brittany, it's so lovely to see you. How are you? Keeping well? I hope Margo's not been working you too hard.'

'Um, no, I'm fine,' I say with a forced smile.

'Good grief! What's happened?' She stares at my hand wrapped in a tea towel.

'I'm so sorry,' I say. 'I had an accident in the kitchen and was then told you needed to see me right away, so I haven't had a chance to sort it out.'

Margo grabs my hand and, before I can stop her, she's unwrapping it and inspecting my finger. 'Hmm, it doesn't look too deep. It's a nice, clean cut. There's a first aid kit you can use in the kitchen.'

'Thank you,' I say, feeling stupid that I hadn't thought about that before. There's always a first aid kit in professional kitchens.

'Good. Good. I won't keep you long. I wanted to check in and make sure everything was okay. That's all. Other than your finger, of course.'

'Everything's fine. Thank you.'

Angela takes off her sunglasses and tips her head back to look at me under the rim of her hat. 'I wanted to say I'm sorry about what happened to your sister.'

Her words feel like a punch to the stomach. 'H-How do you know about her?'

'Whenever we hire a new member of staff, we always conduct a background check.'

That's news to me. She didn't say anything about a background check during my interview or at any stage in her emails. It wasn't in the contract either.

'Oh,' I say.

'It's just to make sure we don't hire any criminals or anything, you understand.'

'Of course.' I want to retort that it's surely illegal to run a background check on someone without their permission, but I hold my tongue. That means she must also know about my surgery, but she doesn't bring it up, luckily.

She reaches out and strokes my arm. The gesture gives

me goosebumps. She's showing me kindness and love and it's making me yearn for my sister's arms wrapped around me. When we were young, I'd sometimes wake up with nightmares, sweating and trembling. Even though she was only twelve minutes older, she hugged and sang me to sleep, like I was her little sister.

'Losing someone we love is one of the most painful experiences we can go through.' Her eyes glisten as she speaks. Has she lost someone too?

My mind flashes back to the child's room I saw a few days ago. Oh God. She even mentioned grief at my interview.

'I lost a child once,' she continues, answering my question for me. 'She was only five days old.'

A lump forms in my throat and I'm completely lost for words. 'I... I'm so sorry.' Despite not being a baby person, I can still understand how traumatic and difficult it would be to lose a child. Grief comes in all shapes and forms.

She inhales slowly, then holds her breath for a moment. 'Luckily, I was blessed with a rainbow baby only a few months later.'

A small smile crosses my lips, but I'm still unsure where this is going. She's opening up to me and I don't know why. She lost a baby, for crying out loud. Why is she telling me this? I am the last person to be talking to about babies.

'Ma'am, I don't mean to overstep the mark or be rude, but... did you wish to see me just to ask if I was okay?'

'Yes and no. I wanted to ask if you could make a special dessert for me. My daughter, Faye, is coming back from boarding school tomorrow and her favourite dessert is chocolate cake. Simple, I know, but would you be able to make a large chocolate cake to celebrate her arrival?'

Her request takes me off guard for a moment. 'I'd love to. Chocolate cake was always my favourite when I was a kid.'

'Wonderful.'

'How long has she been away?'

'Too long,' replies Angela, donning her sunglasses again. 'Thank you, Brittany. I can't wait to see the look on her face when she sees the cake.'

'I'll make it extra special.'

'I know you will.'

I head back to the kitchen, find the first aid kit and fix my finger. Then, I finish the meringues and make a start on sourcing the ingredients for an elaborate and indulgent chocolate cake. I know the perfect recipe.

While mixing the chocolate cake, a wave of dizziness makes me stumble sideways. It's just occurred to me that I haven't eaten since breakfast and it's now almost six in the evening. I've been so busy making the desserts and cake that I've forgotten to eat.

I head to the sink and pour myself a glass of water. The cool liquid instantly makes me feel a bit better, but if I'm to keep going, I'll need to eat something soon. I need to look after myself better. I can't risk getting ill or mess up in any way. I need this job.

CHAPTER TWENTY-ONE

The next day, I keep an eye out for Faye's arrival, but either she doesn't turn up or she hides herself away. Even at dinner, I don't hear the chatter of a child's voice, but Angela catches me two evenings later when I'm leaving the kitchen to turn in. I've come down with a cold, either that or a stomach bug, because I can't bring myself to eat anything, yet the less I eat the worse I feel.

'Brittany!' she says, jogging to catch up with me. 'I just wanted to thank you for the amazing cake you made Faye. She absolutely loved it! As did we all. You truly have a wonderful talent for baking.'

'Thank you, ma'am. I'm so glad she enjoyed it. I didn't see her at all. Is she still here?'

'Oh, no. She had to return to boarding school. She's not back for very long before she's off again. You know how these things are. Anyway, thank you again. You're a dear. How is your finger?'

I'm touched by the fact she's remembered. It's still

wrapped in a bandage, and I still have to wear a plastic glove while preparing food. 'Oh, it's fine. Thanks.'

'Good.' She squeezes my arm and walks away, but as she does, I notice that she's limping slightly on her right leg.

I feel too dizzy to ask her about it or put too much thought into it, but over the next few days, her limp gets worse. Plus, I'm almost certain she starts limping on her other leg too. Perhaps I'm delirious from the lack of food. I haven't eaten a proper meal in almost a week, managing to survive on scraps of food from the kitchen that take my fancy.

This is how Clara's illness started.

I brush the thought away almost as soon as it enters my mind. I can't think like that. No, I'm not sick. Just run down. Overtired. Stressed, perhaps. That's all. There's no way in hell I'm visiting a doctor's surgery or hospital to get checked out. I never want to step foot inside one for as long as I live.

I SEE Angela again about a week later and her leg appears to have healed. I'm feeling better too, although I'm still exhausted most of the time. My feet hurt from standing all day in the kitchen, but I can't fault the work itself. I've created so many elaborate desserts, most of which are so perfect they could be sold in patisserie shops.

I'm also delighted to be asked to come aboard their multi-million-pound superyacht, which they plan to take out on the open sea for a week. Honest to God, the kitchen on the yacht is better than those in some top restaurants I've worked in. Margo comes too, along with two other junior chefs to help her out, although it's still only me working on the desserts.

Angela and John spend their days lounging on the deck, sipping champagne or free diving off the boat. During the times I have off, I top up my tan at the back of the ship and take plenty of naps. However, one day, I end up hurling my guts up over the side of the ship. I've never been on a boat before, so my stomach isn't used to the motion.

'Guess you're not cut out for life at sea then,' says Margo with a chuckle as I finish hurling.

I wipe my mouth and take a sip of water from my water bottle I've taken to carrying everywhere now that the weather is getting hotter by the day. It's also to remind me to stay hydrated because I'm still awful at remembering to drink.

'I guess not.'

'Here, take these. They'll help.' She hands me a blister pack of tablets. I take them, but don't recognise the name of the medication. 'It's anti-sickness,' she says. 'I used to take them a lot when I first started working on the yacht. You get used to it eventually.'

'Oh,' I say. 'Thanks.' I swallow one with another sip.

'Could be worse though, right?' Margo gestures all around us.

I glance at the endless blue ocean, the gorgeous warm sunshine, the expensive ship we're on. 'It could definitely be worse.' And we both laugh.

Maybe Margo's not so bad. She's not done or said anything lately to make me put my guard up. For the first time since I've been here, I feel a connection to another human being and as we share a laugh, I begin to feel better. I relax into a happy state of mind. For once, I don't dwell on Clara or the fact my life is empty beyond life outside of work.

. . .

'HOW ARE YOU FEELING?' asks Angela when she corners me down one of the narrow corridors two days later. We're still on the ship and, despite taking the anti-sickness tablets, I'm not feeling much better.

'Better, thanks,' I lie. 'I've never been on a boat before, so...' Why am I telling her this? I look down at her legs, taking note of her gorgeous flip-flops encrusted with sparkling jewels. 'How's your leg?' I ask.

Angela tilts her chin up, ensuring she's looking down at me, but doesn't say a word. Should I not have asked that?

'Sorry,' I say, stepping around her. 'I better get back to work.'

'My leg's fine. Thanks for asking,' she says happily.

I scurry away as embarrassment floods my system. I'm looking forward to returning to the villa tomorrow. As much as I've enjoyed my time on the yacht, I'm still not liking the constant seasickness. I head to the kitchen to find Margo to ask her if she has any anti-sickness tablets left, but when I do, I find John in there by himself.

I freeze on the spot, hoping I can turn and escape before he spots me. Too late. He stops what he's doing. Wait... What *is* he doing?

It looks like he's sprinkling something in a glass of champagne.

'Brittany, right?' he asks.

'Yes, sir. Can I help you with anything?' It's so odd to see him in the kitchen, a place I've never seen either him or Angela before.

'No,' comes his blunt response.

I step backwards. 'I'll... um... just be going then.'

I don't take a breath until I'm on the other side of the ship. As I stand on the deck, looking down into the crystal-clear water below, I get the strange urge to jump and sink down below the waves and never come back up again. I take a couple of deep breaths as I squash down the claustrophobia rising inside me. I'll be back on dry land tomorrow, with plenty of space around me.

John gives me the creeps. I saw him put some sort of powder into a glass of champagne. Was it for him or for Angela? I glace over my shoulder, but there's no one else around.

CHAPTER TWENTY-TWO

After returning to the villa, my stomach settles, but every time I see John, he gives me a look that sends the butterflies swirling again. On my way back from a long shift at work, I decide to take a quick walk around the grounds for some fresh air before heading to bed.

It's dark, but there's enough light from the villa to ensure I don't accidentally trip over anything. But as I walk down some stone steps to the courtyard, my head swims, my vision blurs and I tumble forwards, only just managing to grasp the nearby railing before I collapse against the hard ground.

I don't pass out completely, but for several moments I don't know where I am or what's happening. I retch once as I attempt to pull myself to standing, but my strength has vanished. While I wait for the strange dizzy spell to pass, I think back to when I found Clara passed out on the bathroom floor. That's when I decided enough was enough and took her to the doctor's against her will. I'm glad I did because a few weeks later she was diagnosed with early-onset kidney disease.

'Brittany?'

I hear my name being called, but I'm struggling to respond. Inside my own head, I'm screaming, but nothing is coming out of my mouth, so I wait and hope that whoever is calling my name finds me.

Soft hands grasp my arms, shaking me gently. 'Brittany, are you okay? What's wrong?'

It's a woman's voice, but I can't be sure if it's Margo or Angela. 'John!'

Okay, it's Angela.

'John, come quick!'

Before I know it, I'm being lifted and carried along the path. My head lolls against a hard chest and my eyes slowly close.

DAYLIGHT BLINDS me as I attempt to peel my eyelids apart, but it feels as if they're fused shut with concrete. My head is pounding, my mouth is dry and there's the nausea again. I retch sideways off the bed I'm lying on, but nothing but bile comes up.

'Brittany, just breathe, okay? You're safe. You're in the hospital.'

The word makes my insides turn to ice. No! I don't want to be here. Anywhere but in a hospital; a place where my sister died. A place where everyone dies. I feel as if I've been abducted and taken somewhere against my will. I need to get out of here now.

When I'm finally able to peel my eyes open, a young female doctor is standing next to me dressed in hospital scrubs. I push back the bed sheet, swinging my legs over the side of the bed.

'I can't be here,' I say.

'Brittany, we just need to have a chat first, okay?' She puts her hand out and gently pushes me back down, just as I'm about to stand.

'What about? Oh God, I'm sick, aren't I?' Tears spill from my eyes. 'This can't be happening. Not again. I don't want to die.' The panic is rising so fast that it's too much. I can't control it; I'm suffocating.

'Brittany, calm down, okay? You're not going to die.'

Her words do nothing to quell the surging panic.

'What's happened in the past?' the doctor continues. 'Can you tell me? Have you ever passed out like this before?'

'I... No, not really. My sister used to... when she was sick.'

The doctor nods. 'I see. You're not registered anywhere yet, are you?'

'No, I've only been in the country for a few weeks. I'm working with...' I stop, remembering the contract I signed. I can't tell anyone I'm working for them.

'Who brought me here?'

'A lady called Margo. Is she a friend of yours?'

I shrug. 'I guess so.'

'Apparently, you've been struggling lately with your work. You're a chef, is that right?'

'Yes, but... I've not been struggling. I mean, I haven't had any time off sick or anything. I really need this job, Doctor. Please... just tell me what's wrong with me.'

'Nothing's wrong with you, Brittany.'

I narrow my eyes. 'Are you sure?'

The doctor smiles. 'Yes. You're experiencing all perfectly normal symptoms for someone who's in the early stages of pregnancy.'

The words go in but make no sense. They swirl around and around in my head. She must have the wrong person. There's no way I'm pregnant. It's laughable! I can't be pregnant because I haven't had sex in almost two years…

Oh, wait…

A wave of dizziness engulfs me. The doctor leans forwards, handing me a glass of water. I take it and sip, then hand it back to her.

'You must be mistaken,' I say. 'I can't be pregnant. We used protection.'

The doctor smiles again. I expect she's heard that phrase a thousand times. 'I take it the baby isn't planned?'

'Planned? Are you kidding me? I've never wanted children in my entire life. It was my sister who wanted them. Hell, it should be her who's pregnant, not me.' Huge sobs shake my body. I cover my face with my hands and fall back against the pillow.

This isn't supposed to happen. I'm supposed to be living my dream for Clara, saving money for my own restaurant one day. In three years, I'll have saved up the money to be able to start afresh, build my career, earn a Michelin star.

For Clara.

What am I meant to do now?

Pregnant! Seriously?

PART 2

CHAPTER TWENTY-THREE
ANGELA

Most days always start the same. My husband's alarm blares to life, jolting me out of my heavy sleep, and he hands me a handful of pills, along with a glass of water, and says he loves me. I take them with a smile and then open my mouth wide while he checks it's empty. I can't always be trusted to swallow them all. Apparently, if I miss any of them, for any reason, it could have dramatic side-effects, so he's just looking out for me, something I'm always eternally grateful for.

John is the love of my life, but we've been through hell and back, especially over the past ten years or so. Maybe our living hell started before that. It's hard to pinpoint exactly when it started. In fact, it's hard to pinpoint anything these days. The medication I'm on often clouds my thoughts and causes severe blackouts, but John explains it's all perfectly normal and not to worry. I trust him. He's my personal doctor, after all. Technically and officially, he's a trained neurosurgeon, but he also has a background in psychology.

He tells me he knows how my brain works and knows what's best for me.

After I've taken my medication, I sit up in bed and stretch my tanned arms above my head. We got back from a week on the yacht yesterday, so it feels good to wake up in my own bed this morning. I love the trips we take on the yacht, but it never feels like home to me. The villa does. It's big; too big for two people some might say, but I don't want to move. I can't move. All my memories are here. Most of them are bad ones, but they are all I have of her, of my sweet baby before she… before she…

I hope the medication kicks in soon. I need it to take the edge off before the memories come flooding back and try and drown me. No, not drown… Anything but that…

'Angela.' John's voice echoes in my head.

'Hmm?'

'How are you today?'

'Too soon to tell, I think, darling,' I reply with a smile. It's true. I don't usually reach my stride until around an hour after I take my medication. It's only been about thirty minutes. 'Actually, would you excuse me a moment?' I shuffle out of bed and pad into our lavish ensuite in my silk nightgown. My stomach is swirling this morning, and I have no idea why. Perhaps it was those scallops I had for dinner last night, but John appears to be fine. I do sometimes drink a little too much wine and, combined with the medication, it doesn't always do me a world of good.

Before I know it, I'm leaning over the toilet. Bile, water and some remnants of the pills I took come up, floating on the surface of the water in the bowl. It's not a lot. I'm sure the pills have entered my bloodstream and done what they're supposed to do. The thought of telling John that I've vomited them up is not one I relish. If he gives me more, then he could overdose me, something that's been known to happen on occasion when he got drunk and forgot he'd given them to me.

I flush the toilet. I just won't tell him. I'm sure everything will be fine. What's the worst that can happen if I miss a partial dose of my medication? I'm not even sure what he has me on, so I can't look them up online and check the side effects of skipping a dose. But I haven't skipped it, have I?

I put on my face, adorn my sunglasses and head out for my morning walk. It always helps to clear my head, and, after this morning's escapade, I need the fresh air.

My mind drifts to Brittany, the delightful new pastry chef we've hired. She's fitted into our little family of staff like clockwork, and I can't say enough good things about her desserts. I almost want to skip the main meal and eat only her desserts. I must remember to put her forward for a culinary award or something. She deserves it.

After my brisk walk around the grounds, I return to the villa, but before I reach it, I hear a scuffle and a thud, like someone has dropped something on the stone path. Frowning, I increase my pace and muffle a scream behind my hands as I see Brittany sprawled on the steps below me.

'Brittany?' I rush to her side and grasp her arms, shaking her. 'Brittany, are you okay? What's wrong?'

Panic rises from within as flashbacks flood my vision. Memories. So many of them. Memories of finding my baby dead at five days old. No. I shake my head, squeezing my eyes closed as tight as I can. I don't want to see them.

'John! John, come quick!'

CHAPTER TWENTY-FOUR

The doctor hands me a tissue and leaves me to cry, despite her protests to stay. She says I shouldn't be alone right now, but that's exactly what I am. I am alone. Even if she stays in the room with me, I'm still alone. I have no one to support me. No one to comfort me. No one I can call to come and wrap an arm around my shoulders and tell me that everything will be okay as I sob my heart out. The doctor is a stranger. It's her job to care about me and look after me. As soon as she finishes her shift today, she'll be out of here, back to her family, and won't give two hoots about the poor, pathetic girl who's got herself knocked up after having a one-night stand with an ex-colleague who's three years younger than her.

Once I've composed myself enough to stop weeping like a child, I put the soggy tissue aside and pick up another from the box, blowing my nose. The doctor comes back in carrying a wad of leaflets all about pregnancy and *other* options. Even looking at the leaflets makes me queasy.

'How far along am I?' I ask her, placing the leaflets on

the bed next to me. The words pregnancy and abortion leap out at me and it's just too much.

'When was your last period?'

'Um... I don't really have them.'

'What birth control are you on?'

'I'm not. I don't have sex regularly. I'm too busy. But I mean... it was a one-time thing and... we used condoms.' Shit, I feel like a teenager explaining themselves to disappointed parents. I'm twenty-six years old. I should know better.

'You don't have periods?'

'I mean... I do, but... they're really irregular. My job is highly stressful, and I've been through a lot recently with... donating a kidney to my sister and then she died and then I lost my job and started a new one, and there's just been a lot going on, so... it's been at least six months since I had one, I guess.'

The doctor nods as she writes on her notepad. 'When was the last time you had sex?'

'Seven weeks ago.'

'And before that?'

'At least two years.'

'So, I guess that's your answer,' she says.

'Right.' Now I feel stupid for not having worked that out by myself. It's pretty simple maths. I frown, looking down at my stomach, which is flat and making strange gurgling sounds.

'You still have plenty of time to make a decision, Brittany.'

'Right,' I say again. My brain seems to have frozen, unable to form any sort of solid or rational thought. 'Could we keep this confidential? I mean... I'm not really in the position to tell anyone right now.'

The doctor looks as if I've offended her. 'Of course! As long as you're okay to go, then I'll release you from here with all the information you need to make your decision about how to proceed.'

It's like she's been trained not to utter the word *abortion* out loud.

'Is it legal here?'

'Yes, up to fourteen weeks after conception.'

'So... I have seven weeks.'

'Yes,' says the doctor again.

I blow out a long breath. 'Okay, well... I guess I'd better be going,' I say in a sing-song-type voice, far more enthusiastic and chipper than I feel. It's all a front. I'm dying inside.

'Is there anyone you need to call? Your friend, Margo?'

'No. No one,' I say quickly. Even if I wanted to call Margo, I can't because we've never swapped numbers. 'Thank you. I'll be in touch if... when I... Thank you, Doctor.'

Once I've signed the release forms, I make my way out of the hospital to the taxi area. There's a black car waiting and a man standing next to it holding a sign that says "Brittany Young".

'Um... Hi. That's me,' I say with a little wave.

'Miss Young, it's good to see you looking better,' says the man, who's wearing a cap and a suit. I recognise him as the driver who drove me from the airport a few weeks ago when I first arrived.

'Did you drive me here?'

'Yes, but Margo had to return to the villa to update Mr and Mrs Dalton. You gave Mrs Dalton quite a fright when she found you.'

What the hell must she think of me?

'How long have you been here?' I ask.

'Only five hours. Please, get in. I'll call ahead and let Mr and Mrs Dalton know that I'm bringing you back to the villa.'

I slide onto the back seat and stare down at my feet while we drive out of the hospital car park. I'm so relieved to be out of that hospital. I don't think I could have spent much longer behind those walls.

In less than twelve hours, my life has completely changed yet again, torn apart by a monumental event that leaves me with a decision I'm not prepared to make yet.

Tears sting my eyes during the journey. Angela and John greet me as I get out of the car. John stands back, watching me with a frown while Angela rushes forwards as if she's afraid I'm going to collapse again. She looks a little unstable herself.

'Brittany, oh you had us so worried. Are you all right? What did the doctors say? I'm so sorry I couldn't come with you, but...' She stops and her eyes flick sideways then back to me. 'I'm just glad you're okay.'

I smile, wanting to push her away from me because the smell of her perfume is overwhelming and is causing my stomach to turn over.

'I'm fine,' I say, swallowing a mouthful of saliva—something else I've noticed that's increased, constantly flowing into my mouth at an alarming rate. I need some sort of spit bucket to carry around with me. What's that about?

'You don't look fine. You look positively ill.'

'Just a bit woozy, that's all. The doctor said I need to make sure I eat something and not let my blood sugar drop.'

'What did they say is wrong?'

'Nothing... just...'

'Oh gosh, have we been overworking you?'

'No, nothing like that.'

'Perhaps it's stress then. Grief can catch up with us in the strangest of ways.' I notice this is now the third time she's mentioned grief and how it can affect people. Clearly, losing her child at five days old was traumatic for her and now, even years later, it's still causing pain and suffering. And here I am, contemplating getting rid of a kid while it's still a bundle of cells in my body. If she knew, I bet she wouldn't be so kind and friendly towards me.

'I'm sure I'll be fine in a couple of days,' I say with a forced smile.

'Then I insist you take the next few days off from work.'

'No!' I shout, much louder than intended. 'No,' I repeat, quieter. 'I mean... I just want to work. I need to work. Thank you, though.'

Angela nods. 'Okay, well... don't work too hard, okay? Take the rest of the day off and start afresh tomorrow.'

I nod and say thank you again, even though her gesture is not as kind as she probably thinks it is considering it's almost eight in the evening now. My bed is calling my name as I shuffle past John towards the staff accommodation. He grabs my arm as I'm walking past, a little too hard, and I let out a small yelp.

'Glad you're feeling better,' he says.

I fight the urge not to hyperventilate at his touch. He's too close to me. Everything's too close, too... I yank my arm out of his grasp.

'T-Thanks,' I mutter, then scurry away, sucking in huge gulps of air. By the time I reach my room, I have the hiccups and heartburn.

CHAPTER TWENTY-FIVE

ANGELA

My goodness, finding Brittany sprawled on the ground gives me such a fright I have to be escorted back to the villa by one of the staff members while John sorts out the poor girl. He picks her up as if she weighs next to nothing and puts her in a taxi. He instructs Margo to go with her, since they seem to have formed a friendship of sorts, then he comes and sees me in my room.

Since this morning, my head has been fuzzier than usual, yet in a strange way it's also clearer. I can remember a lot more than normal. Sometimes, I get memories all mixed up and it feels like trying to put together a jigsaw puzzle of pieces all the same colour, but now shapes and various colours are forming and making it a little easier to place the memories into the right order.

Is this because I vomited up the pills this morning? Perhaps they aren't doing what they're supposed to be doing after all. John says they are to help my mind be clearer, but now there's evidence to suggest the opposite. Is John trying to stop me from remembering something? Does he not want me to complete the puzzle of memories in my head?

'How are you feeling, my love?' he asks me, sitting on the edge of the bed.

'Better,' I say. 'My head is a little... funny.' I smile at him, but he doesn't return it. Instead, he takes a deep breath and places a warm hand on my bare leg.

'I think I should up your dose.'

'Oh... okay. If that's what you think,' I say cheerfully.

'Let's leave it another day and if your head doesn't feel better by then, then I'll increase your dose. I don't want you having a relapse.'

To be honest, I don't want that either. The last time I skipped a dose, my mind played all sorts of tricks on me. I began hallucinating and lashing out, even striking John across the face with a knife, hence his disfiguring scar. Every time I look at him, I'm reminded of the damage I can do when I'm off my medication, but this time feels different. I'm not lashing out or hallucinating; at least not yet. I dare not reveal to John about this morning. I'll just take my next dose as normal tonight.

John leaves me to rest. He says that Margo has called and said Brittany is fine, but she needs to get back to the kitchen to prepare for lunch, so John sends our driver to go and wait for Brittany. Once she's back, I'll hopefully be feeling better so I can ensure she's okay. My heart goes out to the poor girl. I know she must be suffering through her grief of losing her sister.

I know exactly what grief can do to a person over the long term if not treated and managed correctly. Look at me now. Only the medication my doting husband provides me keeps me on a level that's manageable and doesn't cause me to turn into a raging lunatic.

That's the last thing I want to happen.

I close my eyes and try and sleep, but my dreams are plagued by running water and screaming. So much screaming.

CHAPTER TWENTY-SIX

I can't do this. I can't. I can't be pregnant. This isn't the plan. This is so far from the plan that it's practically on a different planet. What kind of higher being thought it would be a good idea for the condom to fail and get me pregnant? Me! The woman who doesn't have a maternal bone in her body and never has. The woman who whoops and cheers when she gets her period (even if it is sporadically) despite the pain being crippling because it means she's not pregnant (despite not having regular sex). The woman who avoids children of all ages like the plague and would rather wait for the next bus than get on the same one as a screaming infant. The woman who refuses to hold a newborn baby in case I catch something, or I get those hormone surges people always talk about, and who looks at other women in disgust when they sniff a baby's head or coo over a new baby, gasping at how adorable they are, despite them looking like a shrivelled-up old man.

It's so ridiculous that it's laughable.

I can't do this. Not because I don't want to, but because I

physically and mentally can't. I can barely look after myself right now, let alone a child. Plus—and I can't stress this enough—if I had a child then that poor child would grow up to resent me as their mother. How do I know this? I have solid proof. My own mother did the same. She got knocked up at a young age too from a one-night stand. She didn't even know our father's name, and whether I like it or not, I'm exactly like her (except at least I know who the father is). I have no idea where Clara's kind attitude and mothering instinct came from, but it wasn't from our mother, who, after a year of raising us, at age nineteen, decided we were too much to handle, handed us over to her own mother and ran off to America, never to be seen or heard from again. That's why I don't want kids. I could never do that. What if I can't handle it and run away like my own mother did? How could I live with myself?

Our grandmother told me and Clara when we were old enough to understand that our mother didn't want us, that we were an accident. Some might say she could have kept that information to herself to spare us the grief of learning that our own mother wished she'd had an abortion, but that information turned out to be the catalyst that lit the fire of my desire to prove my mother wrong. Not about having children, but that I wasn't worthless, and I would amount to something one day. I don't know where she is, and I don't care where she is.

Clara always had the opposite dream; to prove that she could be the best mother to a child. She wanted to adopt, if she couldn't have one herself. She wanted to give a child without parents a second chance because that's who she was. Whereas I'm just an idiot who keeps making rash decisions. Wrong decisions.

I am truly stuck between a rock and a hard place. I have no job to go back to in London and no place to live. If I stay here, then eventually I'll have to tell John and Angela about my pregnancy, and then what? It even said in the bloody contract I signed that if I had to take a break for reasons such as illness or pregnancy, I wouldn't be eligible for sick or maternity pay unless I'd worked here for more than six months. I've only been here seven weeks.

They could have grounds to fire me. Granted, I could probably sue them if they did, but with what? The couple of thousand pounds I've managed to save since I've lived here? They're millionaires. I'd have no chance.

I sigh angrily as I stare at myself in the mirror and do the thing that all newly pregnant women probably do and turn sideways, imagining a huge bump. But instead of feeling happy and excited, I just feel angry. I hate myself. Hate. Hate. Hate.

I scream. I scream until I cry and then I scream some more. Then I throw up.

My life is a mess. A complete and utter mess.

I can't have this baby. I can't.

But I do have a choice to make.

I either continue with the pregnancy, have the baby and put it up for adoption so that another family can love and raise it and give it the life and nurture it deserves, or…

I can book in with the hospital and have an abortion.

CHAPTER TWENTY-SEVEN

I lay awake all night, battling against my own mind, but I finally come to a decision. The next morning, I struggle through a horrible bout of morning sickness, then call the nearest abortion clinic during my break, booking an appointment for Monday, my next day off. The thought of going back to a hospital fills me with dread, but there's no other way. I can survive three more days. As soon as I hang up the phone call, Margo appears where I'm perched on top of a low wall outside the back door of the kitchen.

'Hey, Brittany. Everything okay?'

I slip my phone into my pocket. 'Um... yes. Were you just eavesdropping on me?'

She puts her hands up in defence. 'Guilty.'

'How much did you hear?'

'Not much,' she responds sweetly. I don't like her tone or the way she's smiling at me like she knows my biggest secret. We lock eyes for a few seconds.

'Margo, I'd really appreciate it if you didn't tell anyone about what you just heard.'

'I didn't hear anything.'

I stare at her some more. 'Right, but...'

'Remember, what happens in this villa stays at the villa.'

'Right, but...'

Margo reaches forwards and grasps my arm, giving it a little shake. She winks. 'Don't worry, your secret's safe with me. We've all been there.'

My eyebrows rise. 'Oh yeah? You have?'

Margo laughs. 'God, yes! Do you know how many of the cute waiting staff I've shagged here over the years, not to mention the hot, French, rich dudes in town?'

My face heats up. Surely, she can't be telling me what I think she's telling me? 'Oh,' I say.

'Don't worry. A few pills and you'll be right as rain. Just, ah... wear protection next time, yeah? Having gonorrhoea is no walk in the park.'

I almost burst out laughing, but force it back, which turns out to be a snort. 'Sorry,' I say. 'You're right though. I should have known better.'

'Who'd you shag? Just so I can avoid catching it.'

'Oh, no one here. Just some guy back in London just before I arrived.'

'Got it. Don't worry, Britt, I won't tell a soul.' She motions zipping her lips closed.

I breathe a sigh of relief as I hop off the wall and return to the kitchen.

Three more days.

I just need to get through three more days.

CHAPTER TWENTY-EIGHT
ANGELA

After John gave me my next dose of medication last night, I waited ten minutes, then excused myself from the room and made myself vomit in the nearest bathroom. Something wasn't right. Once I'd woken up from my nap, I saw Brittany, who looked quite unwell, bless her, but then I kept remembering things; things that I'd never remembered before. Like, shouting at Faye when she was naughty. I can't remember ever being upset with her. She's always been a perfect child, but my mind is full of screaming. I can't make sense of any of it, but I'm determined to figure it out. The medication is clearly blocking the memories, so I do the only thing that makes sense. I vomit up the pills after he's given them to me. They might be absorbed in my bloodstream a little, but not enough to take full effect. I've got no idea how long it will take for my memories to return.

However, the next day, my mood is fluctuating like a rollercoaster. I can't be around John because he just makes me mad, so I excuse myself and go for a manicure, massage and a facial in town. If I keep myself busy, then it's less likely

I'll lash out at him, but as I lay there on the massage couch with my eyes closed, the memories flood every corner of my mind and I suddenly scream at the top of my lungs, startling the poor massage therapist.

'I'm so sorry,' I say, wrapping the towel around my chest as I sit up. 'I think I need a break.'

'No problem, Mrs Dalton. I'll give you a few minutes. Let me fetch you some cool lemon water.'

'Thank you,' I reply. As soon as the therapist closes the door, I burst into tears and bury my face in my hands. I remember so much, but nothing makes any sense. The grief of losing my first baby hits me like a sledgehammer to the face and I can't breathe. Perhaps the pills were keeping the pain and grief away. God, this is horrible. I can't stand it.

My poor baby.

Five days old. John and I hadn't even got around to officially registering her name yet, but we had decided on what it would be. But... there was a baby later, wasn't there? Faye, my rainbow baby, but... Oh, God...

She looked different than I remember.

I sob into my hands, rocking back and forth. Maybe I should come clean to John and admit I've been vomiting up my pills. He'll be furious, but at least I'll know that the pain will go away. With the pills, I didn't feel it. It didn't feel like I was being burned alive by grief and anger. I just need to let it all out somehow. Instead of the pain being inside my body, maybe I can make it so that it's outside.

I get dressed and tell the therapist that I need to leave, quickly paying up and giving her a big tip for the inconvenience of leaving halfway through an appointment. I head home and rummage through the drawers in the kitchen, finding a sharp knife, then return to my room.

CHAPTER TWENTY-NINE

The morning of my appointment arrives, and I'm sick several times, hugging the toilet as if it's the only thing keeping me from sinking into a pit of despair. I hate this. I hate being pregnant. Is this baby trying to punish me for what I'm about to do? I swear I've felt ten times worse since I decided to get rid of it. Urrgg. I hate that phrase, but I don't know how else to put it.

Despite Margo's mix-up with the phone call she overheard, I'm still not convinced she hasn't told people what she thinks she knows. The men in particular give me sly looks and the women seem to whisper as I walk past. Maybe it's all in my head.

I carry on with my work as diligently as I can, keeping my head down and only speaking to people when I need to. Luckily, as the only pastry chef in the villa, I don't have to interact with many other chefs. I see Angela several times milling about the place, but she looks quite vacant. In fact, I wave to her at one point but she completely blanks me, something she's never done before. She's usually so friendly and bubbly, but she looks a little different lately. But I can't worry about her right now.

I arrive at the hospital an hour early because I can't deal with the anxiety rolling around in my stomach any longer. Dizziness, nausea and a racing heart are keeping me pacing the halls while I wait for my name to be called, like a person being called in for their death sentence.

I'm doing the right thing.

It's for the best.

Then my thoughts turn to Clara. My beautiful, perfect sister who's had her life stolen from her because I forced her to accept my kidney. If she'd had someone else's, maybe she'd still be here. I killed my sister and now I'm about to kill my baby.

Then it hits me.

Hospitals have always been places of death for me. They've been the root cause of my intense phobia with them, and now... now, I'm about to lose someone else in one. It might just be a jumble of cells right now, but it's a life, right? I'm basically going against everything I've thought since I was a child.

My best friend died in a hospital when I was fourteen.

My grandmother died in a hospital five years ago.

My twin sister died in a hospital less than two months ago.

Now, my unborn child is about to die in a hospital.

'Fuck!' I scream into the waiting room.

Several women sitting nearby jump and give me their best shocked expressions. One even stands up and moves further down the hallway to some other chairs.

'Sorry,' I say, turning my back on them.

But there's one difference this time.

I can do something to stop anyone else dying.

I close my eyes, trying to block out the sounds of the hospital around me, but all I see is Clara's disappointed face. If she were here, she'd tell me not to do this. She'd tell me that it's a blessing and that it happened for a reason.

'It's not what I want,' I say out loud, keeping my voice low. 'Help me.'

If Clara were still alive and I was in this position, what would I do? She always wanted children. She wanted to adopt. Hell, if she were alive, I'd have this baby and give it to her to raise as her own, but she's not here, is she?

What am I supposed to do?

'Brittany Young?'

As soon as I hear my name, I know the answer. I sprint down the corridor and down to the taxi rank before I can change my mind.

No one else is dying in a hospital. Not on my watch. Not if there's something I can do about it.

I cry my eyes out during the ride back to the villa while I go over my options. I'm having the baby, but I'm not keeping it. I want to give it up for adoption back in England, but how the hell do I even go about doing that from here? The last thing I want is to give up this job and return home. Plus, I'm sure Chef Andre's reign of terror is still doing the rounds. I suppose I don't have to stay in London, but where would I go? I have very little money, not enough to rent somewhere and keep myself going for the foreseeable future. Who will hire a pregnant woman as a chef? Granted, I wouldn't be going on maternity leave if I'm not keeping it, but there's so many complicated things to think about and my brain just can't focus on any of them. It feels as if I'm drowning, and I can't keep my head above the water level.

Returning to the villa, I can't face going back to my room, so I walk around for a bit, admiring the grounds and the gorgeous plants growing. I keep walking, ignoring my aching legs and my dizzy head. Walking means I'm not standing still. Walking helps me feel as if my thoughts aren't trying to drown me.

My phone vibrates in my pocket. I answer it without even looking at the screen because who the hell would be calling me other than some salesperson? Maybe it's my doctor back in England, continuing to pester me about seeing a grief counsellor.

'Brittany?'

'Hello? Who is this?'

'It's Luke.'

I hang up like the mature adult I am and turn off my phone.

Nope. Not ready for that conversation. I'll be honest and say I haven't even thought about him in all of this, but there's no way I'm telling him. I don't want to ruin his life too.

CHAPTER THIRTY

Two weeks go by, and I've made no attempt to start the adoption process back in the UK, nor have I signed up to see a midwife or made an appointment with the hospital for a scan or check-up. One of the worst things about going through with this pregnancy is the thought of all the hospital appointments, not to mention labour. That's a whole other issue that I can't face right now, so I'm just not thinking about it at all. I'm not ready to do this, but I know I have a time limit on my ignorance.

Work is busy and I'm glad of the distraction, but I'm not sure how much longer I can pretend this isn't happening. I'm not showing yet, other than massive bloat in the evenings, but it won't be long before the baby starts pushing aside my internal organs and making itself at home.

The toilet bowl is still my friend most mornings, and if I open any of the fridges in the kitchen, I often retch and nearly pass out, but other than that, I'm managing to get by with some anti-sickness wristbands I picked up from the local pharmacy. Margo keeps looking at me funny whenever I say I need to step outside for some fresh air.

Then, one day, the world feels like it tilts sideways as John comes into the kitchen. 'Brittany, may I have a private word?'

My mouth opens and closes, and I feel a familiar burning sensation in the back of my throat. Somehow, I manage to hold it together. 'Of course, sir.'

I follow him through the kitchen as dozens of pairs of eyes watch on. Why does it feel as if I'm being led to the gallows or out into the yard to be stoned to death? I catch Margo's eye, and she winks at me. Oh shit. She told him, didn't she? I'm still not sure if she's worked out the truth or is keeping with the version she invented. But either way, it's not going to be good.

By the time we reach a secluded part of the villa—one of the two offices—my mouth is so dry that my tongue keeps sticking to the roof of my mouth. I swallow several times, but it doesn't help. John motions for me to take a seat on the soft, velvet sofa, which I do quickly because I'm afraid my legs might give out any minute and he'll have to rescue me from a crumpled heap on the floor for the second time since I've been working here.

I cross my ankles and place my hands neatly in my nap, picking at my nails as I do so. I know better than to speak first. Why isn't Angela here? I've never spent any time alone with John (apart from the brief encounter in the kitchen) and it's not exactly a pleasant experience. Come to think of it, for the past two weeks, I've barely seen Angela. Maybe she's gone away somewhere, but then again, I've been making desserts enough for two every evening, so she must be around here somewhere.

'Brittany,' he finally says, taking a seat opposite me in a large, leather chair. 'I know we haven't spoken a lot, but I wanted to check in with you and make sure everything is okay.' It's the most words I've heard him say in a single sentence. Plus, he doesn't have his usual abrupt tone, but a calm, kind one, like Angela.

My hands automatically go to my stomach. 'Yes, sir. Everything's fine.'

John looks around, perhaps wishing his wife were here to back him up. 'It's just that... some of the staff have mentioned that you've been... a bit off lately.'

'A bit off?'

'Yes.'

'With my work?'

'Oh, no, not with your work. Your desserts continue to be the highlight of every meal. In fact, we're having visitors over soon, some very high-up, well-known chefs and also some surgeon friends of mine, and we'd like you to create something positively out of this world, but that's for another time to talk about.'

My eyebrows rise. High-up, well-known chefs? Oh my God...

'The thing is, Brittany, we pride ourselves on excellent standards here and the staff know not to speak out of turn. Now, I know a couple of weeks ago you were unwell. How has everything been since then?' Why is he being so nice to me when previously he's been nothing but blunt and, quite frankly, rude?

My eyes sting with tears. Do. Not. Cry.

'F-Fine.'

'Good. All healthy and back to normal, I hope?'

'Y-Yes.'

I bite down hard on my tongue, but it's no use. The emotion washes over me like a tidal wave and the dam of emotions I've been holding back for the past few weeks comes crashing down. My body vibrates with sobs as I fight to control them, but it's like all the pent-up emotion is being released all at once. My body can't handle it.

I don't look up at John. My eyes stay firmly on the floor in front of me until several minutes pass and the sobs gradually fade to sniffles.

'I-I'm so sorry,' I say, wiping my nose with the cuff of my jacket because I don't have anything else to use. That is, until John hands me a tissue. I take it, my bottom lip wobbling at the kind gesture. Oh God, he's going to set me off again. I'm a blubbering mess.

'Thank you,' I whisper.

'Okay, I think it's safe to say that something is going on,' he says. 'Am I correct?'

I can't do anything but nod.

'Would you prefer it if I asked my wife to join us? She's not feeling her best, but I can fetch her. Would that make you more comfortable?'

Suddenly I feel anything but comfortable. John has never been kind to me before, barely saying more than a few words in my presence since I've been here.

'I... I'm not sure,' I say.

'Perhaps Margo?'

'No.'

'Is there a problem with Margo?'

'No, not really. No, not at all.' I sniff and blow my nose with the tissue. I just need to come out and say it. There's no point trying to hide it any longer. If I tell them now, then perhaps it will give them and me more time to come to some sort of plan moving forwards. It's now or never.

John sighs. 'Brittany, I've never been very good at comforting people, so... if you'd like Angela to join us, then I can fetch her now and...'

'I'm pregnant,' I blurt out.

Then I proceed to hold my breath until he speaks, which takes at least fifteen seconds.

'I see,' he says. 'That is... unexpected.'

'You could say that,' I say. 'I just want you to know that this was completely unplanned, and I had no idea I was pregnant when I took the job.'

John seems to be slowly inching his way towards the exit. I don't blame him. I shouldn't have told him. I should have accepted his offer to fetch Angela and wait for her to arrive, but it's done now. I've ripped the plaster off and now I'm feeling the sting of pain as my wound is exposed to the elements.

John clears his throat. 'This... could pose a problem.'

'I'm so sorry. I know it's not the ideal time, but I fully intend to work for as long as possible and I'm even going to look at getting the baby adopted as soon as it's born back in the UK.'

Just shut up, Brittany. Why are you blurting all this out to your boss?

John just stares at me. 'I see,' he says again. 'While that decision is obviously your choice, I was more referring to your actual pregnancy being a problem.'

'I don't understand.'

John clenches his jaw. 'My wife... has had multiple miscarriages and one stillbirth over the past five years. Not to mention suffered through the sudden death of our first child when she was five days old seven years ago.'

My gasp comes out louder than intended. 'I'm so sorry.' I knew about the baby, but not all the miscarriages. God, I feel like an evil villain right now.

'Thank you. Angela has... struggled to overcome her grief since we lost our first child, and I'm worried that your pregnancy could cause her to spiral. She's already not responding well lately to her medication, and I can't figure out why.'

I think I know what that means.

'Are you firing me?'

John crosses his hands back and forth in front of him. 'No, God no. No. Nothing like that.'

The relief must be evident on my face.

'However, I will ask if you can keep this between us for a bit longer. I shall speak to my wife alone first. Is that okay?'

'Yes, okay. Fine. But... my job...'

'I will have to speak to Angela first,' he repeats.

I stand up and straighten my chef jacket. 'Okay, thank you.' Something tells me it's not going to go well. 'I'm sorry again about crying in front of you.'

'It's perfectly understandable,' he responds, taking a step to the side. I walk past him to the door. 'Oh, and Brittany, I would also keep it a secret from the staff for now, until Angela and I have come to a decision.'

'A decision?'

He doesn't expand on his comment, and I leave the room with my head hanging down, feeling as if I've just been fired, even though he said I wasn't. Surely, he can't fire a woman just because she's pregnant. It's morally wrong on so many levels and quite possibly illegal.

Once the door is closed behind me, it's then that I remember about Faye. They do have a child, right? Angela even said she was blessed with a rainbow baby not long after her first child died, so... I'm assuming that was Faye. It's strange that John didn't mention his daughter just now.

I head back to the kitchen, going over what he said about his wife having several miscarriages and stillbirths and how it will affect her seeing my bump grow each day. I feel awful for the poor woman, but how is that my fault? John can't expect me to hide my pregnancy for the entire duration, can he?

'Hey, Britt. Everything okay?' Margo pounces as soon as she sees me.

'Yes. Fine.'

'What did the boss want?'

I re-tie my apron around my waist and tuck a flyaway strand of hair back into my ponytail. 'Nothing that concerns you,' I answer, not making eye contact.

'You know, it wouldn't hurt to have a friend around here,' replies Margo sternly. 'I'm just looking out for you.'

'By telling John and Angela that I'm struggling?'

'But you are!'

I sigh angrily and squeeze my eyes shut, counting to three. 'I'm not struggling. I'm just... I just need time to sort some stuff out, okay?'

'Fine, but don't come crying to me when it all falls down around your head and you're kicked out on your butt.' Margo storms off down the kitchen towards the huddle of other chefs who are congregating together, most likely hoping for a snippet of gossip.

One thing is for sure; my life and career are now in

John's hands. This could be my last night living at this villa. I suppose I should start researching job opportunities back home again.

There goes my dream of saving up enough money to start up my own restaurant.

CHAPTER THIRTY-ONE

ANGELA

It's been two weeks and two days since my last dose of medication. I've been able to fool John into thinking I'm taking it, but the side-effects are clearly showing, not only physically but mentally. I've been able to convince John that I'm going through early menopause, but I'm not sure he's fully buying into the idea, especially since I'm only in my mid-forties.

The headaches are one of the worst symptoms I'm experiencing. Or, perhaps, the more accurate way of describing them are migraines. The flashing lights behind my eyelids and the thumping pulse in the base of my skull are enough to render me catatonic most days and my brain can't make sense of even the simplest of tasks. Luckily, my husband doesn't pester me, other than to ensure I take my pills, which I continue to vomit up. Although, a couple of times I've been unable to get away before they've been absorbed and, when I've gone to purge them, they don't come up. Therefore, my mood swings are up and down constantly and it's hard to hold a conversation before I keep forgetting what I'm talking about.

 The easiest way to avoid suspicions is to avoid engaging with the staff, so I keep my distance, which is a shame because I usually enjoy speaking to the staff. Mrs Dubois is the only person I can trust and who understands, despite not knowing the truth about why I'm feeling so off-kilter lately. She brings me drinks and sees to my every need when my husband is indisposed or working, which he has been doing a lot lately. I know his work is very important to him, so I don't stick my nose into his business. Over the past few weeks, he's entertained a lot of his work colleagues here over lavish dinners, which Margo and her chefs have prepared. In fact, there's a dinner party scheduled for tomorrow, I believe, so I need to be back on my feet for that. Every party we host, the desserts have been the biggest hit amongst the guests. I'm very happy for Brittany and how well she's doing here, but John has mentioned once or twice that she seems a little off-kilter herself. I don't dwell on it too much, as I have enough to deal with myself.

 I'm sitting in the sunroom, having some quiet time, when John enters, looking a little dishevelled, something I'm not used to seeing in my husband. He's usually the epitome of perfection, but today he has a scowl on his face, and he rubs his chin as he approaches me, a tell-tale sign that he's concerned and needs to talk to me.

 He takes a seat on the lounger next to me and places his hand on my leg. 'I need to tell you something, my love. I'm a little worried about how you'll react, considering how unwell you've been lately. I'm considering taking you to the hospital to get your bloods taken.'

 I plaster a fake smile on my face. 'There's no need for

that,' I say, as panic rises from within. I'm fully aware that a blood test will reveal that I haven't been taking my medication consistently. 'What is it you need to speak to me about?'

'It's about Brittany.'

'Oh?'

John pauses for five seconds. 'She's pregnant.'

At first, the words don't sink in. They float around in the air, hovering in my peripheral vision. My brain races to connect the dots. Pregnant. Brittany, our new pastry chef, is pregnant. I glare at my husband, but I don't get the feeling he's responsible. He's been known to stray from time to time. Not lately, but in the past. I don't blame him. Back then, I'd been almost impossible to deal with.

'Pregnant,' I say slowly.

John takes that as his cue to explain. 'Yes, she broke down in tears and admitted that's why she's not been feeling well lately and the cause of her collapse a couple of weeks ago. She apologised and made it clear she's going to continue with her pregnancy, but that she wants to give the child up for adoption when it's born, back in the UK.'

I inhale through my teeth, making a hissing noise. 'No,' I say.

John frowns. 'What do you mean by no? My love, if her pregnancy is too much for you to handle then we can fire her and give her some money to stay quiet to the authorities. I know it's not legal to fire a pregnant woman over her pregnancy, but if it causes you to get worse, then...'

'No,' I say again. 'No. I need this, John.'

'You... What do you mean?'

I tell him. I tell him everything.

This unplanned pregnancy could be exactly what I need to get better.

CHAPTER THIRTY-TWO

Sleep eludes me, so I start packing my belongings instead. Let's be honest, it'll be easier to leave before they fire me or having to suffer through the next few months trying to hide my expanding body so as not to upset Angela. Maybe I should just quit and return to England and start afresh, yet again. I have no idea where I'll live or what I'll do for work, but I'm sure I can figure that out.

I start work as normal, the nauseous feeling still lingering within. Margo keeps shooting glances at me from across the kitchen while I prepare the dessert menu for this evening. There's a dinner party scheduled to start at six and several of John's surgeon friends are attending, along with their wives and husbands or partners. Since I haven't been fired yet or asked to come for a chat, I carry on as normal, wondering how much time I have left.

Pulling the large freezer door open, I step inside to place the ice cream on a shelf to set. This freezer is big enough to stand in, something that shocked and fascinated me when I first saw it. As I turn to walk out, the door swings shut. The lights go out automatically when it's sealed.

'Hey!' I call out, banging on the door. I pull on the internal door release, but it doesn't shift. It's clearly been locked from the outside.

Goosebumps arise on my bare skin within seconds. Then panic starts to slowly rise, taking my breath away. It's pitch black, not even a sliver of light escaping through the locked door. It's okay. It's fine. Someone will come along in a moment and open the door. The freezer is constantly in use. Someone will be along soon.

Seconds turn into minutes.

I press the button on the side of my digital watch. I've been in here almost five minutes. How long does it take for a person to freeze to death, or start to develop hypothermia? I bang my fists against the door until the pain becomes too much to bear.

'Help!' My voice is weak, croaky. Oh my God, I'm going to die in a walk-in freezer and be found hours from now, curled up in a foetal position like a frozen popsicle next to the ice cream.

I can barely stand. Maybe I should preserve my energy and sit down.

Then, the lights come on and the door opens. Margo walks in like nothing has happened.

'Brittany? What the hell are you doing in here?'

My teeth chatter together as I glare at her. 'You locked me in here!'

Margo laughs. 'Are you delusional?'

'I don't know. Maybe. I have been locked in a freezer for the past six minutes!' I yell, pushing past her into the warmth of the kitchen.

Margo slams the freezer door behind us then places her hands on her hips. 'I warned you on day one about that freezer door, did I not? The internal door release often sticks.'

I rub my hands up and down my arms and stamp my feet on the floor, then blow into my cupped hands. 'I don't know. Maybe.'

'I did. I warn everyone because it tends to swing close, especially if the door at the opposite end of the kitchen is open.'

I blow into my hands again. 'Whatever,' I mutter.

'Do I need to have a word with John and Angela about your attitude?'

I laugh, too cold to care about it. 'You know what? Go ahead.'

Margo huffs. 'Anyway, I was trying to find you to tell you that John and Angela want to have a word in the main office.'

'Great. Can't wait.'

I leave Margo muttering indecencies behind me and make my way to the office in the main part of the villa. I can't seem to stop shivering. Even the warmth of the mid-morning sun isn't enough to warm me up as I walk across the yard.

My feet feel numb as I walk up the stone steps. I feel bad for snapping at Margo, but thanks to my surging hormones lately, I can't seem to control my emotions. I cry at the drop of a hat or get angry for no reason.

Before I knock on the office door, I take a few moments to compose myself, checking my reflection in the hallway mirror. Hair has sprung out from my ponytail and the shadows under my eyes look darker than they did this morning when I got up. I did dab some concealer under my eyes, but it seems to have made little difference.

The office door opens just as I'm readjusting my ponytail. I leap away from the mirror and stand up straight as John looks out at me.

'I thought I heard something. Thank you for coming, Brittany.'

'No problem, sir.'

'Please, come in.'

I shuffle past him with a smile. Angela is sitting by the large window looking over the grounds. There's a silver tray of cups and saucers, along with a selection of biscuits and cakes, all of which I made yesterday. She turns and looks at me as I enter the room, giving me a blank expression. There's nothing behind her eyes. Nothing. Usually, she's smiling and happy and chatty, but today she looks as if she's spent the past twenty-four hours crying.

Is this because of me?

John directs me to a nearby chair. 'Would you like some tea?' he asks.

'Um... maybe just some water, please?'

John nods and pours me a glass of ice water, adding a lemon wedge before handing it to me. I take it, feeling the coolness of the glass against my palm. My body involuntarily shivers again, as if remembering the six minutes I spent in a freezer only moments ago. I don't have the heart to tell him that lemon makes me queasy lately. Another delightful symptom of pregnancy; aversions to random things I normally enjoy.

'As I said, thank you for coming. I hope we're not keeping you from anything.'

'No, sir.'

John clears his throat as he sits next to his wife, placing a hand on her leg. She flinches, barely, but it's enough for me to notice. 'Now, after speaking with you yesterday, my wife and I have come to an agreement.'

Angela makes some sort of gurgling sound.

John flicks his eyes towards her, then back to me. 'While this is upsetting for my wife, she has agreed to honour your contract and keep you on.'

Tears threaten to spill, so I cover my emotions by taking a sip of ice water, which hits my stomach like a dagger to the chest. The lemon flavour tickles the back of my throat. I cough and choke, quickly putting the glass down on the coffee table beside me before I spill water all over my lap.

'Thank you,' I say. 'I really appreciate that, and let me just say again how sorry I am that this has happened. I honestly had no idea, and I wish I could just make it all go away.'

Oh shit. That was the wrong thing to say.

Angela takes a deep breath then breaks down into body-shaking sobs. She covers her face with both hands, leans forwards over her knees and wails. John gives me a stern look but doesn't make any move towards his wife.

'I'm so sorry!' I cry. I stand up, then knock into the table holding the tray of cups and biscuits, sending it flying. What the hell is wrong with me? My body feels weird, and I don't think it has anything to do with being cold.

'Just stop!' shouts Angela.

I halt in place and sit back down, like a scolded child.

Angela finally looks up at me, mascara streaming down her cheeks. 'You have no idea how lucky you are,' she says through gritted teeth. 'You may not want this baby, but I do.'

I open my mouth. Wait... What did she just say?

I look at John for an explanation, but it seems like he's

stepping back and allowing Angela to speak now. She uses a tissue from her pocket and dabs at her eyes.

'Are you quite sure you'd like to put the child up for adoption?' she asks.

'I... Yes.' My mouth is so dry, I can barely speak.

'Then my husband and I would like to adopt it once you've given birth.'

My mouth drops open.

'As my husband has no doubt told you, we have struggled to conceive for many years. Faye was our little miracle baby, but I have always wanted a sibling for her. I have lost several babies in the process. I see this as nothing more than a business transaction. You have something we want. You don't want it. We will purchase it off you.'

So, I take it Faye is real, but it's still odd John has never mentioned her.

Then my brain clicks into gear.

'I'm sorry... *purchase?*'

'In a matter of speaking. We shall adopt your child as our own and, in return, we shall give you as much money as you need and help you open your own restaurant, but after you have given birth, you won't be working here anymore. The three-year contract is now void. That is what you want, is it not?'

'Um...'

'There will be no paperwork involved, do you understand? As in, the child will not go through the normal adoption process. As soon as it's born you will hand it over to me —*us*—and we shall raise it as our own.'

I can't seem to even summon the muscles in my jaw to close my mouth. It just hangs open. Did I hear her correctly?

She did say she was going to adopt my baby and give me a lump sum of money in return, right? I didn't hallucinate just now.

'Brittany, do you understand what we're asking of you?' asks John. I'd almost forgotten he was here. I look up at him and nod.

'Of course, you can disagree to our terms,' continues Angela. 'But I wouldn't recommend it.'

Wait. Did she just threaten me? What will happen if I say no?

I gulp back the lump in my throat that seems to have been stuck there for the past few minutes, since entering this room. The coldness in my veins seems to have been replaced with fire and within seconds I'm visibly sweating.

Oh my God. I'm going to pass out again.

I fan my face as if that's going to miraculously save me, then reach forward and grab my ice water again, taking a sip. The air conditioning is working wonders in the room, but my body temperature is making up its own mind.

'Are you quite all right?' asks Angela.

'Um... hot flush,' I say, taking another sip. 'It's just a bit of a shock. That's all.'

'What is your answer?'

Am I supposed to decide now? I mean... clearly, it's the answer to all my problems and will enable me to open my own restaurant in a year rather than three, but is it the morally right decision? What would Clara say to this if she were alive? Granted, if she were alive, I wouldn't be in this mess.

'I... I have a lot of questions,' I say.

'Like what?' asks Angela. Is it me or has she changed her attitude towards me since finding out I'm pregnant? Before, she was kind and pleasant and I preferred her company over her husband's, but now the roles have reversed and she's making me very uncomfortable.

'Like... um... obviously I'm a British citizen, so how does the healthcare system work over here?'

Angela waves her hand in front of her face, dismissing me. 'You don't have to worry about that. You'll be seen and cared for by our private doctor at the hospital, and all tests, scans and the delivery will be paid for by us.'

'Um... Thank you.'

'Anything else?'

Sweat beads on my top lip. I lick it away and gulp. 'The... The money?' This is awkward, bargaining over my baby for money. She's right though. It does feel like a business transaction, but if I'm going to do this, then that's how I need to treat it. I don't want the baby, but it's still a baby. A human being. The last thing I want is to get emotionally attached to it.

'You're asking how much we'll give you?' she prompts.

'Yes.'

Angela inhales sharply and looks at her husband. 'Will one million euros cover it?'

'Euros?'

'Fine. Pounds. One million pounds.'

'I... Yes. And... um... you said about helping me with opening the restaurant. What will that involve?'

Angela readjusts her position on the chair. 'Whatever you need from us. Recommendations. References. You name it. The only stipulation is that you won't be allowed to see the child.'

'Not even when it's born?'

'No.'

John clears his throat. 'I'm sure we can come to an agreement to allow you to see the child once before we adopt it.'

I nod, satisfied with that answer. If I'm going to spend nine months growing a baby inside my body, the least I should be allowed to do is see them. Although perhaps it's best I don't because seeing it will make it real. I don't know. I'll have to think about it.

'Very well,' I say. 'Is this all going to be put down on paper?'

'You want a contract?' snaps Angela.

'Well... yeah. That way, we're both covered should anything... go wrong.' At this point Angela's eyes become watery again. 'Not that anything will,' I add quickly. 'Just a precaution.'

'We'll have our lawyer draw something up.'

'Thank you. What about the staff here?'

'What about them?' asks Angela, clearly becoming agitated with my constant questions. Did she seriously think I'd just say yes straight away and that would be it?

'What are we going to tell them? Eventually, I'm going to start to show.'

'John and I have discussed it. We shall say that you're our surrogate. That way, it won't seem strange when you just hand over the child when it's born.'

I shrug. 'Seems logical, I suppose.'

'Great.'

'I just have one last question. How will your current daughter feel about this?'

'Why do you care?'

'I don't, but...' I stop, all words failing me.

Angela sighs. 'You don't have to worry about Faye. She's mostly away at boarding school, but I know she'll be delighted to have a baby brother or sister. She knows we've been trying to have another, so this won't come as much of a surprise, especially if we tell her that you're our surrogate. She'll understand.' Angela looks up at John and smiles. He doesn't.

'Okay,' I say, biting my lip. 'It's a deal.'

CHAPTER THIRTY-THREE

As the office door closes behind me, my body freezes on the spot. I feel colder than when I was stuck in the freezer, which is now the least of my problems. What have I just done? What the hell happened? Am I the worst human being on the planet, not to mention the worst mother in the world? But expectant mothers make these sorts of decisions every day, don't they? Surely, it's better for the child in the long run. They wouldn't want me as their mother anyway. What can I offer a child? Nothing.

They'll be happy here with Angela and John, who can provide them with love and anything they could ever want or need. Whereas I don't even have an official place to live and am a single woman with no maternal instinct whatsoever. No. I've made the right choice. Some may call me selfish, but I'm doing this for the child's own good. Everyone's a winner, and Angela gets the baby she's been trying for after so many years of heartbreak.

I return to the kitchen where I find Margo overseeing the

lunch preparations. She glares at me as I get back to work with the desserts I'm making for the dinner party.

'Still got a job then?' she asks.

'Yep.'

A FEW HOURS LATER, I'm up to my ears in pastry, chocolate, flour and fruit. Chopping, dicing, slicing, melting, stirring and kneading. I work diligently and quietly, keeping my head down with my earphones in. I don't always listen to music, but sometimes it helps distract me from the noises in my head being my racing thoughts and constant degrading commentary about myself. Clara used to listen to music all the time. She'd often be found dancing around our house while she cleaned or while she was tattooing her clients. She enjoyed a range of different music styles, from pop to rock to classical and even grunge. I never knew what music would be playing when I returned home. In fact, I could often tell what mood she'd be in by the type of music that was playing. If Taylor Swift was on, then it was usually because she was pissed off with her girlfriend. If classical music played, then she was in a chilled mood. If there was anything heavy metal on, then I knew to stay out of her way and buy her a bar of chocolate.

I'm currently listening to the complete works of Mozart. I'm not in a chilled mood, but it's helping me get there. Since the events of earlier today, my heart's been racing, and my thoughts are still buzzing around my head, making me dizzy. And I still feel like the worse person on planet earth.

A tap appears on my shoulder. I shudder as I pull the plugs from my ears.

'Sorry! Didn't mean to startle you,' says Mrs Dubois. 'You seemed very focused.'

'Sorry,' I say with a laugh. 'Got to get this choux pastry in the oven.' I'm making an elegant croquembouche tower with caramel and chocolate and it is notoriously awkward and difficult to make, let alone have it hold its shape for hours on end. Anything, even allowing the pastry to sit for too long, can have dire consequences.

'I... I hope you don't find this insensitive or forward of me, but... what you're doing for Angela and John is the most selfless thing I think I've ever known anyone to do.'

'Oh!' I feel my face catch on fire, quickly remembering that the staff will have been told I'm their surrogate, not that I'm some knocked-up girl who is giving them her baby in exchange for a million quid. 'T-Thank you. It's nothing really.'

Mrs Dubois smiles, which shocks me, considering I haven't seen her smile at anyone since I got here. 'If you need anything, you let me know, okay? I might even see if I can get you moved to a better bedroom. Something inside the villa, closer to Angela and John. I'm sure they'll want to keep a close eye on you while you're carrying their child.' I'm sure her words are meant to put me at ease, make me feel special, but they do the exact opposite. Keep a close eye on me? Is this Mrs Dubois talking or Angela and John talking through her so as not to seem too controlling?

'Oh, that's okay,' I say. 'I'm happy with my room in the staff accommodation.'

'But you're not really staff now, are you?'

'I... I mean... I still work for them.'

Mrs Dubois's smile fades ever so slightly. 'Well, if you change your mind, let me know.'

'I will. Thanks.'

'So special,' she says, looking down at my stomach, 'to have a baby on the way. They are such a blessing.'

I bite my tongue to stop myself from responding with 'and a curse.'

CHAPTER THIRTY-FOUR
ANGELA

After the conversation with Brittany, I haven't left my room. John took it upon himself to tell the staff about her being our surrogate. I didn't want to be there. I needed some space to get my head straight, although for the past several weeks, I feel as if I've lost it and it's been replaced by someone else's.

I took the pills as normal, but before I could get to a bathroom to vomit them up, I was cornered by Mrs Dubois, who congratulated me on the baby. She then spent almost an hour telling me how much she loves children and how much she misses Faye. Thanks to my brain being as useful as a sieve to hold water, I forgot about the pills I'd swallowed and by the time I did remember, they'd been absorbed by my body. I know how dangerous it is to take these sorts of pills sporadically. John has warned me many times that if I miss a dose, there's a risk of a relapse, but I think I'm managing to hold my sanity together pretty well, especially considering the shock of Brittany's pregnancy, which has now turned out to be a blessing in disguise.

I can't help it. I'm angry. No, I'm more than angry. I'm

outraged that she's pregnant so easily. Even our first child took years of trying, but Brittany has just gone and got herself pregnant just like that. Perhaps it's her youth, I don't know, but it seems unfair that a young woman who clearly has no interest in being a mother should get pregnant so easily, yet here I am, a woman who has dreamed her whole life of being a mother to several children, having to suffer through miscarriages and stillbirths, not to mention the tragic and sudden loss of a young baby.

I feel bad for snapping at her yesterday, but my mind is unable to work or think any other way right now. Now, I must pretend to be happy in front of dozens of important guests for tonight's dinner party. How can I face them? John and I haven't discussed what we'll be telling our friends and his colleagues. Maybe we should keep the surrogacy a secret for now.

I get up from my bed and stand in front of the full-length mirror, studying my svelte figure in my stunning sundress. I run my hands over my flat stomach as tears fill my eyes. I'd do anything to be in Brittany's shoes. Why should she get all the fuss and attention? She doesn't even want the baby.

That's when I remember what's stored under my bed; something I used several years ago when I was struggling with my latest miscarriage. A smile spreads across my lips as my head swims with old memories. It will all be okay now. I have a plan; a plan to make everything right.

CHAPTER THIRTY-FIVE

Several hours later, the desserts are served to the awaiting dinner guests, including the perfect croquembouche tower, and I'm asked to come into the dining room for the guests to congratulate me. I almost don't go in, but I do and am horrified when a round of applause greets me as I enter.

'Here she is!' exclaims Angela. She rushes up to me and gives me a hug. It seems her kind attitude is back. Either that or she's drunk and putting on a show for her husband's work colleagues and their wives and husbands, all of whom are dressed in the most gorgeous white attire. Angela is wearing a white baggy suit jacket over a tight white dress.

'This woman is a goddess in the kitchen,' she says, turning to the room. 'I'm so glad we managed to snatch her up!'

I've never felt so embarrassed in my life.

'Um... thank you,' I manage to say.

'And,' continues Angela, suddenly letting go of me and practically pushing me aside, 'I'd like to take this happy occasion to make an announcement.'

Oh God... Kill me now.

'I'm pregnant!' she exclaims.

There's a collective gasp around the room. John drops his cutlery against his plate and his mouth falls open. The women in white all clamber to their feet, rush to Angela's side, shrieking and jumping up and down, patting her stomach and air-kissing her cheeks as she takes off her baggy jacket, revealing a small, neat bump. I shrink into the corner as I watch Angela revel in all the love and attention. The men stand and offer John a hearty handshake, but his mouth is still open in pure horror. He looks straight at me, and I stare back at him, unsure what to say or what to do. Should I just leave?

He finally takes the lead. 'Thank you, everyone,' he says, walking up to Angela. He grabs her arm and yanks her to his side, a little harder than he probably should do. She beams up at him. 'Yes, it was quite a surprise for us, considering Angela's... health conditions, but... we're delighted with the news... obviously.'

I can't breathe. I shouldn't be here. What the hell is Angela thinking? What about the whole surrogacy ploy? It makes a hell of a lot more sense to tell these people that than to announce she's pregnant, for goodness' sake.

But Angela is beaming like a lightbulb in her stunning white dress. My eyes are drawn to her bump. Clearly, it's not real, which means she's faking it, but why?

When the commotion finally dies down and the women return to the table, still chatting excitedly, Angela glances at me and gives me a wide smile, the first I've seen from her in weeks. I know it's fake because as soon as her eyes leave mine, she slaps on a proper smile and rejoins the party.

John withdraws to the corner and pours himself a very

large glass of whiskey, and that's my cue to leave. Everyone has forgotten about the talented pastry chef hiding in the corner. Angela clearly invited me into the dining hall at this exact moment to humiliate me. I thought she was supposed to be the nice one!

CHAPTER THIRTY-SIX

ANGELA

During the dinner party, after my pregnancy announcement, my husband throws daggers at me for the rest of the evening but smiles and laughs with everyone else. I know I'll pay for my unplanned outburst, but he just doesn't realise how much it will help me during the next few months, especially as Brittany gets bigger. The idea of another woman carrying my child is hard enough, so by pretending I'm pregnant, it will alleviate my stress and give me something to focus on, rather than my growing envy.

As soon as the last guests leave the villa, John slams the door, almost trapping my fingers. He rounds on me, grabs both my arms and shoves me up against the nearest wall.

'What the fuck are you playing at?'

I keep my fake smile plastered on my face. 'John, relax! I'm sorry I didn't tell you, but it's a miracle, isn't it?'

'What's a miracle?' he snaps.

I look down at my bump, then back up at him.

'Wait...' he says. 'You don't *actually* think you're pregnant, do you?'

I laugh. 'Of course I am!' Then I wink at him.

'Angela, enough of this! What the hell is wrong with you?'

'You should know! You're the one medicating me, remember?'

John lets go of me and straightens his cream jacket. 'I think I need to adjust your medication,' he mumbles. 'And watch you for two hours afterwards,' he adds as he walks away, shaking his head, but then he spins around and strides back to me, shoving a pointed finger in my face. 'This stupid idea of yours had better not embarrass me, do you understand? I will not be made a fool of.'

'It won't, I promise. I need this, John. Please. It's the only way I'm going to be able to get through the next few months as Brittany grows our baby.' I cradle my bump.

John rolls his eyes as he turns away.

He leaves me standing by the front door, stroking my fake bump, tears brimming in my eyes. I think back to when I was pregnant with my first child, my baby girl who was taken too soon. But she wasn't taken, was she? Because it's all become clear to me now. It's why my husband has spent the past seven years medicating me, the reason why he doesn't want me to remember.

I killed her.

I killed my baby in the bathtub and my husband has been protecting me for all these years. I don't blame him. I remember how I was back then; a broken shell of a woman, barely able to form a coherent word or thought other than state I wanted to kill myself.

It was the only way.

He did it all for me.

Now, I have the chance to start again with this new baby. Faye is no longer a baby, living away at boarding school. She doesn't need me anymore, but I need this baby. More than I need my next breath.

CHAPTER THIRTY-SEVEN

It's been two weeks since I agreed to give my child to Angela and John to adopt. The paperwork has been drawn up, I've read it and signed it. It's official now. I've reached twelve weeks, which apparently is the time when most people announce their pregnancy because it means the mother is out of the risky first trimester. Angela gave me a book on pregnancy last week, which is still sitting unread by the side of my bed. The less I know about what's going on inside me, the better. That's my take on it, anyway. I don't need to know what type of fruit the baby is the size of or what body part it's growing this week.

Overnight, it seems my stomach has expanded. I have a small bump, but it's still easily hidden behind my chef whites. My trousers aren't even tight yet. Thankfully, the constant nausea and food intolerances have lessened somewhat, although the smell of raw meat still turns my stomach, so I make sure to stay away from the chefs when they're preparing it.

Angela and John are coming with me to my twelve-week

scan. I'm waiting in the yard by the car and am somewhat taken aback when John approaches me by himself.

'Is Angela not coming?' I ask.

John stops next to me. 'I'm afraid Angela is indisposed this morning.'

I glance past him towards the villa, frowning. I'm quite surprised that Angela is missing the first scan of the baby. Then again, her coming to the hospital sporting a fake bump while I have my scan would probably look slightly odd to the midwives and doctors.

I'm a bundle of nerves as I slide into the back seat of the car. I can't believe I'm going to the hospital again. I'm not sure I'll ever get over my phobia. It's probably one of those things that need extensive therapy to get past. Granted, I don't feel like I'm about to implode or have a gut-wrenching panic attack, but the sweaty palms, shortness of breath and dry mouth are all there, like unpleasant sidekicks to my torture.

John and I are sitting in the back of his car in silence. His driver navigates the busy streets towards the hospital.

'Are you excited to see the scan of the child?' asks John.

'Oh, um, I hadn't really thought about it,' I answer truthfully. I don't want to think about it. In fact, I'm not sure I even want to see the scan.

'Angela's very sorry she can't make it, but she'll be there for the other scans.'

'Where is she again?'

John pauses, staring out of the window at the striking coastline. 'A doctor's appointment.'

'Everything okay?'

John turns and smiles at me. 'Nothing for you to worry about. You just focus on growing that baby nice and healthy.'

I suddenly feel like a breeding cow or dog or something, only growing this baby for their purpose. It unsettles me, but once I get out of the car and breathe in the gorgeous, warm air, I feel better.

I can't believe I'm staying in such a beautiful place. Even the area surrounding the hospital is stunning. Everyone is dressed to perfection, wearing stylish clothes, most likely with high-end labels. Whereas I'm wearing a loose-fitting pair of linen trousers and a floaty off-the-shoulder top, which I bought from Primark about five years ago. As I walk towards the building, my bladder alerts me to the fact I'm desperate for a wee, but I've been told it's best to have a full bladder during the ultrasound as it helps to make the picture clearer. Guess I'm going to have to hold it.

John explains that their private doctor has recommended a midwife at this hospital, one who knows the full situation and has signed a non-disclosure agreement. I wonder if they have non-disclosure agreements tucked away everywhere, ready to whip out whenever needed for people to sign. I've never known anyone to use them, not to this extent. I'm sure there are people who work for celebrities who sign them, but it's not something I've ever come across in everyday life.

The midwife smiles at me as she explains the procedure. All I need to do is lie down while she squirts gel on my stomach and moves the scanner thing across it. She says it's still too early to find out the gender, but this scan is to determine how far along I am exactly and estimate the due date, check that the baby is growing and developing normally, confirm if there is more than one baby (my heart rate doubles at the thought of having twins), check the position of the placenta, screen for chromosomal anomalies like Down's syndrome (another heart rate spike), measure the risk of developing pre-eclampsia and asses the baby's heartbeat. All normal stuff, so I'm told, but it's enough to cause my breathing to become erratic. If it wasn't bad enough that my phobia is raising its ugly head, I now have to deal with the dread of finding out if the baby is healthy or not.

She says that the scan is non-invasive, although the gel is stupidly cold and I flinch as she squirts a glob onto my exposed stomach. John is standing on the other side of the room. I must admit, I'm a little uneasy with him being here, but I suppose, for all intents and purposes, it is his child.

'Would you like to see your baby?' she asks me.

'Um... No, that's okay,' I say, turning my head away from the computer monitor. John steps forward and takes a look. A small smile appears on his face, one I've not seen on him before. It softens his facial features, and he looks... happy.

The midwife moves the thing (she called it by its official name, but I can't remember the word) around my stomach, pushing gently, which causes my bladder to almost burst.

Dear God, please don't let me wet myself in front of John.

There's a long silence as she twists and turns the thing on my stomach for several minutes, presses buttons on the monitor and types a few things on the keyboard.

'Just taking some measurements,' she says. 'I'd estimate your due date to be the 14th of February. You could have a Valentine's Day baby.'

I give her a weak smile. She continues with her checks and measurements, but then she frowns and pulls the screen closer. This time, the silence is filled with apprehension. I watch her eyes, frowning, as they flick over the screen, back and forth, back and forth.

I can't take it any longer.

'Everything okay?'

She clears her throat. 'I'll be right back. I'm just going to get the doctor for a second opinion.'

My stomach drops like it's on a rollercoaster and my heartbeat doubles. I can't breathe. I glance at John, who is pale, and he scratches his chin, unwilling to look directly at me.

'I'm sure it's nothing,' he says.

I close my eyes and try and calm my erratic breathing, already knowing that people don't say they need a second opinion unless they think something is wrong.

CHAPTER THIRTY-EIGHT

Two agonising minutes later, a doctor arrives, along with the midwife. He smiles at me. 'Right, let's have a look, shall we?' I know he's trying to put me at ease, but all it does is make me want to burst into tears.

My mind takes me back to that awful moment when a doctor told me my friend died, then when our grandmother died, then when Clara had kidney disease and our whole lives changed. Then it switches to the moment a doctor told me that my sister was dead. All doctors ever seem to do is give me bad news. I want nothing more than to run out the door right now and keep running until my legs can't hold my weight any longer.

The doctor repeats the process with the thing on my stomach, then he takes a deep breath. I swear to God if someone doesn't start speaking soon, I'm going to scream this place down.

'What's going on?' asks John, taking the words straight out of my mouth.

The doctor turns directly to him, ignoring me

completely. 'I'm afraid there's a possibility your child has hydronephrosis. It's a swelling of the kidneys caused by a blockage in the urine flow. You can see from the scan image that one kidney is slightly enlarged, whereas the other is almost non-existent, which means they may also have a missing kidney, known as renal agenesis. I'm afraid I can't offer a full diagnosis until around the twenty-week scan where we'll be able to detect any further developmental issues. Other than that, your baby is in perfect health and is growing normally.'

The men converse back and forth, completely ignoring me. All I can hear is my blood pounding in my ears. My breathing is becoming very laboured. The midwife catches my eye.

'Brittany, are you okay?'

I open my mouth, but I can't breathe. Oh God... I can't breathe.

'She's hyperventilating, Doctor,' says the midwife, rushing to my side and grasping my hand. She squeezes it. The doctor and midwife are talking, reassuring me, telling me to calm down and take deep breaths, but how can I when there's no oxygen in the room? My vision is blurry, but I can just about make out John's shape, standing in the corner. He hasn't made any movement towards me. He's standing there, perfectly still.

This can't be happening. My baby is only the size of a plum (so the midwife says) and yet it's already growing wrong because of me. My body can't even do that right! I scream, not at anyone in the room, but at myself.

I don't know a lot (okay, I know next to nothing) about pregnancy, but surely twelve weeks is too early to detect kidney problems. If the kid is the size of a plum, then the kidneys would be miniscule.

First, my sister died because I gave her one of my kidneys, and now my baby might have a missing kidney, and it's not even born yet. I cry and scream and cry some more, but eventually my lungs breathe in oxygen and things start to return to normal. Whatever the hell that means.

The midwife keeps squeezing my hand while the doctor talks.

'Brittany, there's nothing to worry about yet. There's a high chance the child will be unaffected by this condition. We'll know more at the twenty-week scan.'

'Has this happened because I only have one kidney? Did I do this to it?'

The doctor shakes his head. 'No, the fact you only have one kidney won't have affected the child. It's not caused by anything the parents did or did not do, and it cannot be prevented before or during pregnancy. However, high blood pressure can affect the unborn child, so I suggest we focus on getting that under control.'

The midwife hands me a glass of water, which I sip. The doctor turns back to John, and they lower their voices as they converse in the corner. The midwife offers me a reassuring smile. She probably feels sorry for me.

'Thank you,' I say, handing her back the empty glass.

A few minutes later, the doctor and the midwife leave the room after cleaning the gel off my stomach. I sort myself out and sit on the edge of the bed.

'Brittany,' says John calmly, 'I think it's best we don't tell Angela about this.'

'Why not?'

John pauses, rubbing his chin again, something I notice he does a lot when he's nervous. 'My wife always likes things to be perfect, and when things aren't perfect, she tends to over-react. Besides, like the doctor said, it may not affect the child in the long run, so let's see how the next few months play out with regards to its development before we tell Angela.'

'Okay,' I say quietly.

CHAPTER THIRTY-NINE

Returning to the villa, I go straight to my room. John has given me the rest of the day off to recover from the shock. I'm so exhausted that I grab myself a cold fruity drink from the main kitchen fridge, downing it in one because I feel like I need the sugar, then collapse onto my bed and sleep for five hours before waking up to the sound of shouting. I blink open my eyes, feeling groggy and disorientated as I sit up on the bed and stretch my shoulders.

More shouting. Angry.

A loud bang reverberates around the room as a nearby door slams.

I stand up, creep to my door and open it a crack. The sound intensifies.

'It's all ruined!' It's Margo doing the shouting. 'Where is she?'

Is she talking about me?

'Margo, just calm down,' says Mrs Dubois.

'Calm down? Calm down! How can I calm down when

all my hard work in the kitchen for the past two days in completely ruined, all because she left the fridge door open?'

'I'm sure it was an accident. Brittany wouldn't have done it on purpose.'

'Yeah, right. She's been getting away with a lot lately.'

What the hell?

Rather than hide in my room, I decide to find out what's going on and why Margo is on the warpath for me. I step outside my room and follow the raised voices into the staff lounge.

'You!' shouts Margo, pointing a stiff finger at me.

'What's this about?' I ask.

'You left the fridge door open and now all the meat is spoiled, all the prepared vegetables have turned, and we've had to throw everything away and start again.'

'How do you know it was even me? I haven't been in the kitchen today. I've been at the... I've been... It's my day off.'

Margo frowns at me. 'I saw you go into the kitchen when you got back from your little trip with John. Oh yes, don't think I haven't noticed you spending time with him... *alone*.'

My heart leaps in my chest and my cheeks flush. 'I... I went and got myself a cold drink. I definitely closed it.'

'Well, clearly you didn't. Everything is ruined.'

'It's only been five hours. I'm sure some things are still useable.'

'And risk giving food poisoning to the whole dinner party tomorrow night?'

I roll my eyes, a gesture I instantly regret because not only is it a childish thing to do, but it seems to infuriate Margo even more. Her eyes blaze. 'I expect you in the kitchen to help clean all this up. Just because you're carrying their baby doesn't mean you get away with everything.'

Mrs Dubois steps forwards. 'I think Brittany needs her rest, Margo.'

'No,' I reply quickly. 'That's okay. I'll help.'

Margo narrows her eyes at me before turning and storming away, slamming another door. Mrs Dubois turns to me. 'I'm so sorry about that. Margo can be very... emotional when it comes to her kitchen.'

'It's fine. Maybe it was me who left the door open. I've been a bit absent-minded lately.'

'Well, pregnancy will do that to you, dear,' she replies with a kind smile. 'You just take care of yourself and that little one, okay?'

As she walks away, my body involuntarily shudders. Why does Mrs Dubois give me the creeps every time she speaks to me? I almost wish she'd go back to being standoffish and blunt with me, like she was the first few weeks.

I head to the kitchen to help Margo, who barely says a word to me, other than to boss me around and tell me what to do. The meat does have a slightly weird smell, and it immediately makes me gag, so I'm forced to hold my breath while I dispose of it and have to take several fresh air breaks.

Angela corners me when I'm on my way back to my room two hours later.

'Ah, Brittany! John tells me the scan went well. He showed me the photo. I just wanted to say how happy it made me to see my little one all safe and sound.'

'Oh, um... yes, everything is fine.'

'Good. Good. I wanted to ask you a favour, if it's not too much trouble.' Okay, now she's being all nice to me. What the hell is going on? 'I'd like to throw a baby shower next week and was wondering if you'd design and make the cakes and sweet treats. I'll let you know how many people are coming.'

My mouth drops open. 'Um... sure.' I almost want to start arguing with her and point out that I am the one who is pregnant, but then I remember it's not my baby.

It's hers.

She claps her hands together. 'Wonderful!'

'I'd be delighted to make the cakes. Just let me know the flavours and how many to make.'

'Thank you. You're a doll.' Angela steps forward and gives me a quick hug, one of those hugs where the two people involved barely touch at all, but her fake bump pushes against my real one and it's honestly the weirdest, most surreal experience of my life. I really don't understand this woman. She's either delusional or crazy.

I'm just not sure which it is.

CHAPTER FORTY

I smile and watch her walk away, gently clutching her round belly as she does so. What the hell is going on here? Her eyes are glazed over like she's either high or drunk, and she seems as if she's walking on air. When I first met her, I really liked her. She was switched-on, polite and charming, but lately her attitude and actions have spiralled. I know she takes medication, and John mentioned she was at a doctor's appointment today, which is why she missed the scan, but what medication is she on to make her act so flaky?

I don't know whether to be appalled or worried for her. It's not normal behaviour, is it? She's obviously grieving the loss of her babies over the years, but this is taking things to another level. She's either in denial or mentally unstable and I'm not sure which is worse. Should I ask John about it or continue as if all of this is normal? The last thing I want is to upset the plan in any way and risk pissing her and John off. Then again, we've all signed a contract, but I wouldn't put it past them to have some sort of contingency plan in place in case things go wrong somewhere down the line. Perhaps that's why John is keeping the baby's health condition a secret from Angela. He doesn't want her to overreact too soon. I don't like the idea of hiding it from her. At some point, she's bound to find out, especially if she starts attending my ultrasound scans, which are due to increase to keep an eye on the baby's kidney development. In fact, I have one next week, the day after the baby shower, which I assume she'll be attending with me.

THE DAY of the baby shower arrives. Angela and John make an unplanned announcement in the kitchen that morning, explaining that to the outside world, it is Angela who is pregnant, not me, and they reiterate their non-disclosure agreements. Every pair of eyes turns on me, but Margo avoids my eye contact.

Once they've left, Mrs Dubois thankfully takes over and advises that everyone keeps their opinions to themselves and not ask any questions. It's the strangest thing I've ever experienced. I can practically see the question marks hovering above everyone's heads, yet they keep their mouths closed and just mumble a few words at me, like 'Congratulations,' and 'You're glowing,' and all those other phrases that they assume I want to hear, when in fact I'd rather not.

I finish preparing all the individual blue and pink cupcakes for the baby shower and lay them out on display in the room where the party is being held. There are fifty-two women attending, including Angela, who is flitting about making sure everything is perfect. She's completely ignoring me as if I'm part of the furniture and speaking with Mrs Dubois instead, double-checking the canapés are gluten-free and lining up all the champagne flutes in rows on the tables.

She's wearing a tight-fitted dress, which only emphasises her bump, which is much bigger than mine, still hiding beneath my chef whites.

The guests are due to arrive in less than an hour, so I move the massive four-tiered cake I've also made and place it on the main table, surrounded by all the cupcakes. The cake is lemon sponge with raspberry frosting. Angela said she wanted unique flavours, so that's what she's got. In fact, each layer is a different flavour and the cupcakes are espresso and dark chocolate, with a hint of chilli.

Angela brushes past me carrying a flute of champagne, which she's sipping on. It seems she's more than happy to pretend she's pregnant but stopping drinking alcohol is a step too far. However, I expect she'll stop once the guests have arrived. I can't imagine that alcohol and whatever concoction of medication she's on is healthy, but it's not my place to say anything.

'Will there be anything else, ma'am?' I ask her.

She turns to me, as if surprised I'm here. 'Oh, no, thank you. Everything looks lovely. You've done a wonderful job with the cakes.'

I nod my thanks, secretly looking forward to eating the extra cupcake I made for myself in the kitchen, away from everyone else.

'You may go now. I don't think I need to remind you that you aren't to show your face until all my friends have gone.'

'Yes, ma'am. Um… my next scan is tomorrow at ten. Are you coming with me?'

Angela nods. 'Ooh, yes, I can't wait.'

CHAPTER FORTY-ONE

ANGELA

The baby shower goes off without a hitch. The only issue that arises is that a lot of my friends want to touch my bump. I keep my distance, allowing them to hug me but not to touch. I remember never letting people do that even with my first child.

I know I probably shouldn't, but I drink the champagne that's provided whilst telling everyone that it's non-alcoholic. No one can tell the difference anyway, but I do start to wobble after the first hour passes. I can't recall when the last time I took my medication was; I know I took a full dose a couple of days ago because John stood over me as I swallowed it and then wouldn't let me out of his sight until two hours later, by which time it was too late to purge it from my system.

The memories of that awful day keep coming back to haunt me at the worst possible times, like when I'm making my baby shower speech. I'm halfway through and then all I see is my five-day-old baby face-down in the bath.

I stumble backwards into one of my girlfriends who's

standing behind me. I quickly right myself and smile, nodding that I'm okay. I keep trying to continue with my planned speech, but then the image of my baby blue in the face strikes me and I let out a loud yelp.

John's not here to rescue me, but, thankfully, Mrs Dubois is. She steps in and says that I've been fighting off a fever for a few days and that the stress of entertaining has overwhelmed me. Someone shoves a glass of water in my face, which I take and sip as I'm led to a chair. I sit down.

'I'm sorry,' I say to Mrs Dubois. 'I don't know what's come over me.'

'Don't you worry. Just take a breath. Shall I fetch John?'

'No, it's best not to disturb him. I'll be fine. I've never been good at giving speeches.'

As the baby shower games begin, I force a smile across my face as wave after wave of memories crash into me.

Me screaming at the top of my lungs when I see the baby.

Me jumping into the bath and grabbing her, shaking her like a doll.

John ripping her tiny body from my hands.

Through all of this, there's one thing I can't remember, which is peculiar because anyone would think it would be the only thing I should remember; her name. We'd decided on her name months before, while she was still in my womb, but I can't, for the life of me, remember it.

CHAPTER FORTY-TWO

John meets me at the front of the villa at nine the next morning. He's wearing a pair of grey shorts and a smart shirt, open at the collar. He opens the car door for me and before I can open my mouth and ask, he says, 'Angela is a tad hung over, I'm afraid.'

I don't reply, but the questions pop into my head like pieces of exploding popcorn. So, she was drinking real alcohol during the party? Is she hung over or is she unwell because of the mix of alcohol and drugs? Is John purposely keeping her here so she doesn't attend the scan?

We spend the first few minutes of the ride in silence until, eventually, I can't take it any longer.

'Why is Angela wearing a fake baby bump? I don't understand why she thinks it will make things easier. Surely, it's just going to complicate everything.'

John shifts in his seat. 'Remember, we spoke about this at our initial meeting. To the outside world, it's Angela who is pregnant to keep up appearances, but the staff know you're our surrogate. You, I and Angela are the only people who know the truth.'

I nod and bite my lip. 'I realise that, but I just don't understand the reasoning behind her wearing a fake bump.'

'Does it make you uncomfortable?' he asks.

'A little, yeah. I feel as if she's ignoring me, not taking this seriously. I mean, this is now the second scan she's missing.'

John smiles. 'Trust me, the fake bump was not my idea. One thing you'll learn about my wife is that she tends to think everything is about her and she makes rash and impulsive decisions without thinking it through.'

'And that doesn't bother you?'

John turns his head slowly and looks at me. And then his eyes darken, and it makes my skin tingle and my breath catch in my throat. He may be at least fifteen years older than me, but he's still very attractive. Dark hair, dark eyes and tanned skin.

'It bothers me, yes, but she's been through a lot, especially with her miscarriages. I've not seen her this happy in a long time.'

'But what about Faye? Why is she away at boarding school so much if Angela craves a child nearby?'

'Faye is... a difficult subject.'

'Sorry, I don't mean to pry. It's just...' I stop, unsure what I can say that won't insult his wife or make me sound like an ungrateful bitch.

John reaches over and places a hand on my bare knee. 'Don't worry. She'll come around. Besides, it's probably best that she doesn't attend these scans until we know more about the health of the child. Are you worried about today?'

His hand is still on my knee.

His hand is still on my knee and he's now squeezing it.

I gulp. 'A little. You know what happened to my sister, right?'

'Angela told me. I'm sorry. It must be difficult for you to hear that the baby also has kidney problems.'

'I just wasn't expecting it at all. I feel as if it's my fault.'

He squeezes my knee again. 'Brittany, remember what the doctor said. It's not your fault. It's just one of those unfortunate things that can happen to anyone.'

I turn and stare out of the car window so he doesn't see my eyes brimming with tears. Why am I so emotional about all of this? I'm doing my best to stay emotionally detached from the child growing inside of me, but it's hard, much harder than I imagined.

The scan takes ages because they take more snapshots of the kidneys and confirm that yes, it still looks like they have a smaller than average kidney and a larger than average kidney. My heart sinks again when the doctor says that, but he reassures me and John that the baby is developing fine otherwise and doesn't appear to be suffering with any further health conditions. Another scan is booked for two weeks' time.

When we arrive back at the villa, John opens the car door for me and offers his hand to help me out. I take it, even though my belly isn't big enough yet to cause any issues with getting in and out of cars. I still just look like I've had a big meal.

'Thanks again for coming with me,' I say, letting go of his hand when I see Margo standing outside the staff accommodation. She stops and watches us.

John smiles at me, clearly unaware that we're being watched. 'Any time. You're doing great, Brittany. Let me know if you need anything, okay?' Then he does something which not only causes my skin to prickle, but my heart rate to double in the space of two seconds. He leans forwards and wraps his strong arms around me, pulling me against his body.

But that's not the worst bit.

He sniffs my hair.

He eventually lets me go and walks away, leaving me rooted to the spot. Margo glares at me from across the courtyard, and I see her eyebrows rise.

I need to do some damage control. Quick.

CHAPTER FORTY-THREE

'Margo,' I call out, as I start jogging towards her. 'That wasn't what it looked like.'

'No? Are you sure? Because it looked like you just got out of the car with the man you're carrying a baby for and shared a very intimate hug with him.'

'Okay, the first bit is right, but it most definitely wasn't intimate. Not for me, anyway.'

'What are you saying?'

'I'm saying...' I stop, glance around and step closer to her, lowering my voice as I continue. 'He and Angela seem to have swapped personalities since all this started.'

'All this...'

I glance down at my small bump, gesturing to it.

'Right,' she says sarcastically. 'Maybe you should have thought about that before you decided to be a surrogate for the Addams Family.'

'What do you mean by that?'

'What do you think I mean?'

I shrug. 'I have no idea!' I shriek.

'For goodness' sake, keep your voice down,' snaps Margo.

Tears fill my eyes. 'I'm scared, Margo. All this is just so... so... messed up.'

Margo sighs and rolls her eyes. 'Look, I'm not saying that getting involved with this family was a bad idea, but since you're already committed, let me give you a word of advice. Whatever they've promised you is a lie.'

'That's not advice.'

'Okay, so it's a warning. They've done this before.'

'They *what*? When?'

'Like two years ago.' I don't know how to respond, so I just hold my tongue and listen as Margo explains. 'They entrapped some poor girl into having their baby, but she miscarried at, like, sixteen weeks. They promised her all this money, but she never got it and then they threatened her with legal action because it was written in her contract that if she were to miscarry or lose the baby, then she'd receive nothing.'

'You're kidding! How do you know all this?'

Margo stares at me for several long moments.

'It was you, wasn't it?' I ask.

'Yes, it was me.'

'Holy shit!'

'Now do you see why I'm trying to warn you? We shouldn't even be talking about any of this. They could fire both of us. Well, probably not you, since you're knocked up with their kid, but...' Margo runs a hand through her hair, glancing around the courtyard.

'Should I be worried?'

Margo sighs. 'Let's just hope you carry this baby to term and there's nothing wrong with it.'

My heart drops to my stomach. 'What do you mean?'

'Why do you think Faye doesn't spend a lot of time here?'

'I... I hadn't really thought about it.'

'Well... think about it.' Margo turns and walks away. I want to call after her, beg her to stop and explain more, but then I see the reason why she's abandoned me so quickly.

Angela is now walking towards me, her fists clenched, her eyes wide.

Without warning, she raises her hand and slaps me across the face. The resounding snap makes my eyes water and my teeth bite down on my tongue.

'I saw you getting out of the car with my husband,' she says in a harsh whisper. 'If you so much as touch him again, I'll make sure you never get your precious restaurant. You got it?'

'I... I...' I can't form words because my mouth is filling with blood and saliva from my tongue, and my vision blurs while my brain rattles around inside my skull. She may be fairly petite, but she can pack a wallop.

She turns and storms away, leaving me holding my burning left cheek with my hand.

What the hell have I got myself into?

CHAPTER FORTY-FOUR

Over the following week, I attempt to get back to normal and focus solely on work. I create an elaborate dessert for John and Angela, who both rave about it. Angela's mood seems to swing from one extreme to the other from one day to the next. At one point, during dinner, she throws a plate across the room. I can't keep up. The day after she slapped me, she invited me into the main part of the villa for a cup of tea. She said she was sorry she overreacted, and it won't happen again. Her fake bump seems to have got bigger too. I'm fourteen weeks now, but her bump is much larger than mine, and try as I might, I can't stop staring at it whenever I see her.

I want dearly to ask her questions, but I know how rude it would sound. Something isn't right with this woman, yet I'm too afraid to probe into her life. Then again, I am giving this woman my baby and if she's mentally unstable, then should I really be going through with it? It's the first time the idea of backing out crosses my mind, but I quickly push the thought aside; there's too much riding on this baby now.

Clearly, Angela is just struggling with grief. Hell, if she wants to waltz around with a fake bump, then fine...

AT SIXTEEN WEEKS, I have my next scan, and, to my horror, Angela turns up to accompany me without John present. How am I supposed to keep the baby's condition a secret if she's in the same room as me while I have the scan? Where is he? I assumed he'd come to every scan with me, especially to this one. I'm not quite at the twenty-week stage, where the doctor can confirm the kidney condition, but there's no doubt that he'll talk about it. Unless John's told her and just hasn't told me that she knows.

'Shall we go?' she asks happily as she strolls past me and to the car.

I glance back at the villa, hoping John might make a last-minute appearance, but he doesn't. 'Um... is John coming?'

'He's meeting us there,' she says.

Her words make me feel a little better. She still has her bump, but it's cleverly hidden behind a baggy, flowing jacket, which she can pull across her stomach if need be. I have no idea if the doctor at the hospital knows the details about what's going on.

During the whole ride to the hospital, my heart is thumping so loud that I worry she might be able to hear it. Margo's warning and words echo in my head.

Why would Angela react so badly to the baby having a health condition? I've still not been able to figure out what's wrong with Faye, if anything. There's a lot of mysteries floating around, but my pregnancy brain hasn't been able to comprehend any of them.

We arrive at the hospital doors, but there's no sign of John.

'Let's go in without him,' she says.

'Are you sure?'

'Quite sure.'

By the time I make it into the hospital room and lie down on the bed, I'm almost hyperventilating again. The midwife takes my blood pressure, frowning as she reads the results.

'Your blood pressure is a little high.'

'Um... yeah, it always is when I first arrive. Just nerves.'

'Everything okay?' she asks.

My eyes flick to Angela, who is standing by the door, glancing around the room as if she'd rather be anywhere else. 'Um... it's just I thought Mr Dalton would be here too.'

'I see. Well, I'm afraid I can't postpone any longer.' The midwife smiles as she replaces the blood pressure cuff on the table, then switches on the monitor and picks up the gel.

I close my eyes while she does her checks, awaiting the moment of truth.

'There's a definite decline in the left kidney,' she says. 'But it's still too early to fully diagnose the condition. However, it is looking very likely that the baby has renal agenesis or possibly even multicystic dysplastic kidney.'

I don't breathe, keeping my eyes closed. I still haven't seen the scan of the baby on the monitor, and I don't intend to see it now. I also don't want to see Angela's reaction. I don't even ask what she means by multicystic dysplastic kidney. Should I ask?

'Angela, would you like to come and see the baby?'

I hear footsteps approach.

'Can you see this area here?' asks the midwife. 'One kidney is significantly larger than the other.'

'What are you talking about?' asks Angela.

I open my eyes to find Angela standing next to me. She grasps my arm and squeezes hard. The midwife explains in detail about the kidney condition while I watch Angela's jaw twitch and her face turn pale. Her grip on my arm grows tighter and tighter, but I dare not ask her to stop, or risk pulling my arm away. She looks like a pressure cooker ready to explode.

'Would you like to know the gender?'

'No,' say Angela and I simultaneously. We lock eyes.

'No, thank you,' repeats Angela calmly with a polite smile. 'I'd rather find out when my husband is present.'

'Of course. I shall schedule another scan for the twenty-week point, which is where we'll run some more tests and where we'll also be able to detect structural defects including spinal defects, cleft lip and palate, significant clubfeet, body wall abnormalities, major urinary abnormalities, and major heart defects. It may take some time to double-check the baby's bones, heart, brain, spinal cord, face, and tummy. We'll also check your placenta and the blood flow in your uterus. All normal checks and nothing to worry about. We can tell you the gender then too if your husband is coming.'

Angela nods. 'He will.'

After a further few minutes, the midwife finishes the scan and cleans the gel off my stomach. The tension is palpable as Angela and I walk in silence back to the car and get in. As soon as the door is closed, she shifts her whole body to face me.

'How long have you known about this deformity?'

The harsh word startles me for a moment. 'What are you talking about? It's not a deformity,' I reply sternly. 'It's a possible condition where one kidney is bigger than the other. Didn't you listen to the midwife explain?'

Angela inhales through her nose as if she's just been slapped. 'Don't you dare speak to me like that. How dare you keep this from me? I have a right to know about the health of my child.'

'John asked me to keep it quiet until we knew more about it. Maybe it should be him you're having a go at, not me. Anyway, where the hell is he? You said he was meeting us here.'

'He messaged me and said he got held up.'

I don't believe her. A thought crosses my mind; did she somehow convince him not to come, or maybe told him the scan date had changed?

Angela stares at me as the car pulls away from the parking space. The doors automatically lock. Great, I'm trapped in a car with a mad woman.

'I know you don't want me here, Brittany. I bet that's been your plan all along, isn't it?'

'What? What plan? What are you talking about?'

'You will have this child terminated immediately.'

I'm so stunned by her sentence that I almost choke on air. She cannot be serious. She wants to terminate a baby based on the fact it has a mild kidney disorder?

'No,' I say.

'What did you say?'

'I said no. I'm not terminating the baby.'

'Fine, then the contract no longer stands. John and I no longer wish to adopt your abomination, and you shall be fired with immediate effect.'

This time it's my turn to laugh. 'There's no way that's happening. John seemed fine with the fact the baby has the condition. I know you've done this before. To Margo. She told me everything.'

Angela sucks in a breath. Her whole body goes taut, like she's just been electrocuted. Her fists clench at her sides. 'Margo is a lying whore who slept with my husband and got herself pregnant. She's lucky we didn't kick her to the kerb after she had that miscarriage.'

Wait... Margo slept with John, and he got her pregnant? Funny how she left that little nugget of information out earlier.

I don't respond. The truth is, I have no idea whom to believe anymore. Surely, Margo wouldn't have made that story up? But then, why is Angela so crazy and spinning stories left, right and centre?

'Why are you so opposed to the baby now you know it has a health condition? Chances are, it will live normally and be perfectly healthy.'

'You don't know anything,' says Angela through gritted teeth. 'I shall be speaking with my husband. I suggest you start packing your bags though.'

We spend the rest of the journey in silence.

CHAPTER FORTY-FIVE
ANGELA

I don't know what's wrong with me, but as soon as I hear about the child having a medical issue, I see red, and I can't control my emotions. I don't even mean half of what I say, but the words spill from my mouth, and before I know it, I'm telling Brittany to terminate the child. It's not what I want, but I say it anyway because words make no sense in my head.

The thought of the child having a health issue is unnerving, but it's not the condition that makes me anxious. My whole life I've had to be perfect for everyone—my parents, my husband. Every time I was less than perfect it would give them ammunition to use against me. As a teenager, when I got a pimple on my face, my mother would shout at me and hastily apply layers of make-up to hide it, cursing my youth one minute, but then telling me I should enjoy being young while it lasted the next. My father would scold me whenever I got anything less than an A grade in school. Anything lower than that was a failure in his eyes. As a child, I had asthma and uneven teeth, and my parents wouldn't rest until they were sorted out. During the years I had train-track braces on, I was hidden away or sent to boarding school to hide from the rest of the family and my parents' friends. Nothing I did was ever good enough for them.

Then, when I met John, he accepted all my flaws at first and I thought I'd finally be free from my restraints and be allowed to be me. I was wrong. As soon as we were married, he expected me to be the epitome of perfection, not only behind closed doors, but in public too.

When Faye came along, I was horrified by her appearance. I was drugged up to the eyeballs on whatever John was giving me, and I struggled to bond with her. I hated myself, but I didn't know how to accept her. She didn't feel like my child. She wasn't perfect. John didn't help either, constantly putting both her and me down at every opportunity when we were alone, yet praising his perfect family whenever people came over. My life was a constant rollercoaster of emotion, and now all those strange memories are back. Instead of accepting the child's health condition, I lash out at Brittany because it's the first place my mind goes.

As soon as she's left the car, I cry my eyes out, then go in search of my husband. I can't make sense of what I'm feeling. Despite not taking my medication religiously, I need a dose of whatever it is he prescribes because then my mind is cloudy, and the pain doesn't hurt so much.

I need to forget about this for a while.

Plus, I need to ask him about his relationship with Brittany. It's bad enough he cheated on me with Margo, but now Brittany too. The mother of our child! The man has no morals. My anger is rising within me, and I need a release.

I find John in his study. I burst in without knocking. I'm expecting him to be angry about me lying to him regarding the ultrasound scan. I told him that Brittany told me it had been moved to tomorrow.

'How could you not tell me about the baby's kidney problems?' I scream as soon as I enter.

John wheels around in his chair, a look of horror on his face. He's on a conference call, but I don't care. He quickly mutes the call and turns off his camera.

'What the hell, Angela, I'm on a call... and what do you mean?'

'Don't give me that. I went to the scan with Brittany today and heard everything about the child's health issues.'

John removes his headset and slowly stands up. 'What the hell? Did you lie to me about the change of day?'

'Yes. Obviously,' I snap.

'Why?'

'Because I knew you were hiding something from me, John. In fact, I think you're hiding a lot more than that.'

John's facial expression remains the same—to the untrained eye, at least, but I've had years to study his body language. His left eye twitches the smallest amount and the muscle in his neck tightens. That's it. But I know I've caught him off guard.

'You don't know anything,' he says. 'If I'm hiding anything from you, Angela, it's the truth about your sickness. Do you realise how close you've come to being locked up for your own safety as well as mine?'

'Yes, I do, because you constantly remind me. I'm remembering things, John.'

'What sort of things?'

'Our first baby. Christine.' Her name came to me in a flash while I shouted at Brittany in the car, and now I can't get her out of my mind.

John shakes his head, stepping closer to me. He gently takes hold of my arms, squeezing them. 'There's no need to worry about her anymore. We have a new baby on the way, don't we? Let's focus on her and...'

'Her?'

'Yes, it's a girl,' he says calmly.

'I don't want her, John. She has a medical condition. I can't deal with it.'

'This is why I needed to have been with you today. I knew you weren't strong enough to handle the news. The doctor has sent me through the results. It sounds worse than it is, trust me. A person can survive perfectly well with only one kidney. Brittany is living proof of that.'

I close my eyes as visions of dead babies float around my head. 'What if it happens again?'

'It won't. I promise. You just need to take your medication regularly like I tell you to. You haven't been taking it, have you?'

'I've been feeling better.'

John smiles, his face full of pity. 'No, you haven't. You've been feeling worse, and you're confused, aren't you?'

'I am. I am very confused. Nothing makes sense in my head. Parts of the puzzle are jumbled.'

John pulls me against his chest into a tight hug and holds me, the way he used to before all this happened, before I became a mother for the first time. He hasn't touched me other than to have sex with me in years. He strokes my hair tenderly and my body relaxes against his.

I should have known better than to blame him. He's only been trying to help me for all these years, and he's right, I would be locked up in a mental health hospital were it not for him.

CHAPTER FORTY-SIX

I'm so rattled by the end of the car journey that I run to my room and slam the door. Angela has properly thrown me. I don't know what to think or whom to believe anymore.

I wish Clara were here. I need her guidance and advice. Granted, she'd probably tell me to be nice and give everyone the benefit of the doubt. She was always like that, always seeing the good in people and never thinking the worst of them.

I'm the opposite. I see the bad in everyone and mistrust most people, never letting them get too close. The only person I trusted was Clara, and now she's gone, leaving me to fend for myself and make all the bad decisions. Just look where I am without her already. Living in a different country, knocked up and working for a woman who could possibly be some sort of psycho.

An hour later, a knock appears at the door. I open it.

John stares back at me. 'May I come in?'

I block the space between the door and the wall with my body. 'I don't think that would be a good idea,' I say. 'Your wife has already almost taken my head off, and that was just when you hugged me. What can I do for you?' I ask.

'I just wanted to put your mind at ease. Angela and I have spoken and, while she is a little upset about the baby's health concerns, she's realised she was a bit rash with her outburst earlier. We will, of course, honour our deal and adopt your baby.'

I narrow my eyes at him, scanning his facial features for any signs of deceit. 'She was a bit more than a little upset. She ordered me to... to... get rid of it.'

'I apologise. Angela often speaks before she thinks. What can I do to make you forgive her?'

I stare down at the floor. What I want is an apology from Angela, but I doubt that's going to happen. It's not my place to question John about his marriage, or Angela's health.

John seems to sense my unease. 'I'm sorry again. Please know that we will love and care for this child no matter what.'

'Thank you,' I mumble.

As I close the door, I get the overwhelming urge to take a hot shower. Being around or close to John makes me feel gross, dirty. He acts nice, but it's hard to read him.

THAT EVENING, I finish up some minor preparations for the dessert menu over the weekend, then decide to take a walk. I've never been one of those people who enjoy exercise, but I always notice when I've neglected my fitness. Since I have no idea what I can and can't do now I'm pregnant, I decide that walking is probably my best bet of keeping fit.

I walk for twenty minutes, looping around the bottom

gardens where there's a cute stone building situated between an orchard and an overgrown field. It looks like a little cottage, perhaps where people have stayed. The darkness is closing in, but there's still enough to be able to see my way across the path towards the cottage.

That's when I see a flickering of light coming from the small window around the side. Glancing left and right to check my surroundings, I step quickly to the side, flattening myself against the wall.

Voices.

There's someone inside. No, two people. Maybe three.

Walk away, Brittany. Walk away now.

A sigh escapes, but the second it does, I crouch and then peer over the windowsill into the room beyond. The flickering light is coming from a group of candles on a table in the far corner. There are definitely two people inside.

A man and a woman. It's difficult to make out who they are, because their faces and bodies are in shadows, but there's no mistaking their voices.

I shouldn't be here. It feels as if I'm encroaching on a very serious situation.

They're arguing, almost screaming at each other, gesturing wildly.

The woman slaps the man across the face.

I duck down against the wall, pressing my back against it. My breathing is erratic. I'm not even sure I can get away from here without being seen. It's a miracle they didn't happen to look out of the window as I was walking up the garden path on my approach to the building.

More shouting.

There's no doubt in my mind that the woman inside is Margo and she's just slapped John hard across the face. Why did I decide to go out for an evening stroll? Every time I try and do something around here, I end up getting into some sort of trouble or find myself in a place I shouldn't. I remember that argument I overheard between John and Angela when I first arrived here.

Now, he's arguing with Margo, but it's difficult to understand what they're saying. I can only make out a few words here and there.

Margo: 'Why... tell... that?'
John: 'Because... want... baby... Angela... now.'
Margo: 'Fuck... crazy... bitch.'
John: 'Don't... speak... her... that.'
Margo: 'Why... not... she... deserves... it.'

I'm momentarily distracted by a car driving up the road towards the villa, so I miss the rest of the conversation, but a loud crash jolts me back to the present. Oh God. What's happening in there? Did she just attack him, or did he attack her? Push her over or something?

Another crash.

I need to check to make sure what's going on.

Quickly, I pop my head over the windowsill, then duck down again just as fast. They aren't fighting. They're kissing.

I guess Angela was right about Margo and John.

But what does this mean? Why is John trying to have a baby with Angela if he's having an affair with Margo? Is that what this is or are they in love? Angela clearly already knows that John got Margo pregnant, but then... what did Margo say before? They had tried to adopt the baby as their own, like they're doing to me now. What about Margo? Were they like one, big, happy family, or was Margo being forced to go along with it?

Their passion for each other reaches extreme heights.

There's a lot of grunting and fast breathing. Clothes get pulled off and it's at this point I'm forced to look away, but then they break it off as Margo shoves him away.

Margo: 'No! Can't... not... again. What... Faye? This... wrong... so... levels.'

John: 'I told... nothing... worry... about. Faye... isn't... problem. Never... will... She's... safe.'

Margo: 'Not... worried... about. What... if... finds out... still alive?'

John: 'Won't. Safe... at... hospital.'

Margo: '...no chance... wake... up?'

John: 'No. ...Brain-dead.'

I cover my mouth with my hands, stifling my gasp. Oh my God. Faye isn't at boarding school at all. She's in a hospital somewhere and she's brain-dead.

Worst of all... it sounds as if Angela has no idea. Why is she pretending that Faye is at boarding school? And how the hell has Faye ended up brain-dead?

PART 3

CHAPTER FORTY-SEVEN

I attend the twenty-week scan alone. John and Angela were both supposed to come with me, but John has been called away on an urgent work trip and won't be back for three days, and Angela is feeling unwell, so she's resting. I'm asked again if I want to know the gender by the midwife, to which I say no. It's the most important scan because they'll be able to tell me more about the baby's kidney problems.

The doctor turns to me after taking a long time looking at the ultrasound on the screen while he manoeuvres the thing across my stomach. 'I'm afraid, after further inspection and analysis, there's a possibility your baby has multicystic dysplastic kidney, as we suspected last time. It's a condition in which one or both—but in the case of your baby, one—of its kidneys does not develop normally while in the womb. Often, fluid-filled sacs such as cysts replace normal kidney tissue, which prevents the affected kidney from working as it should.'

I stare at him blankly. 'O-Okay...'

'I know it can be a lot to take in, but there is some good

news. Since only one kidney looks to be affected, it means it's not as serious as if it affected both kidneys. The child has a chance of growing normally and may have few, if any, health problems later in life. Basically, the unaffected kidney will grow larger to compensate for the non-working kidney, and it means it must do the work for both kidneys. The non-working kidney usually shrinks and disappears over time. We will need to keep a close eye on the development of your baby and do several more scans than normal to ensure that there are no further complications. Once the child is born, we will scan to confirm the diagnosis.'

I open my mouth, but nothing but a gargling sound comes out. My brain understands the words, but I just can't comprehend them. He keeps talking, telling me the development of the baby is fine, apart from the left kidney. No other health issues detected. They have a strong heartbeat, which beats a hell of a lot faster than I expect.

As I listen, I close my eyes, listening to the fast *thud, thud, thud*.

Oh my God. It finally hits me like a sledgehammer to the face.

There's a real-life human being growing inside me right now.

How mental is that?

'Would you like to see?'

I shake my head, biting my lip. A part of me wants to see them, but I must continue to keep my distance. I can't risk getting emotionally attached to something that I'm giving away. I can't allow myself to get involved or make it real. I know that doesn't make sense. Of course it's real, but...

'Hmm,' says the doctor.

My head snaps round to look at her. 'What? What's hmmm?' My heart rate doubles again.

'Oh, it's nothing with the baby. I'm just checking your blood work, and it looks like you have a higher-than-average blood glucose level.'

'What does that mean?'

'You could be at risk of developing gestational diabetes,' he replies.

'I... I don't have diabetes.'

'Some women get it during pregnancy. It's all perfectly normal.'

'How is any of this normal?'

He just smiles at me. 'I shall order for you to have a test carried out around twenty-five weeks. It's probably nothing.'

Great. One more thing to worry about.

'I'll send you all the details closer to the time. We're all done here.' He smiles at me again. 'I shall email across all the details we've spoken about today to Mr Dalton.'

ONCE I'VE SAID my goodbyes to the doctor, I have a long-awaited pee then walk towards the exit doors, but a sign makes me stop and pause. *Children's ward.*

No. No. No. No.

I shouldn't. I couldn't. I mustn't.

Before I can talk sense into myself, I take the turning to the children's ward.

CHAPTER FORTY-EIGHT

I pass several rooms, all of which have the doors shut, and I scan the names of the children on their wall charts. This looks like an accident and emergency area. If what I took from John is true, Faye is in some sort of long-term coma, so she'll be in the intensive care unit, I expect. My bump is properly popping now, so it's obvious I'm pregnant. Hopefully, people won't question why I'm here. For all they know, I'm visiting my other child. I scan the signs along the walls and see one for the ICU.

'Hi. Can I help you? Are you lost?' asks a helpful voice. A nurse smiles at me.

'Oh... um... I'm trying to find a patient here. My friend said to meet her on the ward, but I've forgotten the directions she told me to get to the room. The patient's name is Faye Dalton.'

'I'm sorry, but there's no Faye Dalton in the ICU.'

'Are you sure?'

'Quite sure.'

I frown. 'Okay, well, thanks for your help. I'll give her a

ring and find out where she is,' I say with a chuckle as I dig around in my bag for my phone. 'She's probably told me the wrong hospital or something.' The nurse smiles again and walks away.

Well, I tried.

Perhaps she's not being held in this hospital. There are plenty of other hospitals she could be in, but it's not like I can go traipsing across the country looking for her. She's not my child. I won't be allowed access or given details on her condition.

YESTERDAY, when I returned to the villa, Angela asked me how the scan went. I said it was fine and that the doctor should be sending over all the information to John. I decide not to mention the gestational diabetes test or the other stuff the doctor told me about, but it's rolling around in my head, causing my brain to overthink as usual.

She doesn't look well at all. She's very pale and wobbly on her feet, grasping hold of every piece of furniture she can to help her stay upright. She's not wearing her bump either. I suppose there's no reason to when she's alone in the villa.

I CAN'T SLEEP. Apparently, insomnia is normal in pregnancy, but this is ridiculous. My bump isn't even that big yet, but it's still a struggle to get comfortable. I asked Mrs Dubois for some extra fluffy pillows to prop up around my body to support me, but even they aren't helping.

I decide to head to the main kitchen and get a drink of water.

. . .

I FILL my glass from the fancy kitchen tap that takes me several attempts to work out how to turn on, take a drink, followed by a deep breath as the water soothes my dry mouth. I finish the glass, refill it and take it with me back across the kitchen the way I came. I suppose I should head back to my room, back to bed, back to the staff quarters, back to the seemingly never-ending night where I just stare at the ceiling and hope sleep takes me away.

Leaving the vast kitchen behind, I walk slowly and steadily towards the spiral staircase that leads to the staff area of the villa; a separate annex. Grasping the banister in one hand, I take each stair one at a time, still unaccustomed to my unbalanced and stiff frame.

By the time I reach the top, I'm slightly out of breath and stop to compose myself.

That's when I hear a creak of a floorboard up ahead.

I look up, towards the sound, but all I see is the gloomy darkness. I can just about make out the swirly patterns on the tiles in the hallway leading to the staff bedrooms. There's a large window at the far end hall, which overlooks the pool and patio area. There are lights surrounding the pool, which are on throughout the night, casting strange shadows through the window onto the tiles.

But it's not the shadows that catch my attention or make the hairs on my arms prickle.

It's another creaking sound, like someone is opening a door and the hinges need to be lubricated. This time, it's behind me, downstairs. I lean and glance over the banister, holding my breath to listen out for any other sound, but there's nothing.

'Hello?' I call out. 'Is anyone there?'

The glass I'm holding shakes as I wait for an answer.

None comes.

I turn and head down the hall to my room, but as I do, a black shadow darts across the tiles in front of me. I stumble backwards, the hand holding the glass losing grip. The glass slips from my fingers and smashes at my feet, soaking me and the area I'm standing on.

'Hello?' My voice is a little firmer this time, from fear, not annoyance.

My heart rate is so fast that I can't breathe. I put a hand over my heart, praying it calms down because it feels like it could explode. I've been warned several times now that my blood pressure needs to stay low.

Dizziness washes over me and my foot slips on the wet tiles beneath me.

I reach out to grab the banister, steadying myself. That was close.

I'm still off balance as a shadow lunges towards me. I don't even have time to open my mouth and scream because I'm already tumbling down the stairs.

A snap pierces the darkness as my leg breaks, erupting in white-hot pain.

I land with a heavy thud at the bottom and listen to the heartbeat of the villa; the ticking of that damn metal clock on the wall in the kitchen.

But all I can think about is the pain in my leg; that and the dark humanoid shape standing and looking down over the banister at me.

Finally, darkness engulfs me.

CHAPTER FORTY-NINE

The following hours are a blur. Just a haze of beeps, shouts, pain and disorientation. I have no idea where I am or what's going on, and the pain in my leg keeps me from slipping under for too long. I black out, then I wake up, then I pass out, on repeat. I've never been so scared in all my life, other than when Clara died.

I'm ashamed to admit, I don't even think of the baby. Not at first. Finally, I stay awake longer than a minute and that's when my brain switches on. I can't move though. My head is in some sort of brace, so I use my hands and run them over my stomach, feeling a slight bump. Because I'm lying down, it tends to disappear, but I'm pretty sure the baby is still in there. It's difficult to tell though.

Clearing my throat hurts, but I need to know for sure. Before I can ask for help, a nurse approaches the side of my bed and squeezes my hand.

'Welcome back,' she says. 'Before you ask, your baby girl is fine.'

'What did you just say?' I croak.

She frowns at me. 'You... do know you were twenty weeks pregnant, right?'

'Um, yes, but...'

The nurse turns beetroot. 'Oh, my goodness, I am so sorry! You didn't know the sex of the baby, did you? I just blurted it out without thinking.' She covers her mouth with her hands.

'It's fine,' I mumble. But it's not. Knowing the baby is a girl makes everything seem so much more real. I know that sounds strange, but knowing I have a baby girl growing inside me makes me imagine her face, imagine what she'll look like when she grows up. It gives her an identity.

I wonder whether Angela and John have been told too.

'What happened?' I ask. 'My head hurts and my leg is killing me.'

'You have a broken tibia and a concussion. You were extremely lucky, to be perfectly honest.'

'And the baby... they... she's definitely okay?'

'You did bleed a little, but we've conducted several scans while you've been out of it and she's alive and kicking and doing well. However, we'd like to keep you in for observation for at least a week before we release you into the care of Mr and Mrs Dalton.'

'Are they here?'

'I believe Mr Dalton is in the waiting area and Mrs Dalton has gone home.'

'What happened to me though?'

'Mr Dalton found you semi-conscious at the bottom of the stairs. He called an ambulance, and you were rushed here about twelve hours ago. We've performed surgery on your leg. It was a bad break, but it was a clean one.'

I close my eyes, hoping to summon up some memories

from somewhere, but everything is grey and blurry. I had surgery? At least I woke up from it again. In a way, I'm glad I can't remember much because if I had been aware of what was going on, no doubt my anxiety would have been through the roof, stressing both me and the baby out.

'Short-term memory loss is normal for a concussion of your magnitude. It should return in time, but we'll be conducting checks on you to ensure there's no irreparable damage.'

'Can I see John... um, Mr Dalton, please?'

The nurse nods. 'Yes, and I'll fetch the doctor too to let him know you're awake and responding well. He may want to ask you a few questions.'

The nurse leaves the room. I lean my head against the pillow. My lower left leg and knee are in a full plaster cast and my head is swimming, which is either from the concussion or whatever pain concoction they have me on. I doubt it's the strong stuff, since I'm pretty sure you can't give morphine to a pregnant woman, but I could be wrong.

A few minutes later, footsteps wake me from my snooze.

'How are you doing?' asks John. He stands by the doorway. I'm a little shocked at his bedraggled appearance. His hair is messy and he's not wearing a tie.

'Not great,' I say quietly.

John steps further into the room, shaking his head. 'What were you doing walking around the villa in the dead of night in your condition?'

I bite my tongue. 'I was thirsty.'

'What I mean is... What happened?'

I sigh and close my eyes. 'I'm not sure. I can't remember details. I remember getting a drink of water, but after that

I'm unsure. I think... I think I remember someone following me.'

'Following you? Who?'

'I don't know.' I don't say what I really mean and that I think it was Angela who was following me. I have no proof, of course, but she's the only one who'd be crazy enough to push me down the stairs. She openly admitted that she wanted me to get rid of the baby. Maybe she was trying to do the job herself.

John stands by the side of my bed. His fingers twitch by his sides, like he's fighting the urge to reach out and take my hand, which is merely inches away from his.

'I think you should move into the main part of the villa,' he says solemnly. 'The bedroom just down the hall from the master suite is free. That way, we'll be able to keep a closer eye on you, especially as you now need looking after. Clearly, you can't work in the kitchen for the next few weeks, or even months, while your leg heals and you recover from your head wound.'

I hadn't even thought about that. My job! Is my contract with them void now?

Tears fill my eyes. I try and look away so John can't see, but he reaches out and grabs my hand. 'Brittany, please don't worry. Angela and I are just relieved that the baby is safe and alive. And you as well. It could have been so much worse.'

I stay quiet, keeping my opinions to myself. I want to tell him that I know about him and Margo, that I'm worried that his wife is trying to kill me, but I'll just sound crazy.

I feel like I'm stuck between a rock and a hard place with no way out.

He squeezes my hand hard. 'Focus on resting and recovering and then we'll get you home.'

Home. It may be home to him, but not to me. The villa is just my place of work, and suddenly I get a pang of homesickness. I miss my flat. My home. My Clara.

Clara.

I just want to go home.

CHAPTER FIFTY

ANGELA

I've been bed-bound for almost a week now, since Brittany was admitted to hospital after falling down the stairs. I didn't mean to push her. In fact, I didn't even know it was her. John set me up in a different bedroom, the one down the hall from our master suite. I sometimes sleep separately from him, especially when I'm having a particularly bad episode and, since he put me on new pills, they've done nothing but make me hallucinate and have vivid dreams.

I woke up with a start that night, drenched in sweat. I'd been dreaming of trying to save my baby from the water, but the water kept getting deeper and deeper and no matter how hard I tried, I couldn't reach her. I swam down and down into the dark depths, but she was always just out of reach, floating in the water. Eventually, I needed air, and I had to leave her to sink into the abyss below. As soon as my head pierced through the surface of the water, I woke up.

It was so real. My night clothes were drenched, as if I really had been swimming. I got up, confused and dazed as I searched for her. I heard a noise and went to investigate and saw a shadow moving around downstairs in the kitchen area. My brain told me it was an intruder come to steal my baby, so I followed it and then shoved the intruder down the stairs.

It was only when I heard the scream and the snap of bone that I came to and realised what I'd done. I'd killed her. I'd killed another baby. I screamed so loud, and John came running. He dealt with everything, but by then I'd gone catatonic. He sedated me and led me back to bed, which is where I stayed, tossing and turning, attempting to fit everything back together.

John told me that Brittany and the baby had survived.

That was enough for me to realise that I'd taken things too far. I needed to get my head back on straight and that meant taking the pills regularly again. I didn't have any other choice. If I was going to be a mother again, then I needed to be able to think straight.

Mrs Dubois delivered my pills for me, under the strict instruction from John to ensure I swallowed them and kept them down. He was now too busy to deal with me directly and was furious for almost killing Brittany and the child. He can't even look at me; another reason why I'm staying in a separate bedroom.

Perhaps it's better this way.

CHAPTER FIFTY-ONE

The week in hospital drags by. Angela doesn't come to see me, but John visits every day. I'd rather he didn't because every time I see him, I want to bring up the whole kissing Margo thing and the Faye being brain-dead thing, but I force the questions back down.

The cast must stay on my leg for six more weeks, which means I'm basically bed-bound, unless I use the crutches they provide me, or the wheelchair, but my belly is only going to get bigger, so it's going to get more and more difficult to manoeuvre myself around, i.e. harder to escape or run away.

Did Angela really push me down the stairs or did I trip over my own feet and see random shadows that freaked me out? A little of what happened has come back to me over the past few days, but I'm no closer to being certain. I definitely saw a shadow and heard a creak of a floorboard, but if it was a person, then I didn't see them properly.

John picks me up from the hospital and takes me back to the villa. When I arrive at my new room, down the corridor from the master suite, I find my clothes and possessions are already there. I assume it was one of the staff who moved them.

I get myself comfortable on the bed, which is a large double. I must admit, this room is certainly an upgrade from the staff area. Even the sheets are better, an expensive thread count by the look and feel of them. There's a small kitchenette in the room with a kettle and mini fridge, plus a small dining and lounge area and a large flatscreen television mounted on the wall. John leaves me the crutches so I can get around the room, but I decide to rest in bed as much as possible, since I'm still unsteady on my feet and I don't trust my muscles not to collapse.

John leaves the room after providing me a walkie-talkie so I can request help if I need it. I feel like a pathetic invalid.

Margo knocks on my door and lets herself in without waiting for my reply.

'Hi,' she says when she sees me in bed. 'Heard you took a tumble.'

'Uh huh,' I mumble.

'Got yourself a pretty sweet set-up now, haven't you?' She glances around the lavish room.

'What's that supposed to mean?'

'Nothing.' Margo chuckles as she moves closer to the side of the bed. I'm not sure why, but it makes me uneasy to have her so close to me, merely inches away. Helpless, like a little lamb. That's me. I can't even run away. She must sense my unease because she says, 'There's no need to be defensive, Brittany.'

'I know about you and John.'

Where did that come from? I hadn't been planning to bring it up, but now that I think about it, it's probably safer to tell Margo that I know than John. I don't know what I'm supposed to gain from telling her that I know, but I don't like the fact she's acting like she's innocent in all of this.

Margo barely reacts to my words. She stares at me. 'What is it you think you know?'

'You told me that you got pregnant from a staff member, but it was John, wasn't it?'

'I never said that. Besides, it was a long time ago. We're over now.'

'You sure about that?'

Margo clears her throat. She's nervous. Good. I'm fed up with everyone trying to control me and manipulate me. 'What do you want, Brittany?'

'What do I want? I want you to tell me the truth. I could be in real danger here. I'm pretty sure Angela was the one who pushed me down the stairs.'

'How do you know it wasn't me?' She locks her eyes on me, then laughs. 'I'm kidding.'

'Ha ha.'

Margo sits on the edge of the bed. The movement makes the mattress shift, which in turn causes my leg to move. I wince, trying not to show how much pain and discomfort I'm in. Margo doesn't seem to even notice.

'What do you want to know?' she asks.

'Faye.'

'Faye,' she repeats with an exhale.

'I overheard you and John talking about her.'

'Wait... that was when we were... You sneaky little bitch. You were spying on us?'

'For your information, I was going for a walk when I saw the cute building in the grounds and thought I'd take a look.

How could I know it was your and John's secret hook-up place?'

Margo shakes her head. 'Whatever. I don't care. It's not serious this time. It only happened the once. I won't be making that mistake again.'

'Does Angela know? She accused me of having an affair with John just because he gave me a hug.'

'I have no idea what Angela knows.'

'Why are you still sleeping with him?'

Margo is quiet for a moment, as if contemplating her answer. 'I told you, I'm not. It was a moment of weakness.'

I shift my bum up a little higher on the bed as I ask, 'Do you love him?'

'No.'

'Then why—'

'I don't know,' she answers. She's hanging her head. Clearly, she's in two minds about the whole thing. Is John forcing her to sleep with him again? I mean, it's not what it looked like the other day when I caught them in the act, but it's hard to tell what goes on.

'You wanted to know about Faye,' she says.

I nod, biting my lip.

'Faye is in a long-term coma in the Nice University Hospital.'

'What happened?'

'About a year ago, she was swimming in the pool out back. John was working upstairs in his office and Angela was sunbathing nearby, keeping an eye on her. Faye and Angela's relationship was strained at best. On the outside, to friends and family, they were the perfect family, but within these walls, Angela hated her daughter.'

'She hated her? Why?' My hand automatically moves to my bump.

'Faye had a facial deformity. She was born with a cleft palate. She had surgery to correct it while she was a baby and then again as a toddler, but her lip and chin were never completely perfect. Not to Angela, anyway. She's obsessed with perfection. She wanted the perfect daughter, but to her, it wasn't Faye. She kept screaming that Faye wasn't really hers, that she was swapped at birth or something because she couldn't possibly have given birth to something so ugly. Her words. Not mine.'

I shake my head. 'That's... messed up.'

'Anyway, suddenly John hears Angela screaming at the top of her lungs. By the time he gets there, Mrs Dubois is there, doing her best to calm Angela down. Faye is lying face-down in the pool.'

My breath catches in my throat.

'John jumps in and drags her out, performs CPR. An ambulance arrives. She was still alive, but barely. She never woke up. Her brain had been starved of oxygen for too long and she's now classed as brain-dead with no hope of her ever waking up.'

'This might be an insensitive question, but... why are they keeping her alive if there's no chance of her waking up?'

'John isn't ready to let her go.'

'And Angela? Did she try and kill Faye or was it an accident?'

Margo shrugs. 'My guess is she tried to kill her daughter. That's what John thinks too.'

'And what does Angela think of Faye being brain-dead?'

'Oh, she doesn't know. Angela thinks Faye is dead.'

CHAPTER FIFTY-TWO

It takes a moment for my brain to understand what Margo's just said. Clearly, Angela is completely unhinged—for what reason I'm still to find out—but drowning her own daughter in a pool because she had a mild facial deformity is a hideous thing to comprehend. What the hell made Angela be so cruel towards her daughter?

'Let me get this straight,' I say. 'John is keeping the fact their daughter is alive from Angela because what... he thinks she'll try and finish the job?'

'Oh, Faye isn't alive. Not technically. There's no chance of her ever waking up, but he just can't let her go. But yes, John is afraid that Angela will try and finish what she started.'

'So, why the hell does she want another baby?'

'Why do you think? So that she can finally have her perfect family on the inside and the outside. After Faye *died*, Angela had another mental breakdown. She had one way before that too, after their first kid died, but it was never properly treated, not by outside doctors anyway. She clearly had post-natal depression combined with grief. It fucked her up. John's a surgeon. He has access to doctors and medication, whatever he wants. He prescribes all these types of medication for her to keep her sedated, which probably doesn't help her in the long run. She got it into her head that she wanted to start again, try for another baby, but for whatever reason, it never happened for them. Probably for the best, if you ask me. A lot of the time, Angela functions normally, but she has bouts of clarity when everything that's happened comes rushing back and she gets very confused, especially if she doesn't keep up with her meds.'

'And John knows all this and is keeping her drugged up to the eyeballs?'

'Yep.'

'Why the hell would you be involved with a guy like that? He's evil, clearly.'

'I didn't know all that at the start, but now I'm... sort of trapped. He wants me to start sleeping with him again, but I don't really want to. I'm afraid if I don't, then he'll fire me, and I'll end up with nothing.'

'Surely that's better than being controlled by a monster.'

Margo shrugs her shoulders as if that's her answer.

I shake my head, baffled at her choice. 'How did you and John end up getting together?'

Margo sighs and is quiet for a moment before she speaks. 'John found it difficult to handle Angela and her outbursts. She became so fixated on having a baby. She was violent. She'd basically corner him when she was ovulating and force him to have sex with her.'

My eyebrows rise. 'He's a grown man. He could have said no, right?'

'Yes, but you don't know what Angela is like. She's

dangerous and unpredictable. Anyway, one night we ran into each other in the main villa, and he was crying. I stayed to have a drink with him, and I guess things moved on from there. He said he loved me, but then I got pregnant, and he changed.'

'How did Angela find out?'

'I don't know, but one day she pulled me aside and told me how happy she was that I was having a baby.'

'What the hell?'

'It was all an act. She pretended she didn't know it was John's. I told you, she's so confused. They propositioned me with a contract, convinced me to let them adopt the baby as their own when I gave birth, and they'd provide me with whatever I wanted in return. John promised he'd take care of me. He kept saying he loved me.'

I don't respond straight away, but I know what's coming next.

'Then, I had a miscarriage and Angela completely lost it, acting like it was her who'd lost the baby, not me. To be honest, I was glad I lost it. I know that's a horrible thing to say, but I wasn't prepared, and, in all honesty, I didn't want John and Angela to have it, not after what happened to their first two kids.'

'Why the hell do you still work here?'

Margo's eyes fill with tears. 'I'm scared, Brittany. I know too much about Angela. I can't even go to the police because I'm under contract to keep my mouth shut, as are you. John has the power to ruin us. Don't forget that.'

I close my eyes and take a breath. 'This is such a mess. I don't want this baby. I just wanted them to adopt it so I could get on with my life, but now... now I'm worried that she's in danger. My baby. She has a kidney problem. Angela told me to abort her a few weeks ago, but there's nothing wrong with her physically on the outside.'

'It doesn't matter to Angela.'

'Why is she like this? Why is she so hell-bent on having a perfect child?'

'I don't know,' Margo says as she shakes her head. 'I'm sorry you're in this mess, Brittany. I wish there was a way to help you.'

'You can. You can be my eyes and ears. Just keep an eye on things. I'm literally stuck in this room for the next few weeks. Speak to John. I don't know, just... I need someone on my side. You're the only person I have left. Please.' Even as I say the words, my throat closes up and my eyes sting with tears. I keep thinking of Clara and how much I wish she were here, guiding me, helping me. Margo isn't Clara. She'll never be anywhere close to what Clara meant to me, but despite her somewhat icy exterior and our dodgy start, we're both trapped here by John and Angela; we're both being used to serve a purpose.

'Okay,' she says. 'Here's my first piece of advice... Do whatever it takes to get out of that contract. Do not give your baby to those psychos.'

'How am I supposed to do that?'

'I don't know, but I'll help you.'

CHAPTER FIFTY-THREE

Being pregnant sucks. Being bed-bound sucks. Being pregnant *and* bed-bound? They need a whole new word for that. My growing bump makes any position uncomfortable to be in and my broken leg means I can basically only be in one position: on my back. I can't even bend my knee because the cast goes over it, meaning whenever I do hobble around, I look like a wooden soldier boy.

Plus, Margo tells me a couple of days later that as my bump gets bigger it's dangerous for me to lie flat on my back after twenty-eight weeks. I'm only twenty-one weeks, but it's still enough to freak me out. Something about compressing the blood vessels that supply blood and oxygen to the uterus and baby. It can also increase the risk of stillbirth. Talk about stress. How am I supposed to know all these things? I suppose most expectant mothers would have read dozens of pregnancy and baby books by now, which would explain all these things to them in detail, but I've been avoiding reading up on it like the plague. I still plan on giving this baby away (not to John and Angela now, but a couple who aren't psychos) and I'm still under the assumption that the less I know about what's going on inside me, the less attached I'll be to the baby when it's born. I only know what my midwife and doctor tell me. Well, and Margo, although how she knows so much about pregnancy I have no idea, considering she was only pregnant for a few weeks.

Margo brings me my breakfast, lunch and dinner, helps me to the bathroom and washes me. She's basically turned into my personal maid.

'You really don't have to do this,' I say when she's got me back to bed after a trip to the bathroom. 'You're a chef, not a housekeeper or servant.'

'Would you rather I fetch Mrs Dubois? She's busy tending to Angela, but I'm sure she'll be happy to take over from me.'

'No!' We share a quick laugh. Margo pulls the sheet over me, eyeing my bump.

'When's your next scan?' she asks.

'Next week,' I say.

'Have John or Angela been to see you yet?'

'John has, but only to give me another book on pregnancy.'

'Which you haven't read.'

'Which I haven't read,' I repeat. 'Have you found out anything yet?'

'No, only that Angela appears to be feeling better and still has a fake baby bump that she's showing all her friends and family. She's severely deranged. She also lashed out at John the other day. I caught them arguing again.'

'I've been meaning to ask you about that. John's scar across his face... What happened?'

Margo sighs. 'That happened right at the start. John told

me that a few days after their first baby died in the bath, she grabbed a knife and...'

'Yeesh.' We spend a few seconds in silence. 'I need proof that she killed Faye or attempted to kill Faye. If I have that, then I could go to the police and... and... I don't know... They can't be allowed to keep doing this. I thought I was getting a good deal. I wouldn't have accepted if I knew then what I know now.'

Margo opens her mouth to say something, but a knock at the door stops her.

Angela walks in.

'Ah, I see you already have company. How lovely.' She closes the door. Margo and I just stare at her like deer caught in headlights. 'Margo, would you please give Brittany and me a moment alone?'

Margo shifts her eyes sideways to me without turning her head. 'Um... sure.' She squeezes my good leg through the bed sheet. 'Be back in ten minutes.'

I don't want to point out that Angela could probably kill me in less than that time. I hope Margo has the decency to listen in at the door in case she needs to come to my rescue. My eyes shift right and left, looking for something, anything, I could use as a weapon against her.

Angela watches Margo like a hawk without blinking as she walks towards the door and leaves the room. Then she slowly turns around to face me. I've never noticed before, but her movements are almost robotic in nature.

'How are you feeling, Brittany? I'm sorry I haven't been to see you.' She caresses her bump, which is much bigger than mine. 'But you know how it is with pregnancy; it can take everything out of you. I've been resting a lot.'

'Right,' I say, stumped for any other words. This woman is deluded in so many ways. 'Um... Angela... is everything okay?' I decide not to provoke her by pointing out that she's not the one who's pregnant.

Her eyes zone in on me, growing dark. 'Yes,' she says. 'Everything is fine, but I'd like to talk to you about my husband.'

'Okay. What about him?'

'I know what's going on,' she says with a hiss, leaning towards me.

'Huh?'

'You don't think I know about you and my husband? You think I don't notice he comes to bed sometimes smelling of your perfume?'

'What are you talking about?'

Angela grabs my wrist and squeezes so tight that her nails dig into my skin. 'It's his baby, isn't it? You little whore. You're worse than Margo. You think that by throwing yourself down the stairs you could get out of it, earn more sympathy? Well, it's not going to work. You and your abomination of a child disgust me.'

I freeze as my breath catches in my throat. 'Angela, please. You're hurting me. I'm sorry your husband cheated on you with Margo, but as I told you before, I got pregnant *before* I arrived here, *before* I even met your husband. You're getting things mixed up.'

Angela blinks several times. 'I don't believe a word you say.'

'Well, you should. If anything, it should be John who you don't believe.'

'What's that supposed to mean?' she snaps. 'My John has

always looked out for me, always done what's best for me.' She says the words, but her tone tells me she's not sure of what she's saying. I feel sorry for her in a way. I've never been on any sort of medication that changes your brain chemistry, but whatever she's on is doing a number on her.

I don't know how to respond to her.

'You just keep your hands off my husband, you hear?'

'I never touched your husband!' I shout, a little louder than I expect. A shooting pain makes me gasp. Cramp! 'Urrggg!' I lean forwards, yanking my arm out of her grasp, and rub my calf muscle, but the pain is so bad. My good leg feels like a rock.

Angela leaps away from the bed. 'What's going on?'

'I have leg cramp! It's something pregnant women get but since you're not pregnant, you wouldn't know, would you?' Okay, so it's a bit harsh, and I feel bad for snapping, but she deserves to be taken down a peg or two. I block Angela out of my head and focus on breathing and not passing out. A few seconds later, the pain lessens its grip on me and I'm able to take a full breath. Sweat pours from my forehead.

Angela steps closer again. 'I'm sorry,' she says. 'It must be quite uncomfortable for you to be bed-bound right now.'

I reach over to the side table and grab a glass of water, taking a sip. 'Yes.'

'How about I get you a wheelchair and take you for a walk?'

'What, so you can shove me down another set of stairs and finish the job?'

Angela flinches like I've just slapped her. 'What are you talking about?'

Okay, I've had enough now. My temper and hormones are taking over. 'Oh please,' I say with a laugh. 'I know it was you who pushed me down the stairs. You tried to kill me and the baby!'

'Don't be ridiculous. I want the baby. Why would I put the child at risk by pushing you down the stairs?'

'You said the baby was an abomination. She's got a medical condition, and, in your eyes, she isn't perfect, so you don't want her anymore. That's what you told me when you found out. You told me to get an abortion.'

Angela's mouth drops open. 'W-What did you just say?'

'Which part?'

'S-She?'

'Yes, it's a girl,' I say, not caring that I've ruined her surprise, although I'm surprised John hasn't told her, or maybe he has and she's just forgotten, like she forgets everything else.

Angela's eyes flood with tears and she covers her mouth with her hands. 'Oh, my goodness. A girl. I'm having a baby girl,' she cries.

'You're not having anything. I've changed my mind about the adoption. You can't have her. She's mine.' That may have been a mistake. I didn't mean to blurt it out like that, but I can't just sit here and wait for something to happen.

Angela lunges forwards like a woman possessed, her eyes aflame, pinning me against the bed. She digs her elbow into my leg cast, causing severe pain to the point I have to fight to stop from blacking out.

'You can't take my daughter away from me,' she says, her mouth merely inches from my face. Spit flies from her mouth as she tightens her grip on the oversized t-shirt I'm wearing.

Panic is quickly rising within me. I can't breathe and the

pain in my leg is pushing me closer and closer to the edge of blacking out.

'P-Please,' I say. 'S-Stop!'

Angela releases the pressure on my cast and air whooshes back into my lungs. 'I'd think twice about changing your mind, Brittany. John and I will love and adore that child. She'll never want for anything. We can give her a better life than you ever could.'

I blink away tears, then wipe them away with my hand. 'What the hell is wrong with you?' I say.

'You clearly fell down the stairs yourself,' continues Angela. She then turns and heads for the door. I can't let her leave without letting her know that I'm on to her. She thinks she can threaten me. Well, I can threaten her right back.

'I know about Faye.'

Angela stops dead but doesn't glance back to look at me. 'You know nothing,' she says with the emotional depth of a robot.

'I know more than you think,' I say. 'If you don't let me out of my contract, then I'll tell the world that you killed your own daughter because she looked a little different. You're sick.'

I'm expecting Angela to retaliate, defend herself or deny it, but she does none of those things. In fact, she doesn't even reply. She continues walking to the door and leaves without a word.

A rush of relief takes my breath away as I lean against the pillows propping up my exhausted body. I feel as if I've just run a marathon, but my race is far from over. I'm worried I may have pushed Angela too far. Clearly, she's not well and it's not her fault, but she's a threat to me and my baby.

I'm not sure where it comes from, but my maternal

instinct, which I never thought was there to begin with, is surfacing, taking me by surprise. I may not want to keep the child as my own, but it's still my job to protect her until she's with her new family.

I must keep her safe and, for the first time in my life, a glimmer of love for a child I've never even met blooms in my heart.

CHAPTER FIFTY-FOUR

ANGELA

My confrontation with Brittany makes me nauseous. I rush to my room and splash water on my face, an attempt to wake myself from a haze. I don't know what's the truth and what's a lie anymore. Did I push her down the stairs or didn't I? John thinks I did, so I must have done.

But nothing makes sense as I lean against the wall. Even with my eyes closed, the images and memories continue to bombard me, one after the other, everything jumbled together. I need help. I don't have the strength to keep doing this day after day. I wish I'd never stopped taking my pills. I should have listened to John, trusted him, but the more I think about it, the more muddled everything becomes.

I cover my mouth with both hands and scream, muffling the sound as best I can. I'm losing it. No, I lost it a long time ago. I did push Brittany. Of course I did. It's all my fault. The baby could have died. I could have been responsible for killing another child. I'm a child killer.

How could I possibly look after another child? I'm not fit to be a mother. I never have been. John was right in what he said to me all those years ago. I'm not supposed to be a mother. I should have listened to him, rather than force him to keep trying for another baby after losing one after the other.

I killed Christine.

I killed Faye.

And I almost killed Brittany and her unborn child.

Tears sting my eyes as I reach up and grab a razor from the side. Everyone would be better off if I was dead. The only person who deserves to die around here is me.

CHAPTER FIFTY-FIVE

The pain medication I'm on makes my head woozy for about two hours after I take it, so things are looking a little hazy and shaky as John walks into the room a few hours later, followed by a man I don't recognise. Everything is blurry around the edges, like I'm peering through smudged glass. If I didn't know any better, I'd say I was high.

'Brittany,' John says, 'this is Doctor Evans, our personal doctor. He's going to look at you, ask you a few questions and make sure you're okay.'

'B-But... I've already been seen by a doctor at the hospital,' I say, slowly lifting my head off the pillow, but it's such a monumental effort that within two seconds my head flops back down again.

'I understand, but Angela told me some of the things you said to her earlier and, obviously, I'm a little concerned about you and your mental state.'

'My mental state? I'm not the one who killed their own daughter because of a minor facial disfigurement.'

John glances sideways at the doctor for a moment. 'Is that what you heard?'

'Yes, and I know about Faye still being alive, or not alive but brain-dead, and Angela doesn't have a clue about it. What the hell is going on in this villa, because it sure as hell isn't normal. I want to leave right now. I'm done with this whole thing.'

John clears his throat and shakes his head. 'I'm sorry, Doctor. I didn't realise she'd got this bad.'

'W-What are you talking about?' I shout.

The doctor steps forwards. 'It does seem as though she is quite far gone, but I'll do my best to treat her.' He stands by the side of my bed, places his hand on my arm and speaks in a calm voice, as if speaking to a child. 'Brittany, my name is Doctor Evans and I'm here to help you. It appears you're suffering from a severe case of prenatal depression, which is common in women who are carrying a child with a health problem, are dealing with stressful life events, who didn't plan to become pregnant and don't have a supportive network around them, but don't worry because John and Angela will make wonderful parents. We just need to help you get through the next few months, okay?'

I stare at him without blinking. What did he just say? They're treating me like I'm delusional, like I'm crazy and am making all of this up. I'm not crazy!

'Doctor Evans, I promise you, I'm perfectly fine. I'm not depressed. I'm scared for the safety of myself and my baby.'

'What makes you think you're not safe here, Brittany?' he asks, again with the patronizing, calm voice.

'Angela pushed me down the stairs to try and make me lose the baby because she doesn't want to adopt her now that she knows she has a kidney problem.'

John sighs and the doctor looks at him. 'That's not true, Brittany. That night, the night you fell down the stairs, Angela was dosed up on sedatives because she'd had a particularly bad day and needed her sleep. She was nowhere near able to get out of bed, let alone push you down the stairs.'

'And I'm just supposed to take your word for that, am I?' I snap back.

'There's proof. There's a CCTV camera outside of our master suite. I've already checked it, and Angela doesn't leave our room all night.'

'That's convenient,' I mutter, folding my arms across my chest like a moody teenager. 'Look, I know how this sounds, but I'm telling you the truth. I know all about Faye and Angela and I just want out of this contract. I want to go home... *with* my baby.'

'I'm afraid that's not possible,' says John. 'You're our responsibility now. You were injured on our property and you're carrying our child.'

'She's not yours! She mine!' I shriek, slamming my fists down on either side of me. Doctor Evans steps back ever so slightly.

'She may need to be restrained and sedated,' he tells John, ignoring me completely. 'Once she's calmed down, we can look for a more long-term solution to managing her outbursts.'

'Thank you, Doctor.'

Panic and fear wash over me as I realise I'm about to be restrained against my will. 'Margo! Margo!' I fling back the covers and attempt to shift my broken leg off the bed, but it's so heavy and awkward and my bump just makes everything more difficult. The doctor and John restrain me by grabbing an arm each, forcing me down on the bed.

'Margo can't help you,' says John.

'I know about you and her,' I say, glaring at him. 'I saw the two of you. I know everything.'

'Whatever you think you know, you're wrong. Margo has been let go.'

'W-What? When?'

'About two hours ago. She was found snooping around Faye's room. She has no right to be there and it's one of our main rules. Only Mrs Dubois is allowed in there to clean. Margo, being a chef, had no right to be there. She was looking for something, riffling through Faye's things.'

I've got Margo fired. That was the last thing I wanted to happen.

Now what? I'm all alone here. I don't even have Margo around to help me. Did she find something bad, and that's why they fired her? Then it hits me like a slap in the face.

What if Margo found something bad and they did something worse than fire her? How would they be able to make certain that she wouldn't reveal the truth, whatever it may be? I don't have her phone number or any way of contacting her.

Have they killed Margo? Am I next?

CHAPTER FIFTY-SIX

What the hell have they given me? My brain feels disconnected from my body. At least the pain isn't too bad. In fact, I'm feeling pretty good right now. Okay, maybe I'm as high as a kite, but it means I can sleep, something I haven't been able to do before now.

Clara visits me often in my dreams, yelling at me to get out and run, neither of which I can physically do right now. Margo was my only hope of getting out of here and now she's gone too and, worst of all, I don't even know if she's safe. For all I know, John and Angela have killed her and chopped her up into little pieces and buried her in their back garden. Perhaps that's a little too far-fetched, but I can't seem to make sense of the simplest things anymore. Whatever drug they have me on is taking away my logical thought process and ability to even remember what day it is.

That's when a thought occurs to me: Is this how Angela feels? Are these the type of drugs John has her on? How long have I been in bed? How long ago did I fall down the stairs?

How many weeks pregnant am I now? Twenty-two? Twenty-three? I don't know!

I scream into the empty bedroom, then close my eyes as the whole world around me spins faster and faster. Nausea swells and bile rises up my throat. I fight it back down, then open my eyes, focusing on the bedroom door in front of me.

A wheelchair is on the other side of the room, left there in case they need to transport me to places, such as to the car to take me for my ultrasound scans. I'm not even sure when my next one is. I just need to get somewhere so I can call the police. Someone will listen to me. They have to. I'm injured and pregnant. Someone has to listen. I don't know where my own phone is because I haven't had any use for it for weeks. I've no one to call or speak to.

I'm being kept prisoner here now. John and Angela are not who they appear to be and they're dangerous. I must get out and protect my baby. There's no way in hell I'm letting them take her. I still don't want to keep her, but if I can get out of here, I'll return to the UK and go through the proper adoption process. That's the new plan. Yes, I'm throwing away the prospects of a lot of money and owning my own restaurant like I always dreamed, but how do I even know they'll keep their promise after how they've been treating me lately? They think I'm crazy and are drugging me for no reason other than to keep me quiet and sedated so I won't cause trouble.

Every muscle and joint in my body creaks and groans as I manoeuvre myself off the bed and sink to the floor. My muscles are weak and I'm barely able to support myself in a crawling position, let alone standing. Slowly but surely, I crawl and drag myself across the floor towards the wheelchair, using what little strength and energy I have to hoist myself up.

My hand slips on the armrest and my heavy body collapses against the chair, and I knock my chin on the metal. My teeth clamp down on my tongue, causing blood to trickle from my mouth. I wipe it away and try again, finally pulling myself into the chair.

It takes a few attempts to move the chair in the right direction towards the door. I finally figure out how to turn, but when I reach the door handle and push it down, nothing happens.

They've locked me inside my room.

Fighting the panic that doubles in the space of two seconds, I spin the chair around and wheel myself over to the window, pulling back the curtains. It's a lovely view across the villa courtyard below. It's dark outside. I didn't even know it was nighttime. Time seems to have come to a halt lately and because I've been sleeping so much, my body clock is all wrong.

Gentle lights are on in the courtyard below, but I can't see any movement from anywhere. It must be late at night. Perhaps everyone is asleep.

Grabbing the curtains, I pull myself to my unsteady feet and release the catch to open the window. Cool, fresh air pours in, making my head feel a little clearer. At least they haven't bolted the window shut. Maybe they thought I wouldn't be stupid or reckless enough to escape out the window with a broken leg and being twenty-something weeks pregnant.

The window opens quite far, enough that I can squeeze my body through. If I'd not been pregnant and had a cast on, I'd have been able to fit through the gap no problem, but my broken leg makes it difficult to manoeuvre, since the cast restricts my movement and ability to bend my entire leg. But somehow, I manage to sit on the windowsill and shimmy my bottom so my legs are dangling over the edge. Okay, this is a bad idea.

CHAPTER FIFTY-SEVEN

There's a roof about four feet below me. It would be simple to jump down if I wasn't incapacitated, but I can't risk it. One slip and I'm done for, not only risking my life but the baby's life too because below that roof is a ten-foot drop. I could easily fall and bounce or roll off, then crash to the ground, most likely breaking my other leg.

I look left and right, noticing a drainpipe leading to the small roof below. It's within reach, so I stretch my arm out and grab it, giving it a small yank to test its strength. It creaks but doesn't break or come away from the wall. Am I so desperate that I'm about to climb down a drainpipe with a broken leg? Once I'm on the ground, I just need to get myself to the garage where there's an array of cars I could borrow. They keep the keys in a locked box on the wall, which I'm sure I can break into somehow. Again, I don't have all the answers, but I need to do something. I can't just lie in bed and await my doom.

I grab the pipe and pull myself out of the window, my broken leg hanging freely and the other one digging into the brickwork with my toes. Inch by inch, I lower myself closer to the small roof. It's not far now, but my arms are screaming at me, threatening to give up. My muscles appear to have wasted away over the many days or weeks I've been lying in bed.

I finally touch down on the small roof, so I get on all fours in case I lose my balance. I shuffle towards the nearest edge and look down. There's no way I'm making it down ten feet, but there is another window on this roof level, so I crawl over to it, peering inside.

The room beyond is dark, the curtains pulled across. I'm pretty sure it's just a hallway window, not a window into a main room, but I can't be sure. The master suite is on the other side of the villa. Holding my breath, I give the window a shove, but it looks like it's locked tight. Damn it.

Even if I wanted to, there's no way of getting back inside my room, so it's either stay up here all night until someone finds me, by which time I'll be freezing and regretting all my life decisions, or break this window somehow and get inside. However, if I break the window there's a chance that either someone will hear me and alert the police, thinking they've got an intruder, or the alarm system will blare to life, which could also alert the police. Both of those instances mean the police will possibly get involved, which may turn out to be a good thing.

Of course, there's the chance that John and Angela don't have an alarm system in place or have warned their staff not to call the police (which I wouldn't put past them, considering the amount of detail in the non-disclosure agreement), in which case I'll just be caught red-handed and then they might add extra security to my room.

There's only one thing for it.

I grab a nearby loose roof slab and hurl it at the window. The crash is louder than I thought it would be, and my body instinctively ducks as if a huge searchlight is about to come on and find me. I pause for several seconds, waiting for something to happen. Maybe a shout from a scared staff member or a 'Hey!' from one of the security guards. No alarm sounds. Nothing happens.

Now comes the problem of dragging my injured, pregnant body over the broken edges of the glass window. I don't usually make stupid decisions like this. At least I don't think I do (although the one-night stand with Luke is turning out to be a pretty stupid decision), but my head feels fuzzier than ever, and right now, all I can think about is escaping and contacting the police.

Putting the pain to the back of my mind, I awkwardly lift my leg cast over the broken glass, then lean my weight gradually onto it, so I can lift the other. Using the curtains, I pull myself over, managing to get inside without so much as a scratch.

The room I've just crawled into isn't a hallway.

It's Faye's room.

If I'm caught in here, I am one hundred per cent dead. Just like Margo may be.

CHAPTER FIFTY-EIGHT

I shuffle slowly towards the door, towards freedom, but then stop as my hand touches the door handle. I may not have another chance to investigate. This was where Margo was caught. Had she found something in here?

The light from the moon and the outside yard lights are enough to highlight the general areas, such as the bed, wardrobe and small desk. My curiosity overrides my desire to escape, and I head straight for the desk. When I was a kid, I always hid stuff in my desk drawers or under my mattress, which is where I'm going next.

I pull open the desk drawer to find lots of drawings and pink items. They are several drawings of gardens and animals, but nothing else.

The mattress is next and lifting it up is rather awkward and much harder than I'm expecting. My biceps immediately burn as I keep the mattress lifted with one arm while I use the other to search for anything underneath.

Nothing.

Come on, Margo, what did you find?

My brain is screaming at me to get the hell out of this room because someone could have heard that crash and be here any moment, but my heart is telling me to keep searching. I'm so close. I can feel it. I don't even know what I'm looking for, but there must be something here. Something. Anything.

My heart feels like it's trying to break my rib cage as I hobble over to the wardrobe, pulling the doors open. The light outside is enough to shine on the array of perfectly hung children's clothes, mostly pink or lilac. Without warning, my eyes sting with tears as I think of my own little girl growing inside me.

I'm going to have a daughter...

No. No, I won't. Yes, I'll give birth to her, but just because a woman gives birth to a child, it doesn't make them qualified to be their mother. My own mother is a prime example of that. I shouldn't be a mother either. I know that. My own didn't want children and I'll be damned if my kid ever finds out I didn't plan or want her. She'll be better off being adopted by loving parents who'll be able to love her and give her everything she needs. Not me. And not these two psychos who live here.

A creaking floorboard makes me freeze in place.

I spin around just as the doorknob turns.

Before I can even take a breath, I make my decision and squeeze myself into the wardrobe, amongst the tiny pink clothes. It's a tight fit, made harder by the fact I can't bend my broken leg. I hold my breath, afraid that whoever is coming into the room will be able to hear my ragged, heavy breathing.

I listen as footsteps sound just outside the door.

But something is digging into my back. Something sharp.

Swallowing back the hard lump in my throat, I reach around behind me, feeling for whatever it is that's poking me. It's a loose wooden panel at the back of the wardrobe with a nail sticking out. I can't lean forwards away from the sharp nail because there's not enough room. If I move even an inch, the door could burst open. I can't even close it properly as it is because my bump's in the way, so I'm having to grasp the edge of it with my fingertips, pulling it towards me as hard as I can to keep it closed.

The footsteps disappear.

I think they're gone.

I wait a few extra seconds to be sure, then gradually push the door open. The room is shrouded in darkness. I turn and investigate the loose nail, the sting of pain from where it was digging into my lower back still lingering. I peer through the hanging clothes and pull on the loose wooden board at the back of the wardrobe. It comes away, making a loud crack. There's a dark crevice behind. I stick my hand inside, my fingers touching a hard surface. Grabbing whatever it is that's inside, I yank it out.

A diary.

An old diary. Well-worn and written in.

Looks like Faye didn't want her parents to read her personal thoughts. Did they keep a close eye on her? Did they...

Another floorboard creaks from outside the bedroom.

This time, I don't make it back into the wardrobe before the door bursts open.

CHAPTER FIFTY-NINE

Since I can't move fast enough to hide again, I do the only thing I can think of; hide the diary in the waistband of my stretchy underwear (thank God for pregnancy pants) and press myself against the wall beside the door as it opens and a beam of light pierces the darkness.

John enters and immediately locks eyes with me.

'You'd better have a good reason for being in here,' he says.

'And you'd better have a good reason for locking me in my damn room,' I answer back, sounding much more confident than I really am. The thing is, I know that by snapping back I'm at risk of pissing him off, but I'm at my wits' end. I can't just roll over and let them do this to me. Besides, I know he wouldn't hurt me because I'm carrying precious cargo.

We're locked in a stalemate, neither one of us making any move to open our mouths next. I've never been good at staring contests. Once, Clara and I decided to have one and she had the stare of a freaking eagle. I broke every single time. John doesn't blink. In the end, it's my leg that gives out and I wince in pain. He darts forward to support me just before I collapse against the wall.

'You shouldn't even be out of bed. What if you'd fallen down the stairs again? How the hell did you even get in here?' That's the moment he notices the broken window. 'What the hell?' He steps further into the room, the door swinging closed behind him.

'You're lucky you didn't fall to your death!' he shouts. 'Do you realise how reckless that was?'

'What choice did I have? You locked my door. Am I a prisoner here or something?'

'No, of course not.'

'Then why would you lock my door?'

'For your own safety, but it seems that's gone out the window...'

We lock eyes again. He's probably wondering the same thing; whether it's the right moment to laugh at his perfectly timed joke. I reach for the door handle, grasp it and twist, but nothing happens. That's when the realisation hits me.

Even if I'd managed to get to the door, I wouldn't have been able to get out of the room. It seems the door can't be opened from the inside. Did they lock Faye in here?

John steps around me, pulls a key from his pocket and unlocks the door. Okay, what the hell?

'Let's get you back to your room,' he says, like I'm a pathetic child who's had a nightmare.

'Look, I'm no longer comfortable with being here,' I say. 'Please, may I have my phone back? I need to call someone.' I don't mention that I have no one to call.

John narrows his eyes at me. 'I don't have your phone.'

'I haven't seen it for days.'

John opens the door wider, grabs my arm, wrapping his

whole hand around it, and gently pulls me towards the door. Oh, no, he did not just manhandle me. I yank my arm away.

'Get off me!'

'You're being irrational.'

'Irrational? Irrational! You've drugged me against my will, taken my phone, locked me in my room and your wife tried to kill me. I think it would be more of an issue if I *weren't* being irrational.'

John sighs heavily, taking a step back so I can walk past him into the lit hallway beyond. Mrs Dubois appears, rubbing her eyes, dressed in a long, silk dressing gown.

'What on earth is going on?' she asks. She looks from me to John then back to me again. 'Why are you in Christine's room?'

Christine?

'Who the hell is Christine?' I ask.

Mrs Dubois turns white in two seconds flat. 'Sorry, I meant Faye's room.' She looks to John, who closes his eyes and takes a deep breath.

'Please can you escort Brittany back to her room and we'll sort all this out in the morning,' he says.

Mrs Dubois nods and stares at me, a silent order to follow her and not say another word. I do exactly that, scurrying past John as if I'm afraid he's suddenly going to chase after me. She grabs my arm and supports me as I hobble along. Just before we turn the corner, I look back at John, but he's gone.

'You just couldn't keep your nose out of it, could you?' she hisses.

'What?'

She stops dead. 'There are some things you just don't say

around here. Did you not read the non-disclosure agreement?'

'I am fed up with hearing about the non-disclosure agreement.'

'I suggest you rethink your tone.'

I hang my head like a scolded child. She's right. I need to calm down. My temper isn't helping my blood pressure, which apparently is too high as it is.

We start walking again. While I can put weight on my cast to walk, it's by no means comfortable and within a few steps, the pain starts building again.

'Where is Margo?' I ask.

'Margo has been let go.'

'Yes, I understand that, but *where* is she?'

'I believe she's gone home.'

Great. She's gone and left me here. That's the last time I trust anyone around here. 'Who's Christine? I thought their daughter's name was Faye?'

Mrs Dubois stops outside my room. 'Their first daughter. The one who died at five days old.'

'Then why does she have a room that looks as if it belongs to a young child of six or seven?'

'It was Christine's room before it was Faye's. It was merely a slip of the tongue on my part. Besides, Christine didn't even sleep in there. She was too young. They decorated it ready for her, but it wasn't to be.'

I look at the ground, contemplating what else I could question her about.

Mrs Dubois turns to me, looks me dead in the eye and says, 'Angela is not a well woman. After Christine was born, she suffered from severe post-natal depression to the point she began hallucinating and making reckless decisions, putting Christine's life in danger several times within the first couple of days. Christine drowned in the bathtub. Angela had no idea it even happened until John found the child several hours later.'

'I... I don't even know what to say. Why is Angela still... still... unwell? She can't still be suffering from post-natal depression. I thought women recovered from that within a few days. Margo said... said that John was prescribing her medication to keep her calm and level-headed.'

Mrs Dubois shakes her head. 'Yes, that's true, but you have a lot to learn. What you're thinking of is usually known as the baby blues. All women go through it after giving birth. It's completely normal and natural, but post-natal depression is something else entirely. It can take weeks, months, even years to go, and, in Angela's case, it's still keeping a firm grip on her mental health. She's never been treated properly for it.'

'But why has no one helped her? Why has John not taken her to a therapist?'

'If you ever found out you killed your own baby when it was five days old, would you want to know about it? Angela would be traumatised. John and his business would be ruined.'

'You're not telling me that John is lying to her and keeping her drugged up on purpose so that his life isn't ruined? That's barbaric.'

'Maybe so, but it's for her own good. She tried to kill Faye too.'

'I take it you also know that Faye isn't really dead.'

Mrs Dubois nods once. 'Now, you already know far more than you should, so I'd like to offer you some advice. I suggest you take it. Stay out of their way. Give birth to the child and let them have it. Then take whatever it is they've offered you and leave and don't ever look back.'

I shift awkwardly and lean against the wall. 'Yeah, I can't do that,' I say. 'I need to get out of here.'

Mrs Dubois narrows her eyes at me. 'Brittany, you're in no condition to go anywhere. I'm afraid with the security measures in place around the villa, there's no way of leaving without John being alerted. Do yourself a favour and just stay in your room and take care of yourself.' Then she turns and walks away down the corridor, leaving me to hobble inside my room.

My body is so exhausted, I barely make it to the bed before collapsing onto it. I need an escape plan. Where do I even start? Mrs Dubois' threat about the security isn't enough to put me off. I need to regain my strength and start again tomorrow. Besides, I do have something up my sleeve, or, more appropriately, tucked into the waistband of my pants.

Once I've found a semi-comfortable position on the bed, I pick up the diary and read. Most of it is cute, anecdotal ramblings from the mind of a child, none of it making a lot of sense. Her writing changes shape and size on every page and most of her i's are dotted with a heart. There are drawings of pink hearts and flowers on every page and even yellow stars dotted in the corners for decoration. She talks about her favourite things to do (horseback riding), who her most recent crush is (mostly a boy called James) and why she enjoys school (because she gets to see people her own age).

However, the vibe starts to change around halfway through. She's taken out of school and taught at home. She misses her friends. She has a lot of arguments with her parents, mostly her mother, who keeps calling her ugly. My heart breaks the more I read about this poor little girl whose mother calls her ugly and who keeps saying she wishes she were dead. Whether that means Angela wishes she herself were dead or that she wishes Faye were dead, I can't be sure.

As I read closer to the end, the writing on the page becomes darker, more foreboding. There are little sketches of black broken hearts and even one of a hangman. It's a vast difference to the tone of the start of the diary with the little hearts and pink flowers. Whoever this girl is, she's not the same as the one at the start of the diary; not mentally, anyway.

My first thought is that she was being abused. Maybe not physically, but if a child hears she's ugly from her mother enough, it's bound to have a long-lasting effect on their self-confidence.

Then, on the final page, everything clicks into place.

There are just a few sentences, but they hit me like a punch to the gut.

My mummy isn't my real mummy.
Mummy and Daddy have been lying to me.

Wait...
Does this mean that Faye isn't Angela's biological child?

CHAPTER SIXTY

I turn my room upside down but can't find my phone. When did I use it last? Then I remember the day Luke called me and I switched it off. That was weeks ago. I don't think I've used it since then. My leg starts throbbing so bad that I bite back tears. I need my pain meds, but I've missed the last dose thanks to my nighttime activities and chances are I doubt Mrs Dubois or John will be in any hurry to administer them after finding me trespassing. John wouldn't allow me to keep them by my bed, as if he thinks I'm some sort of junky. He clearly likes to be the one in control of handing out medication.

The morning arrives, by which time I'm delirious from pain and hunger and in no position to start my escape attempt. I lean against the pillow, but then my eyes fly open as I feel a weird fluttering in my belly. Holy crap, what was that? Is that my stomach gurgling with hunger or is it... could it be the baby moving for the first time? Am I supposed to feel its first kicks at twenty-something weeks?

I lie completely still and hold my breath, waiting for it to happen again. It takes a couple of minutes, but then... There! That's definitely not my stomach gurgling or gas. It feels like tiny bubbles popping. I place my hands flat on my belly, close my eyes and lean back, feeling the tiny movements, almost as if she's talking to me. Probably telling me she's hungry and I need to eat something. She's not wrong there. This feels so weird and surreal. I still can't quite get my head around the fact there is a real human being growing inside me, moving and squirming about.

A few minutes later, the bubbling stops. I can't just lie here and fade away, or I'll feel worse and worse as time wears on. If I had my wheelchair or the crutches, I could get about easier, but John's had both removed from the room, meaning I have no way of getting myself around. Have they forgotten about me?

Rather than risk feeling any worse, I get up, use the facilities, then shuffle/hop/hobble to the door. It's locked.

I clench my jaw and bang my fists against the door over and over and over, even shouting for someone to come. It takes several minutes, but eventually the door opens and Mrs Dubois pops her head around, as if shocked that I'm making so much noise.

'Good morning, Brittany,' she says happily, as if last night never happened. 'Is there something you need?'

'I need painkillers,' I say, slightly out of breath. My brain is so muddled that I can't think straight. I just need the pain to go away.

'Oh, yes, John will be along soon to administer your medication. Is there anything else?'

'Have you seen my phone lately?'

'No, I can't say that I have.'

We stare at each other for a moment. 'Is Angela okay?' I

ask. I'm not sure why, but after our confrontation yesterday, it's made me realise that she's probably just as trapped as I am here. The whole thing with Faye has thrown me.

'Angela is resting today.'

Footsteps sound in the corridor and John appears beside Mrs Dubois, looking rather dishevelled. I'm pretty sure he is wearing the same clothes he was last night.

'You've missed your dose of medication. Here.' He hands me my medication and a glass of water. 'You have a checkup in two hours. The doctor will be coming here.'

'For my leg or the baby?'

'The baby.'

I swallow the painkillers and hand him back the glass. 'Fine,' I say.

Mrs Dubois smiles and backs away, leaving us standing together by the open door of my room.

'Also,' he continues, 'once the doctor has seen you and confirmed the baby is okay, how would you like to get out of the villa for a bit?'

'I thought you wanted to keep me hidden?'

'We do, but we thought that since you've been cooped up since breaking your leg, you'd want to get out and get some fresh air. I've organised a couple of days out on our private yacht. We'll be leaving once the doctor has given you the all-clear.'

'Um... I'm not sure...'

'I thought you'd jump at the chance to get out of here for a few days. Everything will be handled. You're our guest, Brittany.'

I don't ask him how I'm supposed to get about on a yacht with a broken leg. Also, the idea of being on a boat in the middle of the ocean, alone with the psycho couple from hell, is not my idea of a good time. It would be too easy for them to just shove me overboard. My plan of finding a way to escape is very quickly slipping through my fingers.

'I appreciate the kind gesture, but I don't think it's a good idea. I get seasick easily, and that was before I was pregnant.'

'Are you sure?' he asks, looking a little hurt.

'I'd rather not spend the whole time throwing up over the side,' I say with a smile.

'Very well. I guess Angela and I will see you in a few days then.' He nods. 'Get some rest. The doctor will be here soon.'

I feel like I've just hit the jackpot. A few days without John and Angela will give me the perfect opportunity to find answers and escape.

CHAPTER SIXTY-ONE

The doctor arrives just as I'm drifting off to sleep. The pain meds John gave me earlier well and truly kick in, allowing me to relax and get some rest.

'Hello, Brittany. How are you feeling this morning?' asks the doctor, the same one as before.

'Tired,' I say.

'Well, growing a human being is hard work. Did you know that it takes the same amount of energy as running a marathon every day for nine months?'

'I did not know that. I've never been great at running.'

I remain silent while he checks my blood pressure and measures my bump. 'Have you eaten anything this morning?'

'No, not yet.'

'Good. I think I'll give you the gestational diabetes test today then. I'm going to take some blood. Then, all you need to do is drink a liquid containing glucose, wait an hour, then I'll take some more blood again. Does that sound okay?'

I shrug. 'Sure.' I decide there and then that once he's taken blood from me a second time, I'll make my escape.

John and Angela will be leaving soon, so once I know they've gone, it's the perfect time to leave. My thoughts turn to Angela alone with John on the yacht. I'm sure she's fine... I hope she's fine.

I lean back and close my eyes while he takes some blood. He gives me the drink, which I drink as quickly as possible because it tastes disgusting and makes me gag several times.

'Oh, and here are your next set of pain meds,' he says, placing them in my palm. 'John says to take them now.'

I nod my understanding and swallow them with a sip of water.

The doctor assures me that he'll have the results of the test soon and that he'll be taking care of me while John and Angela are away. Who even is this doctor? I'm sure I remember him from one of John's business dinners.

I'm so weak that I can't even get out of bed. Plus, the pain is so bad that I'm seeing stars. What kind of painkillers am I taking? They don't seem to be doing anything.

If I'm going to try and escape, I need the pain to be more manageable. I wait several minutes for them to kick it, but then everything goes black as I get to my feet. I don't even make it to the bedroom door.

CHAPTER SIXTY-TWO

At first, when my eyelids flutter open, I have no idea what's going on, but then things start to click in place like pieces of a jigsaw. I'm not in my room, but I am in a very posh, very lavish room, much smaller, but better than any hotel room I've ever stayed in.

I'm clearly on the yacht, but I only know that because it's obvious that's where John wanted me and, since I said no, he took it upon himself to get me here via other means.

It's weird though because it doesn't *feel* like I'm on a yacht. Granted, I've only ever been on one once a few weeks ago. Last time I remember feeling a bit seasick but maybe that was because I was in the early stages of pregnancy at the time. I feel fine so far. Is that because the sea is calm or because the boat is so bloody big that you can't even feel the waves beneath? Who knows.

My throat is sore, so sore that I can barely swallow. I manage to sit up, shuffling my bum up the bed a bit more, but then a wave of nausea hits and I retch over the side of the bed. Nothing comes out. I don't think it has anything to do with being at sea. Probably more likely to do with whatever they put in that damn glucose drink and the concoction of drugs I've taken. Clearly, they weren't merely paracetamol.

'Hello?' I call out, my voice croaky and weak.

I glance at the bedside cabinet and see a walkie-talkie. I reach over, pick it up and talk into it.

'Hello, is anyone there?'

A few static crackles appear.

'Ah, you're awake. I'll be right in,' comes a female voice.

A few minutes later, Angela comes in. Her bump is now very noticeable, almost double the size of mine. She even moves like she's pregnant and constantly touches and caresses it like I've found myself doing over the past few weeks.

'How are you feeling?' she asks.

'Um... I've felt better. How are you?'

Angela's smile wavers for a moment. 'What do you mean?'

'How are you, Angela?' My eyes focus on her left wrist, which has a tight bandage around it.

'You know, no one's asked me that before,' she replies. 'John says you were giddy with excitement at the prospect of joining us for our little sea adventure. It's always so lovely to get away and spend some time out on the open ocean. The fresh air is enough to rejuvenate even the most stressed-out individual. I promise it will do you the world of good. Why don't you join me out on deck for a little sunbathing?'

'I'll pass, thanks. I didn't want to come, but clearly John had other ideas.'

'He's only doing what's best for you.'

I keep my mouth shut.

'Oh, that reminds me. We've passed the gestational

diabetes test, so everything is well.' She rubs her belly and smiles.

'You mean *I* passed the test.'

Angela continues to smile. 'Yes, of course.' She looks drunk. Her eyes aren't focusing on anything, but constantly flicking from one thing to another, never settling.

'Angela,' I say slowly. 'Is everything okay? What happened to your wrist?' I'm not quite sure where I'm going with this, but it's now or never. She's unwell and somehow, I need to make her understand that.

'What do you mean?'

'I'm worried about you.'

'About me. Why?'

'You... I mean...' I stop, re-thinking my original plan. This woman is clearly unstable and confused. She's been lied to and is dangerous. John is doing this to her. It's likely she was never pregnant at all, not with Faye anyway, and this post-natal depression is almost like a placebo effect, covering up her real mental health issue.

'Do you know who Christine is?' I ask, changing tactic slightly.

At the mention of the name, her eyes stop wandering around the room and she zeros in on me, like a lion stalking its prey. 'Christine,' she repeats.

'Yes,' I say. 'Christine.'

'Faye.'

'No... not Faye. Christine. Who is she?'

Angela takes a step backwards. 'How do you know her name?'

'I'm just trying to understand what's going on. I was in her room last night.'

'You were in whose room?'

'Christine's.'

Angela takes another step backwards. She closes her eyes for several seconds, then opens them. 'I didn't mean to do it,' she whispers. Her words send a jolt through my body.

'What didn't you mean to do?' This is it. She's on the verge of telling me the truth. If I can get her to trust me, then perhaps she can help me to escape. Margo's gone. Angela is all I have left, but I'm worried that she's too confused and unstable to put anything into context.

Despite her icy exterior, I feel sorry for her. Whatever medication she's on is clearly not only altering her brain chemistry, but combined with the lies she's been told, it must be so confusing inside her head right now. She's had to put on a brave face, be the perfect front woman for the family, while under the surface she's been slowly drowning.

'I didn't mean to kill her.'

'I know you didn't. It was an accident, right?'

She nods. 'I was so tired. She'd had me up all night. She wouldn't stop crying. John wouldn't help. He said that she was my responsibility, and I needed to keep her quiet because he had a lot of business meetings and needed his sleep.' Angela's eyes are flooded with tears as she continues. 'I gave her a nice warm bath and...' She stops and furrows her brow.

'What is it, Angela?'

'Memories have been coming back to me. I keep trying to piece them together, but none of them quite fit.'

'Okay...'

'I remember Christine in the bath, sitting in one of those tiny bath supports. At five days old, she wasn't old enough to be in the bath without one. It was pink, I remember. But...

when I found her... in the bath... she wasn't in the bath support. In fact, I never saw the bath support anywhere.'

Now it's my turn to frown because I have no idea where she's going with this.

Before she can continue, the door bursts open and John storms in.

CHAPTER SIXTY-THREE

ANGELA

It's like a light bulb has switched on, dazzling me, and the memory of that night has come into focus for the first time in seven years. I can see her now, my sweet Christine, kicking and cooing in the warm water as I use a soft sponge to wipe her delicate skin. She'd had a huge nappy explosion, and wet wipes weren't going to be enough to clean her, so I decided to give her a bath instead. Her first one.

Her umbilical cord hadn't fallen off yet, but it was becoming dry and shrivelled. The midwife had told me not to bathe her until it fell off, but I was being careful not to get the cord too wet. I really was tired. I hadn't slept properly since she'd been born, and I was somehow getting by on only an hour or two of sleep a night for the past five days.

I didn't care though. She was my baby, and it was my job to take care of her. She stared up at me with her milky blue eyes and trusted me. I promised her that I'd never let anything bad happen to her, but I was so tired. I could barely keep my eyes open.

I sang to her as I cleaned her tiny body, then picked her

up in a soft towel and held her close to me. I took her into the bedroom, put a fresh nappy on her and started to get her dressed.

That was it. That's all I can remember, but it's enough to make me realise something. Christine was out of the bath and in the bedroom, so how did she end up face-down in the bath without her bath support?

I'm startled back to reality by John bursting through the door.

CHAPTER SIXTY-FOUR

John's face is tomato red, and his body is practically vibrating with fury. I can't be certain about what he's put Angela through, but I know he can't be trusted. He's been drugging Angela for years and lying to her. There may be no way back for her. How much psychological damage can the human brain take before it's irreparably broken?

Clara and I used to watch true crime dramas about childhood trauma, and Netflix shows about psycho killers. It always made for interesting discussions between us. Clara always believed that there was good in everyone and people who killed only did it because they were damaged inside. I thought the opposite. I believed that if people were bad, then they were just bad. There was no saving them.

I'm not sure if Angela can be saved, but at least I can save myself and my baby.

'What the hell is going on in here?' he shouts.

Angela doesn't make a move, not at first. Her eyes flick between me and John until she finally chooses John and rushes to his side like a trained dog. 'John, this woman is dangerous. I no longer want to adopt her child. Give her money and send her away.'

I keep my mouth shut because that could work in my favour, but it's clear John has no intention of following through with his wife's wishes. He takes her arm and guides her towards the door.

'Angela, darling, you're confused. We are adopting Brittany's child, remember? That's what you wanted. That's what you've always wanted.'

'No,' she says. 'No.'

John turns to me. 'What did you say to her?'

'Nothing!'

John drags Angela towards the door, but she fights back, trying to pull her arm away. 'No, John, stop. I need to know the truth. Please. I can't take it anymore. I remember taking Christine out of the bath. She didn't drown. She didn't.'

John closes his eyes and takes a deep breath. 'You see what you've done?' he asks me. 'My wife is so confused, and you've been filling her head with lies.'

'*I've* been filling her head with lies?'

John grabs Angela and shoves her out the door, slamming it in her face before throwing the small lock. Angela bangs on the door, crying and shouting.

John is quiet as he turns to look at me. 'You've ruined everything. Do you know how long we've been waiting for another baby? The adoption agencies won't touch us because of Angela's mental health. This was the only way we could have a child again, and now you've gone and ruined it.'

All words fail me. The truth is, I'm terrified. There's no way off this ship now. I can't see how I'm going to get out of this. My breath is coming in short, sharp gasps and my heart rate is so high that my heart is banging against the inside of my chest hard enough to feel it.

'Please,' I say, lowering my tone of voice. 'I'll leave and you'll never hear from me again. I promise. Just let me go and I'll take the baby and run.'

John sighs. 'It's too late, Brittany. You know too much. That baby belongs to us. You'll find I have some very powerful friends in very high places. We're taking that baby whether you're on board with the idea or not. If you're not, then...'

'What? You'll kill me?'

John doesn't respond.

'Or will you keep me locked up and drugged up like you have your wife?'

Then, the answer smacks me in the face.

Oh my God.

I know what really happened to Christine.

CHAPTER SIXTY-FIVE

'It was you,' I say slowly.

'What was me?'

'You killed Christine.'

John barely reacts. In fact, his shoulders drop slightly, as if the tension releases itself all in one go. Am I right? Did I just figure this all out?

'It wasn't Angela who killed Christine,' I repeat. 'It was you.'

John won't make eye contact with me as he talks. 'Angela was a wonderful mother, and Christine was a healthy baby, but she wouldn't sleep. She cried all through the night.'

I can't breathe. I just sit and listen, frozen to the spot.

'Angela needed some sleep. I told her to take two sleeping tablets and go to bed. I'd take care of Christine. I admit I hadn't been pulling my weight as a father. I had a lot of important work on, but I let Angela get some sleep. Christine wouldn't stop crying.'

My heart leaps. Oh my God. It really was him. The

thought of that happening is more than I can bear. No wonder Angela had a breakdown.

John's eyes are watering and his Adam's apple bobs up and down. 'She wouldn't stop crying,' he says again.

'What did you do, John?'

'I shook her.' He stops and turns to me. 'It was an accident. I shook her too hard.'

My eyes also fill with tears. Dear God, I can't even...

'She was found in the bath,' I say.

'I moved her. I couldn't go down as a father who killed their child after only looking after her for less than an hour.'

I see red. 'So you framed your wife and told her that *she* killed her?'

'I put Christine in the bath face-down, removed the bath seat thing and carried Angela's sleeping body into the bathroom so when she woke up, she'd think she fell asleep. Angela woke up thirty minutes later.'

'You're a monster,' I whisper.

John wipes his eyes, then straightens up, brushing off his moment of weakness. 'It was better her than me.'

'She had a breakdown,' I say.

'That's one way of putting it. She fell apart from the inside out. I had no idea that she'd take it that badly. I had to medicate her. She became irrational. Dangerous. No one could help her.'

'Why was she not arrested for the death of Christine?'

John breathed in through his nose and held his breath for several seconds. 'Because we never told anyone that Christine died. I obtained another baby of roughly the same age. We hadn't registered Christine's birth yet, so it was easy enough to swap the babies.'

My mouth drops open. I had not been expecting that response. 'Hang on a minute. You... *obtained* another baby.'

'It wasn't too difficult. In fact, it was easier than I thought. The hospitals around here really need to improve their security.'

'You stole a baby,' I say flatly.

'Yes, but I couldn't exactly be picky, so I grabbed the first baby girl I came across. Unfortunately, she had a facial deformity, so Angela knew she wasn't hers. It took a lot of convincing and a lot of medication before she accepted Faye as her own. I gave her a fake baby bump and made her believe she was pregnant. Desperate people will believe anything. Faye became known as our rainbow baby.'

'Why did you change her name from Christine to Faye?'

'Ah, now that was Angela's decision. She knew she wasn't Christine, so we named her Faye. It did over-complicate things to start with, but in the end, people accepted it. Luckily, no one had seen Christine yet, because she was so young and we wanted to get settled into a routine first.'

'So... what happened to Faye?'

John sighs again. He seems to be on a roll, so I allow him to spill his guts. 'Well, we had her operated on to correct the cleft lip, but it was never perfect. Angela and Faye never bonded properly. Angela has always had this need for perfection. Before she became unwell, she told me it was because of her upbringing. Her parents wouldn't accept anything less than perfection. She refused to accept Faye as her own and became more and more depressed. In the end, no amount of medication could control her, so I decided to step in and get rid of the problem. With Angela drugged up to the eyeballs, it wasn't exactly hard to convince her that Faye had a tragic accident in the pool. But, to save face, she told everyone that Faye was away at a special boarding school for the exceptionally gifted.'

I snort and roll my eyes. 'And you let her continue to believe that.'

'She got better, didn't she? Without Faye in the picture, she started becoming more like her old self again, but she still wanted a fucking baby. What is it with you women and needing to have a child to feel as if you're making a difference in this world? I was never enough for her. I'd do anything to make her happy. Anything.'

'Even kill your own children, it seems. Where does Margo fit into all this?'

John takes a step towards the bed and sits on the edge. He's only inches away from me now. He places a hand on my broken leg, placing just enough pressure through it to ensure I feel pain.

'Margo was a happy accident. Angela pulled away from me, wanting a child but not understanding why the adoption agencies weren't agreeing for us to adopt one. We also had several failed attempts at IVF, and she was now tired of going through the treatments, so adoption was our only option.

'I'm a man. I have needs. Margo fulfilled those needs. Lo and behold, she told me she was pregnant, and it presented me with the perfect opportunity to give my beloved wife a baby. I spun Margo a lie, convinced her I was in love with her. She agreed to give us the baby to adopt, but sadly she miscarried. It did, however, plant the seed of an idea. I just needed to find the perfect someone. It didn't matter if the child wasn't biologically mine, as long as it was perfect for Angela. That, my dear, is where you came in. Another happy accident, but one that worked to our advantage.'

He finishes his story, keeping his hand on my leg, gently pressing down. 'But now... we have a problem, don't we, Brittany?'

'What are you planning on doing with me?'

'Sit tight, Brittany,' he says, patting my leg harder than is needed. He rises to his feet. 'Then again, it's not like you can do anything else right now.' He chuckles and leaves the room.

I close my eyes and try not to scream.

CHAPTER SIXTY-SIX

ANGELA

John slams the door in my face and all rational thought leaves my head. The cloud of confusion lifts, eliminating the constant weight on my shoulders. My fists pummel against the wood, then I bash my forehead against it several times before realising that it's useless.

I sink to the floor, leaning up against the wall opposite the door. It's a narrow hallway, which means I have to pull my knees against my chest. I can't hear anything except muffled voices from both John and Brittany. Loud then quiet. Strong then weak. I have no idea what they are talking about, but the door remains shut.

I didn't kill my baby.

I know that now. There's only one logical explanation for finding her dead in the bath.

My husband.

He's been behind all of this. I don't know the details of what happened, but I know he did it. I know he killed her. Whether it was an accident or not, I don't care. The only thing I care about now is punishing him for what he did and what he's put me through.

There's no reason or justification good enough to excuse what he's done to me, to her, to my Christine, who was too tiny and weak to fight back. I must hold a part of the blame though; I did agree to take sleeping pills so I could sleep. I shouldn't have done that. I should have realised my husband wasn't up to the task of looking after her. He hadn't shown her any sort of attention since she'd been born, other than to complain about her smell and the noise.

Why did I allow him to let me do it? I should have said no, that I was fine, that I didn't need his help or any sleep... Am I as bad as him in all this?

I bury my face in my hands as the memories swarm inside of me.

No, I'm not the one at fault here.

John must pay for what he did.

Brittany and her baby are in danger. I cannot allow another person, another baby, to be manipulated or killed because of my husband.

But what can I do?

CHAPTER SIXTY-SEVEN

My only priority right now is getting off this ship. I'm a good swimmer, but with a broken leg and pregnant, it's not even worth attempting. Plus—and maybe this is more of a reason not to swim to shore—I am in the middle of an ocean.

I have no idea how many staff members are on board. If I came across them, would they be on my side or are they brainwashed by John? I'd also be able to move a hell of a lot easier if I didn't have a massive cast on my leg, but there's no chance of getting that off. Thankfully, my bump is small enough that I can still get around.

Shuffling on my bum towards the edge of the bed, I get to my feet, find some clothes to pull on over my t-shirt and then hobble to the door, pressing my ear against it. I can't hear anyone. I know this yacht is huge because I've been on it before, but I didn't take a lot of notice where everything was. All ships have life rafts, so all I need to do is find one and hightail it back to shore, except I have no idea which direction that is, but that doesn't matter right now. I just need to get off this ship.

Suddenly, flashbacks to shipwreck films come to mind. Clara and I loved watching those too. She always said she'd be great in an emergency or a catastrophe and I wouldn't have to worry about anything because she'd always get me out of whatever state we found ourselves in. But she's not here now. I've got myself into this mess and now I must get myself out of it.

I slowly turn the doorknob, raising my eyebrows when it turns smoothly. I guess John isn't bothering to lock me in my room, since there's nowhere for me to run. John thinks he has me right where he wants me. The hallways are narrow, but everything is exquisitely decorated. This ship is something else. I shuffle along a few more halls, eventually coming across a T-junction with a map of the ship on the wall, highlighting the emergency exit routes and, more importantly, the location of the life rafts.

They are up on the deck, which isn't ideal since it means I'll probably be visible, but it's all I have to go on. I'm only on level two, so I just need to climb a few stairs to get to the deck. I find the stairs further down the hallway. There's a very slight movement from the waves, but otherwise if I didn't know I was on a ship, I wouldn't be able to tell at all.

Just as I'm climbing the last set of stairs, my legs and arms burning from the exertion, footsteps sound behind me. This makes me move faster, but my movements are clumsy and uncoordinated as I emerge onto the next level, panting like I've just sprinted round a track.

The footsteps get louder.

There's no possibility of outrunning whoever it is, so I need to find a place to hide. Seeing a random door ahead and to the left, I open it and duck inside. It's some sort of storage cupboard and my awkward body only barely fits inside. I dare not close the door all the way in case I can't open it from the inside, so I pull it to as far as I can and hold my breath, fearing my rapid breathing can be heard from miles away.

The footsteps get closer. Closer.

They are now right outside the door. I close my eyes tightly and say a silent prayer to whatever gods are listening.

A few seconds later, the footsteps fade away, but I stay in my hiding spot for a few extra minutes just in case. My leg is beginning to throb with pain as the blood rushes down to it. I really need to keep it elevated to stop the swelling in my ankle, but there will be time for that later.

Pushing open the cupboard door, I step out into the hall and make my way further along it, pausing at each corner and door in case something or someone jumps out at me. My stupid heavy leg makes a *thump, thump, thump* against the floorboards as I walk. I feel like some one-legged pirate.

One more set of steps leads me to the upper deck. The ship is enormous. Is that a swimming pool? I didn't see that last time. Why would you need a swimming pool on a boat when the ocean is right there? That has got to be one of the craziest things I've ever seen. There's light music coming from somewhere. I crane my neck to search for the source, but as far as I can tell, the music is coming through speakers dotted throughout the ship.

There's another map situated just ahead of me, so after reminding myself where the life rafts are, I head in that direction towards the back of the ship, keeping as quiet and low as I can. The more I walk, the harder it becomes to move. My energy is fading fast, and the pain is building to the point I want to scream, but I bite my lip and keep going.

I reach the life raft. It's the fanciest life raft I've ever seen, and I have no idea how to use it or drive it. That's the moment I catch sight of the ocean around me. It's the most beautiful blue and seems to sparkle under the sun. There's not a piece of land as far as the eye can see.

Great.

'I commend you for making it this far.'

John's voice makes me jump. I spin around on the spot, but he's too fast. He lunges forwards, grabs a fistful of my hair and yanks me towards him. Several hundred of my hairs rip from my scalp as he drags me away from the life raft.

'Stop! No!' I scream, as I grab his fist and attempt to loosen his grip.

'You're just determined to piss me off, aren't you?'

We're almost at the edge of the deck now. The deep ocean looms below me.

Oh my God, he's going to throw me overboard. He really is going to do it. This is the end.

I'm fighting and kicking as hard as I can, but my leg is basically acting like an anchor, weighing me down. John is super strong, but I'm not making it easy for him. He shoves me up against the railing, grasping my throat as he leans in close.

'You and your bastard child aren't even worth it,' he says with a snarl, spitting in my face.

My mouth opens, but only a gargling sound escapes. I'm done. I'm dead. The only positive is that I'll join Clara wherever she is, but what about my baby? She hasn't even had the chance to live yet. And that's all the motivation I need to somehow find the strength to ram my hard cast into his balls. John's eyes bulge and his teeth clamp down on his tongue, drawing blood. He retches, the pressure around my throat finally releases, and I fall to the side, collapsing on the deck.

On hands and knees, I scramble towards the nearest

object I can use to defend myself—a paddle—but I'm not quick enough and John has recovered quickly. He grabs my ankles and drags me backwards. I do my best to stop him, digging my fingernails into the wooden deck, and scream in pain as they break and bleed, leaving a trail of blood in the grain of the wood.

From behind me, a loud crack sounds, followed by an almighty scream that makes my insides turn to ice. What the hell...

I crane my neck to look over my shoulder. John's no longer grabbing my ankles. He's collapsed against the railing, the side of his head bleeding. Angela is standing over him with an emergency axe, holding it like a woman possessed.

Angela lowers the axe, glaring at her husband as his head wound oozes and bleeds. There's so much blood on the deck that his feet can't get a grip, and he keeps slipping, but he's determined not to fall and is grasping the railings for dear life.

John growls as he attempts to hold himself up, but the life and strength left inside him are almost gone. He slips one last time and crashes to the deck. His hand reaches out towards his wife.

'I... I gave you everything,' he splutters.

'No,' she says, shaking her head sadly. 'You took everything from me. You lied to me, John. My mind is finally becoming clear again. You killed my baby. You probably killed Faye. And you've been drugging me for years and blaming me for all of it. I won't let you kill another innocent child.'

Angela steps forward, raises the axe over her head and brings it crashing down.

I close my eyes at the last second before blood and brain spurt across my face.

CHAPTER SIXTY-EIGHT

My eyes remain closed for a long time. It feels as if I'm floating underwater, deep underwater. I can hear voices, but they are muffled. I dare not open my eyes. Eventually though, I'm dragged upwards, and I break the surface, my eyes fly open, and Angela is standing in front of me, shaking my shoulders.

'Brittany!'

'Yes, what?' I say automatically. For a moment, I forgot where I am.

'Are you okay?' Her face is splattered with blood. Her eyes are like saucers, the whites shining in the glaring sun. The warmth is almost too much. The blood. Heat. It's all too overwhelming. I lunge sideways over the railing and hurl my guts up as the metallic smell enters my nostrils.

'Give me a minute,' I say, holding my hand up as I retch again.

Angela stands and watches me.

Once my stomach calms down, I wipe my mouth with the back of my hand, spit out the bile in my mouth and turn to face her. John is lying just off to the side, one leg caught in the railings, twisted awkwardly. The puddle of blood has expanded somewhat and is creeping in every direction as the ship bobs and sways against the current.

'What are we going to do now?' I ask her.

'The only thing we can do,' she says calmly.

I wait for her answer. I'm expecting her to say that we're going to push him overboard and watch him sink below the waves, then scrub the blood off the deck and cover the whole thing up, but that's not what she suggests.

'Leave this to me.'

'What?'

'I'm going to inform the staff of what's happened. I'm going to take the blame. We're going to return to shore, then once I've been arrested, you'll disappear and return to the UK.'

Her willingness to take the blame for everything is enough to take my breath away.

'What about...' I glance down at my bump.

'She's yours. She was never mine. I'm in no position to take her now.'

Tears bubble behind my eyes and I openly weep because I don't know what else to do. The flood of emotion comes pouring out. Damn these pregnancy hormones.

'T-Thank you,' I say. 'I'm sorry about everything that happened to you. I misjudged you. You're unwell and I didn't realise. I wish I'd seen the signs earlier. Even the first time I met you, I saw small things that make so much more sense now.'

'I brought a lot of it on myself. I don't remember a lot, but maybe that's for the best. My mind is still very foggy, but I'm hoping that, with time, I'll be able to heal.'

I give her a weak smile. She turns and walks away slowly towards the middle of the deck, leaving me alone with John's body. I could easily shove him overboard, try and help Angela in some way, but the thought of lying about all this makes me queasy. She's going to go to jail or perhaps a psychiatric hospital for the rest of her life. Does she deserve it? She's just murdered someone in cold blood, but what John did to her, what he put her through is unforgivable. I do know that she's damaged, quite possibly beyond repair, and she's just risked her life to save me and my baby.

John has got what he deserves. Maybe she'll tell the authorities that he killed their baby, that he stole a child, but maybe she won't. It's her decision though, not mine, and I'll respect her choice. She's not been able to choose for herself for a long time. The least I can do is allow her this one.

CHAPTER SIXTY-NINE

The next few hours are a blur. I wash the spatters of blood off my face and then join the small handful of staff in the main living area of the yacht, where Angela explains about John. She explains that John attacked her on deck, and she killed him. She doesn't mention that I was there. Her eyes don't even flick over to me, but she does mention that I will no longer be giving them my baby.

We arrive back at shore three hours later. The police are already there waiting for Angela, who is taken away in handcuffs. She gives me one last look, a sad smile, before turning and walking away with two police officers either side of her. The yacht is cordoned off and each member of staff is questioned, including me.

Thanks to John and Angela's insistence that there be no official paperwork regarding the adoption, my baby isn't mentioned, other than one of the officers asking how I'm handling the shock of my employer murdering her husband. I explain that I was alone in my room resting before the evening's food preparations. They believe me and my whereabouts isn't questioned any further. I didn't hear or see anything.

After I'm questioned, I am dropped off at the villa, feeling at a loss. I don't know what to do now. Angela said I'm free to go back to the UK with my baby. I have some savings from working here, so it'll have to be enough to start again, but there's no way I'll be returning to London.

A fresh start is exactly what I need. There's still time to contact the adoption agencies and get the process started.

As I'm walking through the yard, my head swims. The pregnancy, heat, combined with the lack of food and the drugs leaving my system, not to mention the shock of seeing a man murdered in front of me, is enough to make my legs wobble. I don't make it much further before my body collapses to the ground and I fade to black.

I WAKE up in hospital an unknown amount of time later. Again. Deja vu hits me hard. My head is woozy, and it takes me a moment or so for my brain to catch up with what my eyes are seeing.

Wait... that can't be right. There's a person sleeping in the chair next to my bed, their neck at an awkward angle resting on a folded-up jacket, but they're the last person I ever expected to see.

It makes no sense.

No sense at all.

'Luke?'

He stirs and sits bolt upright when he sees me staring at him. The jacket he'd been sleeping on falls to the floor. 'Brittany! Thank God you're awake.' His chin is unshaven and there's a sheen of sweat on his forehead.

'What the hell are you doing here?'

'Looking for you,' he answers.

'But... But...'

'I tried calling you so many times, but you never replied. Then your phone was switched off and disconnected. I was worried.'

I just continue to stare at him.

He continues. 'I asked around if anyone had heard from you. Chef Andre finally told me that you'd got a job overseas as a private chef on the Cote d'Azur, so finally I managed to track you down. I flew over here. There was a bit of commotion at the villa, and I ran into a friend of yours who told me you were here.'

I blink rapidly. 'A friend of mine?'

'Margo, I think her name was.'

'Margo's alive?'

'Alive? Well, yes, but...'

'Where is she?'

'I'm not sure. She helped me find you and I haven't seen her since. Brittany, what the hell is going on? Apparently, the woman you were working for murdered her husband on a boat. You have a broken leg and... and you're...'

'Pregnant?'

'Well... yes.' He holds eye contact, which is a sure-fire way for me to feel uncomfortable.

'Please stop staring at me like that,' I say quietly.

'Is it... um...'

'Yes, it's yours. *She's*... yours.'

'It's a girl!' He stands up and runs his hands through his hair, turning his back on me, then rubbing his chin as he looks at me. I look back at him, wondering how many more seconds he's going to hang around before sprinting out the door and forgetting he ever saw me here.

But he doesn't. He eventually sits back down. His eyes are glued to my stomach.

'Seriously, Luke, enough with the staring. Didn't your mother ever tell you not to stare?'

'Sorry,' he says, his eyes looking down at the floor. 'Just... a bit of a shock.'

'Yeah.'

'Why didn't you tell me?'

'Because I was going to give her away.'

'Why?'

'Because I'm not cut out to be a mother, okay? I'm not. My own mother ran off and abandoned me and my sister when we were tiny and never came back. She couldn't handle it, so that means I can't handle it. No one wants me as a mother. Trust me. I'm selfish and boring and grumpy. Clara, she was supposed to be a mother, but no, she had to go and die, didn't she?' I close my eyes, tears blurring my vision. I can't stop the floodgates now. They've burst open. 'I can't do it, okay? I can't. I don't need your help, and I don't need your pity. I'm going to return to the UK and get her adopted via the proper authorities and forget this whole nightmare ever happened, and there's nothing you can do or say to make me change my mind.'

A silence fills the room after my speech. I look anywhere but at Luke, who slowly stands up, walks to my bedside and grasps my hand.

'I'm sorry you had to go through this alone, but I'm here now and...'

I snatch my hand away, too afraid of his touch in case it

makes me crumble into a thousand pieces. 'I've made my decision. She'll be better off without me as her mother.'

Luke looks as if I've just slapped him. He nods and steps away.

'Okay, I'll honour your decision, but it doesn't mean I agree with it. I care about you, Brittany. Just remember that, okay?' He walks out of the room and closes the door, and I spend the next hour and a half crying my eyes out until my head feels like it's about to explode and the nurse gives me more pain medication.

MRS DUBOIS VISITS me a day later and fills me in on what's happened. She tells me that Angela has been arrested and charged with John's murder. Angela will be undergoing a psychiatric assessment soon, which may mean her sentence is lessened, but it's hard to tell. She told the truth about what John did to Christine and to Faye and the police are looking into it, but it's going to take a long time to unravel all the lies and deceit.

Mrs Dubois also tells me some very sad news, something I wasn't expecting. Faye died yesterday. After seven years, her brain signals finally stopped firing. My heart aches for her and for her real parents who have only just found out what happened to their baby who was stolen. I hope she's in a better place now.

'Angela would also like me to tell you that you have been compensated for your time here. All the staff have been given some money to tide them over until they find new jobs, but you've been given a larger sum.'

'I-I have?'

Mrs Dubois sighs and hands me my phone. 'Here.'

So, she did take it! Probably under John's orders.

'I want you to know that I had nothing against you, Brittany. I was only following my orders from John. I had no idea what a monster he was, not until I started to see the signs of Angela's mental health decline. For what it's worth, I'm sorry. John told me to keep giving Angela the medication, but I swapped them so that Angela wasn't taking them regularly. It took time for them to leave her system.'

I nod, taking the phone. 'Thank you.' I turn it on and wait while it erupts to life. Messages, texts, voicemails flood in, including a notification from my banking app, informing me that I have twenty-five thousand pounds in my account.

It's not a million, but I couldn't care less right now.

EPILOGUE
ONE YEAR LATER

I'm so freaking nervous, but I've also never been more excited in my whole life. My body is practically vibrating with nervous energy, but it's the most alive I've ever felt.

My new restaurant opens tomorrow, and I'm fully booked every night all the way till the end of the year. Sometimes I worry I'm going to wake up one day and realise the past year has been nothing but a dream, but I never do. I keep living my life, day after day, and yes, there are hard days when I still mourn Clara, where her face is the only thing I see, when the pain is so bad that I can barely breathe, but there are other days when I'm so deliriously happy that I want to shout it out loud. I wish she were here to experience all this with me. It's unfair that she's not. I still blame myself partly for what happened to her, but I'm working my way through my grief a day at a time with the help of a grief counsellor, whom I see once a month. I did see him more regularly at the start, but I'm doing a lot better now and I didn't have to go on anti-depressants.

There are times when the guilt almost eats me alive

about experiencing happiness when it comes at such a cost. I want Clara to be alive, yet here I am living my life, living my dream without her. I don't deserve it, but I hope that wherever she is, she's proud of me and all I've accomplished in the past year. It's what we always talked about.

Dessert Heaven is a new fusion restaurant on the outskirts of the Lancashire borders. A quaint country cottage-turned-restaurant, which serves only dessert. What's not to love? But I add something extra by including spices and savoury flavours alongside the sweetness of the desserts, each one tailored and designed by me. Some of the recipes took me months to perfect, but with the help of my new friend and sous chef, Margo, we've created the ultimate dessert menu, one which even Gordon Ramsay approves of (he came and tasted my menu a few weeks ago and has given me a shining review to use for promotional material). Take that, Chef Andre. I heard several months ago that Chef Andre had been fired from his latest job for groping a young sous chef. I doubt he'll be working in another high-profile kitchen anytime soon.

Margo was paid off by John to leave and never come back or he'd ruin her, but she came back anyway, even before she found out that John was dead. At that point, I was in hospital after fainting. The staff told her where I was. She saw Luke wandering around the villa looking for me and helped him find me in the hospital. She left again, too ashamed to face me, but I found her about two months later, once I'd bought the old cottage with the money Angela gave me as a deposit. I knew I needed Margo working with me. We're business partners because she's also put her payout money into getting the restaurant up and running, marketing it heavily and gaining a hugely popular following on TikTok thanks to the reels she forces me to film as I create and design my intricate desserts from scratch.

She's a good friend and we've spent many hours over the past eight months going over the designs and plans for the restaurant. No one will ever replace Clara, but Margo is slowly helping to mend the giant hole in my heart.

I'm in the kitchen creating the red berry spicy sauce for tomorrow. My leg is twinging a bit, so I pull over the stool I use when I need to take the weight off for a moment. It was a bad break and I'm still having weekly physiotherapy, rebuilding the muscles that had faded away to nothing after being in a cast for so long.

'You're needed upstairs,' says Margo, popping her head round.

My head snaps up to the clock on the wall. It's six o'clock already. Damn it, time keeps flying by. I've had the upstairs of the cottage renovated into a place to live. It's not large, but it's more than enough room for me. Margo lives in the nearest village, but she often stays over here, especially if we're both working long into the night.

'I'll be right up. Can you take over for me here?'

'Sure thing.'

'Thanks.' We exchange smiles, then I quickly wash my hands and wipe them dry on my apron as I head out of the room and head upstairs, taking two steps at a time.

I pop my head round the nearest open door. 'Did Auntie Margo give you a nice bath? You all ready for bed, Milly?'

My eight-month-old daughter grabs her feet and smiles up at me from her cot. 'We've got a big day tomorrow, so you'd best sleep straight through or Mummy's going to be a walking zombie in the morning.'

I tickle her feet, then read her a bedtime story.

Milly's eyes slowly close as she clutches her blanket tightly in one hand.

It seems I was wrong. She has no issue with me being her mother, even if I am useless and had to ask a midwife for help the first time her nappy needed changing at the hospital after I gave birth. I don't do the fancy voices when reading her book like her daddy does either, but she doesn't seem to mind. I also sometimes make her milk too hot. She used to scream long into the night because I couldn't soothe her. Those times were hard, but Margo was there to help and reassure me that I am a good mother.

Luke and I aren't together. He still works in London. In fact, he's worked his way up to being a sous chef now, but he comes to see us every month, spending time with us and playing with his daughter. It's the cutest thing to see them together. I'm not sure if anything more will happen with me and Luke, but right now it doesn't matter. We may be slightly broken as a family, but we're happy.

I never did file for adoption. As soon as I returned to the UK and had my first scan, I looked at her picture on the screen and fell in love. It was like a lightbulb moment. Her kidney condition was confirmed. She has one normal-sized kidney and one tiny one, which doesn't work. In a way, we're kidney twins. I can't help but think it was written in the stars.

THE NEXT DAY, the restaurant opens on time, everything goes perfectly, and Margo, Milly and I even make the front page of the local newspaper, posing outside of Dessert Heaven. Milly is propped on my hip and I'm beaming like a Cheshire cat.

Luke has come over especially for the open evening and takes care of Milly while Margo and I flutter around the restaurant ensuring everything is perfect. The guests are smiling and, other than a spilled saucepan of cream, nothing goes wrong.

Margo is taking some pictures and videos for social media, so I leave her to it while I go and see to a table I've been keeping my eye on for a while now.

'Hello. My name is Brittany Young. I hope you've enjoyed your meal tonight.'

The woman looks at me and smiles. 'It was delightful,' she says. She licks her lips and gulps as her eyes shift sideways.

'Is everything okay?' I ask.

'Yes, everything is fine. Thank you for the dessert. I've never tasted anything quite like it. Now, please, can you bring us the bill?' asks the husband, a tight-lipped smile on his face.

I look at the woman. She's no longer smiling. Her eyes are shining with tears that haven't yet fallen. 'Ma'am, is everything okay?' I ask again, this time directly to her.

She nods once and looks at her lap.

'I'll be right back with your bill,' I say.

As I walk away towards the small reception area, I glance back once at the couple. The husband is gently stroking his wife's arm and whispering close to her ear, a loving smile on his face. She nods and smiles back at him, placing her hand over his.

Something is wrong. Or at least, it feels like something is. After what I went through with John and Angela, it's like my senses are on high alert for any abuse or bullying, especially having experienced my own share of it during my time working with Chef Andre.

My eyes land on the phone at the front desk.

If I call the police, it will ruin my perfect restaurant opening night. Someone being arrested is not the type of marketing I need. But then again... I've never been one for following the rules.

I think back to when I first met Angela and John. The signs were there—that he was controlling her—but I didn't see them. But now it's like I'm seeing small signs everywhere I look. Is the man controlling his wife, or isn't he?

I pick up the phone and hold it to my ear, but as I do, the husband appears at my side, making me flinch.

'Apologies, but my wife and I are in a bit of a hurry,' he says.

With a trembling hand, I return the phone to the desk. 'Of course,' I say, turning to the computer and bringing up their bill. While the husband swipes his card, I risk a glance at the wife, who is still at the table. She's gathering her things and soon joins her husband.

'Thank you,' she says.

'Have a nice evening,' I reply.

I watch the couple leave.

My eyes flick back to the phone, then up at Luke as he approaches me, carrying our daughter.

'Everything okay?' he asks.

'I'm not sure. I have a funny feeling. Can you just stay here and hold down the fort? There's something I need to do.'

Luke frowns. 'Do you need my help?'

I shake my head, already heading for the door. 'No, thank you. Just stay here with Milly.' I jog outside into the cool evening air, searching left and right for any sign of the couple. The car park is over to the left, so I head in that direction.

Goosebumps prickle my skin as I round the corner. Raised voices echo from ahead just as the husband shoves his wife against a car and she collapses to the ground.

I don't even think. I just react.

'Hey!'

The husband looks up, his eyes ablaze. 'This doesn't concern you.'

'Actually, it does. You're on my property. I know a bully when I see one.'

The man clenches both fists at his side. 'You don't know anything.'

'Look, this can go one of two ways. Either you walk away right now and leave her alone so I can take care of her, or you put up a fight and the police will arrest you when they arrive. I've been keeping an eye on you all night. From the moment you walked in here, I knew something was wrong.'

The man huffs loudly. 'You're bluffing. The police aren't coming. You wouldn't risk ruining your perfect opening.'

'How can you be so sure? You don't know anything about me.'

We lock eyes. My body may be trembling, but there's a fire inside me now. I am determined to protect this woman. She's still shaking on the ground. I don't think she's seriously hurt, but it's only a matter of time before he could take things too far.

It's just him against me now.

Either he believes me about me calling the police, or he doesn't.

I guess we'll just have to wait and see.

THANK YOU FOR READING

Did you enjoy reading *The Good Parents*? Please consider leaving a review on Amazon. Your review will help other readers to discover the novel.

ABOUT THE AUTHOR

Jessica Huntley is an author of dark and twisty psychological thrillers, which often focus on mental health topics and delve deep into the minds of her characters. She has a varied career background, having joined the Army as an Intelligence Analyst, then left to become a Personal Trainer. She is now living her life-long dream of writing from the comfort of her home, while looking after her young son and her disabled black Labrador. She enjoys keeping fit and drinking wine (not at the same time).

www.jessicahuntleyauthor.com
Sign up for her newsletter on her website and receive a free short story.

ALSO BY JESSICA HUNTLEY

Inkubator Books Titles

Don't Tell a Soul

Under Her Skin

The Good Parents

Self-Published Titles

THE DARKNESS SERIES

The Darkness Within Ourselves

The Darkness That Binds Us

The Darkness That Came Before

THE MY…SELF SERIES

My Bad Self: A Prequel Novella

My Dark Self

My True Self

My Real Self

STANDALONES

Jinx

How to Commit the Perfect Murder in Ten Easy Steps

COLLABORATIONS

The Summoning

HorrorScope: A Zodiac Anthology – Vol 1

Bloody Hell: An Anthology of UK Indie Horror

Printed in Great Britain
by Amazon